I0614728

Judge Not

by

Suzanne Rossi

This is a work of fiction. Names, characters, places, and incidents are either the product of the author's imagination or are used fictitiously, and any resemblance to actual persons living or dead, business establishments, events, or locales, is entirely coincidental.

Judge Not

COPYRIGHT © 2019 by Susan Peek

All rights reserved. No part of this book may be used or reproduced in any manner whatsoever without written permission of the author or The Wild Rose Press, Inc. except in the case of brief quotations embodied in critical articles or reviews.
Contact Information: info@thewildrosepress.com

Cover Art by *Kim Mendoza*

The Wild Rose Press, Inc.
PO Box 708
Adams Basin, NY 14410-0708
Visit us at www.thewildrosepress.com

Publishing History
First Mainstream Thriller Edition, 2019
Print ISBN 978-1-5092-2762-4
Digital ISBN 978-1-5092-2763-1

Published in the United States of America

The detective returned, closing the door behind him.

"I've just had a little chat with Mr. and Mrs. Garrett. According to Mrs. Garrett, you threatened to kill your husband on numerous occasions."

"She's nuts. The stupid bitch just attacked me in your lobby. I might sue."

"Mr. Garrett claims you constantly tried to extort money from him and demanded the same from their son."

"He's lying. All I wanted was Danny out of my life."

"You succeeded in doing that. Now about that missed history class."

That first sentence sounded ominous. I'd seen enough *Law & Order* episodes to know when to shut up and ask for an attorney. I shut up. I should have done it a long time ago but was convinced I had things under control.

"I want a lawyer."

"Sure, no problem. Please stand up and turn around. Theresa Lennox, you're under arrest for the murder of your ex-husband, Daniel Garrett. You have the right to remain silent…"

The handcuffs closed with a loud click. The steel on my wrists was damned cold.

Previous Titles by Suzanne Rossi
Published by The Wild Rose Press, Inc.

Along Came Quinn
All in the Family
A Tangled Web
Nearly Departed
Hear No Evil
The Reunion
Deadly Inheritance
Death is the Pits
Through My Eyes
A Novel Death
Rendezvous with Death
The Good Twin
The Assassin
Killer Conference
The Murder of Grace Bryant
Point of View
A Taste of Death

~

The Good Twin won
the 2016 Maggie Award for Single Title

Dedication

I wrote this book many years ago but was told by several other authors it would never get published. Being relatively new to writing, I put it on the shelf. But something kept drawing me back. It was a story that needed to be told. Eventually, I submitted. The manuscript was turned down. I continued writing and after a while thought now was the right time to give it another try. It worked.

Judge Not was a hard book to write. I once knew a Theresa who was in an abusive relationship. The results were not pretty. Eventually, she managed to leave the situation and move on. I haven't heard from her since but can only hope she found happiness.

I dedicate this book to all the Theresas out there who have found a Matt or the courage to take control of their lives, and also to all women, especially those with children, who desperately want to end the abuse.

May God guide you and keep you safe.

Chapter One

A dead man on my bedroom floor really screwed up my day. The corpse sprawled at my feet was my abusive ex-husband. The two holes in his chest—made with my gun, now lying next to him—told me my life had taken a turn for the worse. I'd be the first person the cops would suspect. My heart slammed against my chest, and I found it hard to breathe.

Instinct said to run like hell and put as much distance as possible between the late Danny Garrett and me. Acting upon that sensible idea, I turned and ran on trembling legs only to stop with my shaking hand poised to yank open the front door. At last, a kernel of common sense germinated in my frozen and panic-stricken mind.

Where would I go? I didn't have many friends. When you get beaten to a bloody pulp every few months, you tend to hide and avoid giving people an explanation. I was still in therapy, trying to figure out why I had allowed Danny to pound on me.

I gathered my scattered wits. I had nothing to fear. I'd been in class at the University of Memphis from ten in the morning until three in the afternoon. My panic subsided.

"I have an alibi."

Hearing my voice helped steady my nerves. I dragged in a deep breath, turned from the door, and walked into the kitchen where I did what all innocent people would do—called the police.

The police responded in a few minutes. Now my apartment was choked with cops, photographers, and paramedics—although why the latter I couldn't imagine. Danny was dead, and no amount of resuscitation would bring him back. I gave up trying to keep track of who was who and stayed out of the way, sitting on the edge of the sofa. A detective stood next to me.

"Mrs. Garrett, let's go over this again. I want to get everything straight," he said, his pudgy fingers flipping through a notepad.

I sighed, prepared to launch into my story one more time.

"It's Lennox—Theresa Lennox. I took back my maiden name after the divorce eighteen months ago."

"Was the divorce amicable?"

"No. It was nasty as hell. Danny beat the crap out of me on a regular basis. I still had a restraining order out against him."

"What time did you leave your apartment this morning?"

I couldn't remember the detective's name and didn't care. I wanted everybody—especially Danny—out of here.

"Quarter to ten or so. I'm not sure exactly."

"Where were you going?"

I explained about my university classes.

"Did you see your ex-husband or his car in the parking lot as you left?"

"No. I was running late and didn't pay any attention to who was parked where."

"And you came straight home after your classes?"

"I stopped to refill my Xanax prescription."

"That's a tranquilizer," he said. "Why do you need a tranq?"

"You would, too, if you'd lived with Danny," I retorted, tempted to tell him it was none of his business.

"Did you stop anywhere else?"

"I told you—no. I came home, walked into the bedroom, and saw…"

My stomach turned over. I had never seen a dead person before and hoped I'd never see one again.

"Why would your ex-husband break into your home?"

"Danny still pursued me."

"Why? Did he have hopes of reconciliation?"

The mere thought of reconciling with Danny made my skin crawl. "Hell no. He probably wanted a slice of revenge for daring to divorce him. Danny was big on revenge."

The detective nodded and jotted something in his notebook, then asked, "Why do you have a gun?"

I licked my lips, and my nerves jumped. I saw where this line of questioning was headed.

"For protection, of course. After the divorce, Danny beat me so badly I had to be hospitalized. I bought it shortly after that."

"Where did you keep it?"

"In the top drawer of my nightstand."

"Fired it lately?"

"I spent an hour at the firing range last night. When I got home, I put it back."

I knew forensics would find my fingerprints on it. Why not? It was my gun.

"Anyone else know it was there?"

"No, why should they?" I started to sweat. I smelled it—the scent of fear mixed with anxiety.

A man came out of my bedroom and spoke to the detective. "I'd say the guy's been dead at least six to eight hours, maybe a little more. Probable cause of death is two shots to the chest with a large caliber gun, most likely the thirty-eight on the floor next to him. One of the pillows on the bed has two holes in it. Probably used to muffle the sound. I'll run the usual tox screens and get back to you as soon as the autopsy is done."

"Thanks, Doc." The detective nodded and then looked at me again. "Danny Garrett. Any relation to State Senator Hamilton Garrett?"

"His son."

"Which makes Diana Worthington Garrett his mother?"

"I'm afraid so."

The cop looked like he'd just bitten into a lemon. His eyes narrowed, and his lips puckered. I sympathized. I had the same reaction whenever I was forced to talk to my ex-mother-in-law, too. Luckily, I hadn't had that particular displeasure in a long time.

"Damn." He turned to a uniformed officer. "Go to Senator and Mrs. Garrett's home. The deceased is their son. Break it to them as gently as you can. This one's gonna be messy."

He put it mildly. The Garrett union had been made in heaven—or hell, depending on how one looked at it. Diana Worthington came from old money preceding generations had squandered. Hamilton Garrett replenished the family coffers in exchange for help with his political ambitions. The merger had worked well with the exception of Danny for whom the words "trouble" and "scandal" would undoubtedly be chiseled on his headstone.

The detective turned to me, his eyes sharp and suspicious. I stared back, trying not to show fear even though my heart rate accelerated and my breathing quickened. I was nobody, and the Garrett name moved mountains, so to speak, in Western Tennessee.

"Miss Lennox, you claim to have been at the university all day. If I call, will I find you attended your classes?"

Uh-oh. I had skipped my eleven o'clock history class to study for a math test at noon. Not wanting to be disturbed, I'd found a quiet spot under a large oak tree in an isolated corner of campus. To the best of my knowledge, no one saw me, but then that had been the whole idea.

I figured it would be better to admit I'd missed a class than to have him find out about it from my professor. I told the truth. He wrote in his notebook again.

"I see. Anything else I should know about?"

Before I could answer, the paramedics wheeled my late husband through the living room. I watched the gurney roll past and for the first time realized I would never again have to fear the bastard. He was dead, and the person who killed him deserved a medal.

I couldn't take my eyes off the procession. They had stuffed Danny's stiff body into a bag, but I vividly remembered my encounter with him two weeks ago.

Drunk and high, he had created a scene when we bumped into each other on campus. He wasn't enrolled, and I had no idea why he was there. He'd called me the usual assortment of vile names and then threatened to kill me. His exact words being, "You'll get yours, bitch!"

Fortunately, two security guards had taken him down, shipping him off to jail on a drunk and disorderly.

The paramedics rolled the gruesome cargo out the door.

"When did you last see your ex-husband?"

I shrugged and lied, not wanting to admit I'd seen him on campus. "Not since I moved here."

"And when was that?"

"Seven or eight months ago."

"No phone calls or emails?"

"I told you—no."

"Excuse me for a moment, Miss Lennox."

He walked into my dining room and made a call on his cell. I should have told him about the campus meeting, but it supplied a motive for me killing him. Self-preservation kept me mute. I shivered. It's never a good idea to lie to the cops.

The detective returned and asked, "Miss Lennox, do you have a place to stay for the next few days? This is a crime scene, and we'll need to go over it."

"No, but I guess my credit card will survive a night or two in a motel."

"Fine, but first I'd like you to come downtown to the station with me. I have a few more questions, and forensics wants to get started."

Downtown? The station? A huge boulder settled on my chest. Oh, God. They suspected I'd done it. I didn't buy that forensics bullshit for a minute.

"Of course. May I pack a few things?" I asked, rising on trembling legs. How could I sound so calm? My insides shook. Nausea churned my stomach. A small dart of pain slashed behind my dry, itchy eyes.

"Let me come with you so you don't disturb anything."

He walked with me. Even though the murder had taken place on the opposite side of the bedroom from my dresser and closet, we were handed little bootie-type things to place over our shoes and walked carefully under the eagle eye of a man with *Forensics* printed on the back of his jacket. Blood stained a portion of the carpet. I supposed they would go over the room like human vacuum cleaners once I left.

I packed a bag with the necessities, returned the booties once outside the door, and even remembered to pick up my backpack from the coffee table where I'd dumped it earlier. Then the detective, with his hand on my elbow, carried my suitcase and escorted me to his car.

****

The small, airless interrogation room suffocated me. Scuffed, light-gray linoleum with little flecks of black and white in it made me dizzy. The drab, gray walls inched closer with every passing minute. A table and two chairs were wedged in opposite the single door. Fluorescent lights threw a harsh glare over the Spartan contents. An intermittent buzzing told me one of them would soon blow. My head pounded. No wonder people confessed. After three hours of sitting in the hard, plastic chair, it sounded like a good idea.

The detective asked the same questions he had at my apartment, repeating them over and over until I wanted to scream. The pain in my head intensified, and my mouth was dry in spite of the water I'd drunk. I also had to go to the bathroom.

"Miss Lennox, are you sure about the last time you saw your ex-husband?"

"Yes, I'm sure. Look, I have to use the restroom."

"In a minute. Our records show Daniel Garrett was arrested two weeks ago on the University of Memphis campus on a drunk and disorderly."

A stupid lie. Of course they knew. Nothing to do now except brazen it out. "I forgot."

"Forgot? How? The report says he accosted you."

"I didn't think it was all that important." I squirmed and bounced a little on my chair. "I have to go."

"Soon. Why lie?"

"I didn't lie. I just didn't think it mattered."

"Come on, give me the truth. He was an abusive son of a bitch. He threatened you, didn't he? You ditched a class, came home, found him there, and shot him. It was self-defense—right?"

The detective leaned in close, his face inches from mine. Hard, unrelenting blue eyes squinted, and thin lips drew into a stern line. His breath smelled of strong coffee and onions. I glared back and squeezed my legs together.

"No, I didn't. And if you don't want a puddle in the middle of the floor, you'll let me go to the bathroom now."

"Did you arrange to meet him at your place?"

"Certainly not!" I had to go—bad. "I have no idea how much the average human bladder holds, but we're about to find out, and I refuse to clean up the mess."

My situation had reached critical mass both physically and emotionally. I had to get out of this room.

The detective, ignoring my request, smiled and wrote in that damned notebook again. So that's how they wrung confessions out of people. I wondered about the legality of refusing a simple call of nature. A good defense attorney would call it duress and get the confession tossed.

"I didn't do it and will not confess to anything in exchange for bathroom privileges. I have to go, and if you don't let me out, I won't be responsible for the consequences."

He couldn't stop me from leaving. I hadn't been charged with a crime. I stood, jerked open the door, and tore down the hallway. The restrooms were located in the waiting area. I ran into the ladies' room, barely making it.

When I finished, I washed my hands and gazed at my reflection in the mirror over the basin. I looked like hell. My dark blonde hair hadn't seen a comb in hours, and the wavy mass hung to my shoulders in a tangled mess. Maybe it was the lighting, but the face staring back at me presented a pasty white complexion, and my gray eyes took on a deeper hue from the dark circles under them. I resembled a raccoon. I rubbed my finger over the skin. Mascara.

I needed a repair job, but my purse was in my backpack in the interrogation room. Using a wet paper towel, I scrubbed the mascara away and then tried to tame the snarled locks on my head with my fingers.

I massaged my neck and stretched my arms over my head. I couldn't put off returning to that room any longer. If the detective—I'd discovered his name was Simmons—didn't charge me, I was out of here.

I inhaled a couple of deep cleansing breaths, opened the door, and came face-to-face with my former in-laws as they entered from the street.

"You murdering bitch!" Diana screamed.

She lunged at me, her thin, bony fingers wrapping around my neck like the claws of a vulture. I staggered and slammed against the wall while two cops and her husband tried to pry her off.

"You piece of trash! I warned Danny not to marry anything from a trailer park. He never had any problems until he met you. I hope they stick a needle in your arm," she ranted.

Her fingers tightened. Flashes of light danced in front of my eyes. I grabbed her wrists and jerked. She held on with superhuman strength, squeezing harder.

"Diana, no! Not in public!" Hamilton shouted.

The death grip loosened, and they finally pulled her away. I clutched my throat, coughing and sucking in air at the same time. I braced my legs and, by the grace of God, didn't collapse on the floor.

Diana, however, wasn't finished. She kicked, her well-shod foot making contact with my knee. A scream of pain came out as a mild croak. My leg crumpled, and I sagged to the floor.

"You whore! If the state doesn't kill you, I will." Diana kicked again but missed.

I realized the flashes of light came from cameras. The media had followed the Garretts through the front door. I crouched on the floor, clasping my knee and trying to shield my eyes from the glare as they shouted.

"Did you kill your husband, Mrs. Garrett?"

"How did it happen?"

"Why'd you do it?"

The cops tried to hustle them back outside.

"Bitch! Murderer!" my ex-mother-in-law screamed, spittle flying from her mouth.

"Diana, control yourself!" Hamilton shouted again. He grabbed his wife and pulled her to the far side of the room, then turned to glare at me.

I pushed myself up, leaned against the wall, and massaged my sore knee. The shouted questions from reporters now being shoved out the door and Diana screaming filthy names sent me limping back to the relative safety of the interrogation room where I found the detective calmly going through my purse and backpack.

"I take it Mr. and Mrs. Garrett have arrived," he said, flipping open my agenda book.

I snatched it out of his hands. "It's polite to ask first, and if you can't do that, get a goddamned warrant."

His eyebrows rose. "Wait here. I'll only be a few minutes." He left the room.

I collapsed in the chair and stuffed the book back into my purse with shaking fingers. Diana had always hated my guts, but the disdain had been refined. Today, I'd seen a whole new side of her and understood where Danny had gotten his temper. My ex-mother-in-law sounded as crazy as her son.

I needed to regain my composure. Closing my eyes, I forced my mind into visions of meadows with wildflowers and slow-moving streams. My therapist had taught me that trick to combat anxiety attacks. Now seemed like a good time to use it.

I rubbed my throat. Tomorrow bruises would form. My knee hurt like hell, and I wondered if I had grounds for a lawsuit. There were plenty of witnesses with cameras.

The detective returned, closing the door behind him.

"I've just had a little chat with Mr. and Mrs. Garrett. According to Mrs. Garrett, you threatened to kill your husband on numerous occasions."

"She's nuts. The stupid bitch just attacked me in your lobby. I might sue."

"Mr. Garrett claims you constantly tried to extort money from him and demanded the same from their son."

"He's lying. All I wanted was Danny out of my life."

"You succeeded in doing that. Now about that missed history class."

That first sentence sounded ominous. I'd seen enough *Law & Order* episodes to know when to shut up and ask for an attorney. I shut up. I should have done it a long time ago but was convinced I had things under control.

"I want a lawyer."

"Sure, no problem. Please stand up and turn around. Theresa Lennox, you're under arrest for the murder of your ex-husband, Daniel Garrett. You have the right to remain silent…"

The handcuffs closed with a loud click. The steel on my wrists was damned cold.

****

I clutched a scrap of paper with a scribbled address in sweat-dampened fingers and walked along the cracked sidewalk in a seedy part of downtown, scanning store fronts. I stopped for a moment, set my suitcase down, wiggled my cramping fingers, and then readjusted the backpack on my aching shoulders. The annual Memphis in May Festival was in full swing, and the scent of burning pig wafted over the city from the barbeque contest being held in Tom Lee Park.

I ignored the mouth-watering aroma and my discomfort as I searched for the address on South Third Street. No self-respecting woman would be caught dead in this part of town alone, even in broad daylight, but getting mugged or raped was the least of my worries.

I finally found what I sought. My heart sank. The building was old and decrepit, the paint having long since peeled off. Even the bricks looked tired. Gang graffiti decorated the plywood in the street front window. Only two windows on the upper floors remained unbroken. A hand-printed sign tacked to the front of a narrow door read, *Matthew Summers, Private Investigations, Second Floor.* I assumed the intact panes belonged to him.

I had no choice but to open the door. Straightening my shoulders and gathering my courage, I turned the knob and pushed. The hinges screeched in true horror movie fashion. I could almost hear the audience crying, "Don't go in there!"

I forced myself to climb the stairs, each step protesting with squeaks of ancient nails rubbing against old wood. The narrow stairwell smelled of musty mold, dust, and odors I didn't want to identify.

A door at the top of the steps had the same hand-printed sign as downstairs. I knocked, then opened it and stepped through.

A miniskirted woman wearing a tight, low-cut, red top and fuck-me, leopard-print stilettos idly shoved papers into an open file drawer. Her plastic bangle bracelets clanked against the metal. She looked surprised to see me.

"Is Mr. Summers in?" I asked.

"Are you a bill collector or an honest-to-God client?"

That didn't sound encouraging. "I'm a client."

"In that case, he's in there." She thrust her chin in the direction of an open doorway and continued filing, boredom already replacing the surprise on her face.

I stepped through the door and almost fled.

A scarred desk stood in the center of the room with a straight-backed wooden chair in front of it. Behind the desk, a table with a laptop was crammed between the two windows. Several beat-up file cabinets nestled in the corner. A framed private investigator's license hung on the wall above the computer. Tan-colored walls had long ago degenerated into a neutral smudge. The place ran a close second in the depressing category to the Shelby County women's lock-up.

A man sat at the desk, supporting his head with his hands. Bracing his elbows on the desktop, he clutched his hair and groaned. He reeked of cheap booze and looked as if he'd slept in his navy-blue golf shirt.

"Are *you* Matthew Summers?"

"Who wants to know?"

I answered with a question of my own. "Are you drunk?"

"Not anymore. That's the problem. What do you want?"

"Common sense tells me to say nothing, but I need

a private investigator, and your ad in the phone book said reasonable rates. I haven't got a lot of money."

He finally raised his head and, bloodshot or not, the eyes I gazed into were the bluest I'd ever seen. His brown hair was in dire need of a trim, and his face demanded reacquaintance with a razor. He looked as seedy and rundown as the building.

"How much can you afford?"

"How much do you charge?" I countered.

He paused for a second and then replied with a figure that sounded just a tick under the national debt.

"Do I look stupid?" I stared around the room. "This isn't the Taj Mahal. I'll pay a third of that, and I want receipts for the expenses."

"I haven't said I'll take the case yet." His voice turned rough and challenging.

"You haven't heard anything *about* it yet. Now do I write a check?"

"Sit down. Tell me your story—and it's cash only."

Not having much of an option, I did as he asked, looking over my shoulder, conscious of the receptionist hovering just outside the door.

"I'm not sure if you remember me. My name is Theresa Lennox. We met when I was your sister's roommate in the hospital a couple of years ago. My husband had beaten the hell out of me. You gave me your card."

He stared at me through his bloodshot eyes and nodded. "Yeah, I remember. I think I told you to file charges and then divorce the son of a bitch."

"I divorced him before the beating but took your advice and filed charges. Unfortunately, I came home the other day and found him dead on my bedroom floor.

Shot twice in the chest. With my gun. The cops arrested me. I didn't do it. I made bail and now need a private investigator to find out who did." I gave him a hard look. "No offense, but you don't look so hot. Are you up to it?"

"Yeah, I'll be fine as soon as I get some coffee. Carleen," he shouted to the girl out front. "Get some coffee in here."

"Yeah, yeah. Gimme a few minutes."

"So tell me what's on your mind," he invited, leaning back in his chair.

"I just did."

"So tell me again. I got a short attention span today."

Swell, just what I needed—a frigging wiseass. I repeated what I'd just told him in more detail. "I was jailed for three days and don't want to repeat the experience."

"No, I don't guess you do."

I resisted the urge to smack him. The receptionist returned with the coffee, slapped a chipped mug in front of me, and then tossed a couple of packets of sugar and non-dairy creamer onto the desk.

Summers grabbed his mug and set it on the blotter before him. From a drawer, he snatched a bottle of aspirin, popped three into his mouth, and washed them down with the hot liquid. His hands shook so badly I was surprised the contents reached his mouth without splashing all over.

He drained the mug, and I wondered if he'd scalded his throat. I added the sugar and creamer to my cup and then cautiously sipped some of the best coffee I'd ever tasted.

"More?" Carleen asked him.

"Of course." She left with the mug. "So your former father-in-law is State Senator Hamilton Garrett. I hear he's been making noises about running for governor."

"I wouldn't know. I don't concern myself with Garrett's political ambitions."

"That name pulls a lot of strings in this part of the state. I'm surprised you made bail if Diana Garrett wants you in jail."

I shrugged. "I caught a lenient judge. With no passport, I'm not a flight risk. Bail was set at two hundred and fifty thousand."

"How'd you pay it?"

"I cashed in some CDs I'd bought with my divorce settlement. It took a couple of days."

Carleen sashayed back in with another mug of coffee for her boss and set it in front of him, shooting me a sidelong glance.

"So is she a client?" She stood with her fists balled on her hips.

"Maybe," he replied.

"Well, if she pays anything, just remember you owe me fifty bucks wages from last week." On that parting shot, she flounced from the room. The door stood wide open.

"Close the door," Summers shouted after her. She ignored him, slamming a file drawer instead. He turned his attention back to me. "Sounds like the cops have a pretty good case—means, motive, and opportunity. What does your lawyer say?"

I glanced back at the open door, and he took the hint.

"Leave your things here." Rising, he jerked his head, and I followed, noticing his khaki slacks were as wrinkled as his shirt. His shoes, however, looked first class, comfortable with thick rubber soles.

"We're going to lunch, Carleen. Lock up when you're done. Take the rest of the day off."

"I intended to," she replied.

Out on the sidewalk, he squinted in the bright sunshine and fished a pair of sunglasses from his pocket. Settling them on his nose, he looked up and down the street.

"You're being followed."

I swung my head in that direction, staring past a couple of homeless men hunkered down in the meager shade of a nearby recessed doorway.

"Don't look!" he barked. "See the tan car parked at the end of the block?"

"What about it?"

"They're cops."

"How can you tell?"

"Only idiots or someone doing surveillance work would sit in a car in this neighborhood. Where do you want to eat? I'm hungry. A burger will do, but I prefer steak. Your treat."

My jaw dropped. "You expect me to pay for lunch?"

"If I'm working for you, I want to be well fed. I know a great little café on Front Street. Where's your car?"

"At my apartment. I just got out of jail. Remember? I rode the bus. Does this mean you're taking the case?"

"Haven't decided yet. I'll tell you after lunch.

Money is a great motivator. I got bills. Come on. I need exercise."

"What about those guys in the car?"

"They'll tag along. They'll also be pissed. It's a bitch following someone who's on foot when they're in a car."

"Speaking of cars, don't you have one?"

"Yeah, but it's been a slow month. I'm saving on gas."

"Has anyone ever told you you're a smart-ass?"

"All the time. I've learned to ignore it."

He cupped my elbow in his hand. We crossed the street, walking at a brisk pace. I was proud of myself. I didn't deck the son of a bitch.

Chapter Two

From outside, the Starlight Diner looked like any other hole-in-the-wall restaurant, but the interior was retro—straight out of the fifties.

The gray walls had a red stripe accent just below the ceiling. Chrome, so shiny I could use it as a mirror, gleamed everywhere. The counter, located along the back wall, ran the entire length of the restaurant while booths surrounded the perimeter. Wrap-around windows in the corners let in abundant natural light.

It was not quite eleven thirty, but already a substantial crowd gathered. Tourists, most likely staying at hotels in the downtown district, ate lunch before the bus for Graceland left. The woman wearing everything Elvis tipped me off.

Most of the clientele had chosen booths or counter space near the front door. The noise level had not yet reached critical. Conversation and the clinking of silverware on china were minimal. Waitresses and the cooks in the back shouted out orders and pick-ups to each other.

Jail didn't have the best cuisine, and the homey aromas of frying bacon, hamburgers, and onions made my stomach rumble.

We slid into a red vinyl booth in the corner, away from prying eyes and ears. A waitress glided up, slapped a couple of menus on the Formica table top, and then asked, "Coffee?"

Summers looked at me, and I nodded.

"Two coffees. Give us a few minutes to look at the menu, okay?" he said to the woman. She left and returned in less than a minute with two huge mugs of steaming, dark-brown liquid. I sniffed the heavenly aroma. Jailhouse coffee sucked.

As I studied the menu, two men walked past and sat in the booth behind ours. I glanced at Summers who grinned, winked, and cast his gaze out of the window. I looked and spotted a tan car parked in an end space of the parking lot. I didn't like being followed and wanted to tell the bastards just that, but my companion laid a hand on my arm and shook his head. No way could we conduct business with them hanging onto every word.

Our waitress returned. Summers kept his part of the bargain and ordered a steak, medium rare, fries, and a salad. I settled on a burger with all the trimmings and fries. While the coffee tasted as delicious as it smelled, I couldn't resist a chocolate shake.

"Tell me about your lawyer."

I shot a glance over his shoulder at the two men.

"Mr. Summers, don't you think…?"

"Matt. My name is Matt. What do people call you? Terry?"

"I prefer Theresa."

"Okay, Theresa. Now who's your lawyer?"

"Don't you think this is kind of a public place to be discussing such things?"

"Don't worry. No time like the present. Besides, if we don't talk about your case, what will we talk about? I like conversation with my meals."

I didn't want to talk about a damned thing in front

of cops, but as long as we kept to generalities, I guessed it would be all right. After all, Matt was the professional.

"I was assigned a public defender named Warshovsky. He's an idiot. We met with the DA after my arraignment, and Warshovsky advised me to take a plea bargain of man one. I told him to drop dead. I didn't do it. I met with him again yesterday, and the moron suggested I go for self-defense or temporary insanity."

"And what did you say to that?"

"The same, only in more colorful language. If I had any ready money, I'd hire a real attorney."

"Don't blame the public defender's office. They're overworked and understaffed. Tell me about your ex-husband. Where did you meet the son of such powerful parents?"

Sipping some of my coffee, I wondered where to start. My shrink had finally convinced me I bore no blame for Danny's behavior, but I still winced at my grass-green naivety at age twenty-one. I had been ripe for plucking by someone like my ex.

"I worked as a cocktail waitress in an East Memphis bar called Newton's. I was fresh out of the trailer park in Walls, Mississippi, and for the first time earning a decent wage. I'd been working two months when I met Danny. He drifted in one night full of flattery and flirting. He was good-looking with dark hair and dark eyes. I fell for his you're-the-most-beautiful-woman-I've-ever-met line. The funny thing is—he was a perfect gentleman all the time we dated."

Matt scowled and curled his lip. "Let me guess. He impressed you with expensive gifts, fancy restaurants, and his condo on the riverfront."

I bit my lip and nodded. "He made me feel like a princess. Mike Harper, the bartender at Newton's, warned me. He said Danny was notorious for drinking, carousing, and landing in jail, but I never saw any of that. I ignored Mike, too dazzled by Danny's attention to believe him."

"When did you meet the Garretts?"

The waitress brought our food, and it was several minutes before I answered. I didn't like remembering *that* first meeting either. Tall and slim to the point of emaciation, Diana Garrett had smiled, offered a limp handshake, and looked me up and down like a prize cow at a cattle auction, her eyes cold as the wind in January. I'd been intimidated down to my toes.

Hamilton, also tall with a long face and lots of teeth, reminded me of a horse. He hadn't offered to shake hands but bowed his head as a form of greeting.

"Danny took me to their house on East Parkway near Overton Park about three months after we met. I almost had a panic attack when I saw the place. I'm not a political person, so I never made the connection between State Senator Garrett and Danny's father."

"I'll bet they were charmingly polite yet made you feel insignificant and unworthy." Matt chewed a piece of steak and shoved several ketchup-laden french fries into his mouth.

"Absolutely."

I slathered all the mayo I could find on the bun, mashed it down onto the meat, bit in, and tore off a hunk of hamburger, savoring the greasy, grilled flavor mixing with that of the lettuce, tomatoes, pickles, and onions in my mouth. After three days of that crap served in jail, I thought I'd died and gone to heaven in the Starlight Diner. I sampled a fry. Oh, my God—fantastic. I came close to passing out sucking the thick chocolate shake through the straw. I wondered if the management would let me live here.

"How the hell did you end up married to the creep?"

Matt's voice brought me out of my gastronomic daze. "He said he loved me. I needed to hear those words. Silly, huh?"

He stopped eating, stared into my eyes, and said softly, "No, not at all."

His words sent a warm glow throughout my body.

"What was Diana Garrett's reaction to your engagement?"

"She was the soul of discretion. She smiled, congratulated us, and immediately began planning the wedding. Even though she appeared gracious, something in her eyes told me she'd rather see her son dead than married to me. Rumor has it, after we left the house, she broke every lamp and vase in the den."

We ate in silence for a few minutes before he asked, "When did the beatings start?"

"About six months after we were married. He'd come home drunk, and when I asked where he'd been, he let loose. I was terrified but had nowhere to run for help. My mother had died the year before, and I'm an only child. My closest relative is an aunt in Biloxi. I haven't seen her since I was ten."

Matt finished his meal and signaled the waitress for more coffee. "Why didn't you get out? There are shelters for abused women."

I shrugged and crammed the last of my sandwich

into my mouth, then cleaned up the rest of the fries.

"Over the years, Danny and Diana kept repeating that it was my fault. After a while, I believed them."

For the first time since I'd begun talking, I remembered the two men in the booth behind us. They'd been served and to the best of my knowledge hadn't spoken a word. One appeared to be writing in a notebook. Now the waitress cleared away their plates and gave them the check.

Matt rested his elbows on the table, sipping his refill, clearly in no rush to leave.

"How long were you married?"

"Nine very long years."

Matt looked at me over the rim of his cup. His gaze was sharper, and he didn't look as haggard as he had earlier. The food must have helped his hangover, although his hands still trembled.

"It sounds like you've had a hell of a time." He paused for a moment. "Okay, I'll take your case on one condition. I expect clients to lie. Look me in the eye, and tell me you didn't kill him."

The man sitting behind Matt leaned back against the seat and turned his head to catch my answer.

Not wanting him to miss anything, I gazed over Matt's shoulder, and said in a raised voice, "I did not kill Danny Garrett."

Matt waved at the waitress who brought the check over. He passed it on to me.

"You've hired yourself a private investigator. Let's go back to the office. I need more information along with times and names."

I followed him to the cashier, stifling a laugh as the two men scrambled out of the booth. I'd never been this important in my life.

****

Carleen had taken Matt at his word and vanished by the time we returned to the office. We resumed our seats from earlier. While I filled out paperwork, he fished around in a desk drawer, extracted a tape recorder, placing it on the blotter, and then changed the batteries with shaking fingers. I hadn't seen a cassette player in years and wondered how hard up he really was.

For some reason, the tape recorder made me nervous. My words would be forever preserved. He looked up and caught me staring at the thing like it was a live snake.

"What? Expecting me to memorize everything you say like on TV?"

"Well, yeah—kinda."

"Pure Hollywood crap. Some PIs take notes, while others use tape or a digital recorder if they can afford it. Occasionally, I do both. With tape there's never any question about what was said. It helps trip up liars."

He stared hard, and I swallowed.

"I never thought about the inner workings of something like this before. I assumed you all used tiny cameras and microphones to spy on people, and slithered through the dark with night vision goggles."

"Nothing so dramatic. Most investigative work involves talking to people and asking questions. When I use a camera, it's a high-def, zoom-lens digital. That way I can download the pictures onto the computer and print them out." He finished with the batteries and pushed the record button. "Now let's get back to your ex-husband. Tell me the same thing you did at lunch."

He was as bad as the damned cops, but I repeated my life-with-Danny horror story.

"Any ideas on who'd want him dead—besides you, I mean?" he asked.

Trembling fingers fiddled with a pencil. His hangover must have been a beaut. I'd never had one, so I couldn't relate or sympathize. After viewing Danny's mornings after, it was not something I wanted to experience.

"When he was drunk, he got belligerent—lots of barroom brawls and arguments. Someone he had a fight with could have done it."

"But why at your apartment?"

"I have no idea. Maybe he arranged to meet someone there, knowing I'd be at school."

"What about his friends?"

"Most were like him—drunks. They used to come over to the condo, drink, snort coke, and hatch all kinds of get-rich-quick schemes."

I leaned back and rubbed my forehead. I had the beginnings of a headache and took a moment to visualize a meadow.

"Why would your ex-husband need a get-rich-quick anything? He came from money."

"Yeah, but he hung out with definite low-lifes who didn't have beans. He loved to egg them on and brag about how much influence he had."

"Did any of these schemes ever work?"

"Hell, no. The plans were usually illegal, and they always got caught. His shit-for-brains friends did jail time, but Danny got off. The Garrett family can afford the best lawyers. Do you think one of them could have done it?"

Matt shrugged and scribbled something on a notepad. "His friends? It's possible. I'll need the names of this brain trust to check them out."

I gave him three possible suspects and then said, "You know, Danny was in jail a couple of weeks ago. Maybe he met one of his friends, and they hooked up. Danny would get a kick out of using my apartment for a drug deal. If they were drunk or high, the friend could have found my gun and accidentally shot him."

It sounded plausible to me. The damned thing had been an accident. The more I thought about it, the more sense it made. Had I solved the case on my own? Matt threw instant cold water on my theory.

"One shot, maybe—two shots, not a chance in hell. Plus your gun is a revolver. It won't go off without a hard squeeze on the trigger. And you said a pillow had been used to muffle the sound. Sorry, but it was no accident."

"Maybe they got into an argument or something."

"It won't wash. How many sets of prints did the police find on your gun?"

"Just mine," I replied, my enthusiasm deflating.

"Where did Danny get his drugs?"

"I don't know. I never knew his connection, but I overheard him on the phone one night, referring to someone he called The Juice. I assumed it was a street name."

Matt frowned as he doodled on a note pad. I kept quiet and let him think.

"The Juice," he muttered. "I've heard that somewhere before. I can't remember now, but I will. Did Danny owe money to a drug dealer?"

"I have no idea."

"If he did and couldn't pay, that would make a good motive for murder."

It certainly would. My spirits rose, then plummeted.

"Mommy and Daddy would have coughed it up. If you and I are figuring this out, why didn't the cops?"

"As far as they're concerned, the case is closed. You've been arrested, arraigned, and will stand trial. They don't give a damn."

Swell. The cops didn't give a crap about finding another suspect. Not even my lawyer believed me.

Matt turned a page on the pad. "Tell me about your classes at the university on the day of the murder."

I groaned. I was so sick of telling this story I could scream but went over it again. Matt took occasional notes.

When I finished, he remarked, "Okay, you fidgeted through a ten o'clock English Lit class, cut World History at eleven to study for a math test at twelve, ate lunch at one, and kicked yourself to stay awake during Economics at two. Where did you eat?"

"The cafeteria. It's in the student union and was crowded. I went through the line, and no, I didn't talk to anybody."

"Not even a simple hello to the cashier?"

"I don't remember. What does it matter? According to the coroner, Danny had been dead six to eight hours before I got home at three forty-five."

"How far do you live from campus?"

"Not far. Maybe a ten-minute drive."

"Why did it take forty-five minutes to get there?"

"I stopped to fill a prescription."

"The police think you left campus at eleven, drove

home, killed your ex, and returned for the math test." He shook his head. "I gotta tell you, it takes one cool customer to murder a man, take a test, and then eat lunch."

"But even if I did leave campus and go home, why would Danny be there?"

"Well, *someone* lured him to your place. The cops will say it was you for obvious reasons. And withholding that information about the confrontation in front of the history building two weeks ago didn't help your case. Now let's go over when you got home that day. Didn't you notice the patio door had been forced?"

"No. The drapes were closed. I came in, dropped my backpack on the coffee table, flipped through my mail, and headed for the bedroom to change clothes. I never looked."

My headache had blossomed like the meadow wildflowers I imagined. I wanted to go home, take a shower, and sleep for a hundred days.

A drop of water splashed on my hand. I stuck out my tongue and caught a tear as it rolled down my cheek. The salty taste broke my control. Hiding my face in the crook of my arm, I laid my head on his desk and bawled.

The storm was short-lived. Within a few minutes, I sat up and wiped my cheeks.

Matt shoved a box of tissues in my direction. "I'm sorry. It's been a long day—for both of us. Why don't I take you home? I've got enough information to get started. I want to see the crime scene anyway."

He punched the stop button on the recorder, removed the tape, and dropped it into his pocket. I finished blowing my nose while Matt unplugged his laptop, jammed it into a carrying case, slung it over his shoulder, and then hoisted my suitcase and backpack in one hand. Out in the hall, he locked the office door. I followed.

Home. It sounded wonderful.

****

I had expected Matt's car to look as slovenly as he did. I was surprised to find a clean, well-cared-for Ford parked behind the building.

He opened the back door and tossed my suitcase and backpack onto the seat, then laid his laptop on the floor behind the driver's side. I got in and fastened my seatbelt.

A few papers littered the dashboard along with two or three pairs of sunglasses and baseball caps. He removed several file folders from beneath my feet and chucked them into the back seat, then started the car. It turned over immediately, telling me he also maintained the engine.

"Nice car," I commented.

"Thanks. I spend a lot of time in it and like my comfort."

"I thought all private investigators drove either souped-up sports cars or rolling wrecks."

"There's that Hollywood thing again," he said, driving down the alley and then pulling into the street. "The smart PI will drive a car that blends in. Stand on a corner and count how many white cars pass."

"I see your point."

"Have the police released your apartment yet?"

"Yes, according to Warshovsky."

Twenty minutes later we swung into the parking lot of the Quince Garden Apartments. Vans emblazoned with the call letters of the various local news stations and sporting satellite up-links on the roofs filled every parking place near my unit.

Matt made a hard left turn.

"What the hell is this?" I asked.

"The jackals have obviously heard of your release. Damn. I don't want anyone to know I'm working for you yet."

"Can they do this?" I didn't want reporters breathing down my neck. My brief encounter with them at the police station had been enough to last a lifetime.

"They can until somebody complains. This is private property."

I bent out of sight. Matt passed by the reporters interviewing one of my neighbors and drove to the far end of the lot where he slipped into an end space. The car next to us shielded me from view.

"Can we get in your patio door?"

"I don't know. Danny forced the lock, but my lawyer said he'd make sure it was repaired."

"You can't stay here tonight. Give me your keys. You wait while I go in the back way and pack a few things for you."

"Like hell," I snapped, still irritated at the presence of the media. "I don't want you rummaging through my underwear. I'll go with you."

Not giving him a chance to protest, I opened the door and exited, trying to act nonchalant. Matt joined me, positioning himself between me and the gaggle of reporters. We walked up the sidewalk until the end of the building gave us shelter from prying eyes.

We both stuck our heads around the back corner. No one had staked out my patio. The coast was clear.

We ran for my apartment. I fished the keys out of my purse, slipped one into the repaired lock, and turned. Nothing happened.

"Damn. What do we do now?" I whispered.

"Let me try."

He wiggled the key and jiggled the door handle until it clicked and slid open. We squeezed through, batted the drapes out of the way, and closed the door behind us.

I'd left the curtains in the dining room partially open, so we ducked low until reaching the safety of the hallway and then hurried to my bedroom. I pulled up suddenly. Matt rammed me from behind, thrusting me into the room. I stared at the bloodstain. Fingerprint dust marred every surface.

The stuffy apartment made my stomach queasy. Someone had turned off the air conditioning, and a sick, sweet smell permeated the room. "Yuck. It stinks in here."

"Never mind. Just pack, and let's go."

I agreed. The place gave me the creeps. Who was responsible for clean-up? Me? The apartment complex? Either way it was going to cost me money.

I snatched a large duffle bag from my closet and threw in some jeans, tops, a couple of skirts, underwear, and a nice pair of shoes. Then I raided my bathroom for an extra tube of toothpaste and other toiletries.

I shoved the duffle bag into his hands, exited the bedroom, and tiptoed along the short hallway to the dining room. Peeking around the corner, I spied my book where I'd left it on the table, dropped to the floor, and scooted on my belly like a snake to retrieve it.

"Are you nuts?" Matt hissed from behind me.

"They'll see you."

With my gaze glued on the window, I raised my hand, groping until my fingers closed around the novel. I pulled it off and wiggled back to the hallway just in time. A sudden dimming of light told me someone had decided to investigate the interior.

We flattened ourselves against the wall, and I inched my head around the doorjamb, then whipped it back. A woman, her hands on either side of her face, peered in. I held my breath. A few seconds later, the light returned, and the curious reporter was gone.

"What was that all about?" Matt demanded in an exasperated whisper. "You were almost spotted."

"My English Lit reading assignment—*A Tale of Two Cities*," I replied.

"For crissakes. You could have bought another one."

"Hey, three days in jail put me behind with my studies. Besides, I made notes in the margins for a report due next week."

I heard him mutter something unflattering as we made our way to the patio door, walking bent over like coal miners. I left first. Matt followed, shoving the duffle toward me, then closed and locked the door.

We scurried back the way we'd come and stopped to catch our breaths before the final dash to the car.

"Shit! What about my car?" I'd forgotten I would need transportation, especially if I wanted to see my lawyer.

"Give me the keys."

I complied and asked, "What are you going to do?"

"Which one is yours?"

"The dark green Grand Cherokee. What are you

going to do?" I repeated.

"*You* are going to walk to my car, throw the duffle into the passenger's seat, and drive out like you don't have a care in the world."

"But I'll have to go right past them. They'll see me."

"No, they'll see *me*. Give me a minute to get back to your place and then leave. By that time, I should be at your car and the center of attention. Meet me in the grocery store parking lot on Mt. Moriah."

"What if they follow you?"

"They won't have time. We'll both be long gone."

Matt disappeared around the corner. I counted to twenty, walked with my head down to the Ford, tossed in my bag, and then slid behind the wheel. I heard my car alarm beep, unlocking the doors.

I shoved the key into the ignition with trembling fingers and twisted. The car started instantly. I put it in gear, backed out, and drove away.

Matt was right. The horde of reporters gathered around him as he got into my car. I passed without anyone noticing, swung onto the street, and took off.

A few blocks later, I parked in an isolated spot near the grocery, rolled down my window, and waited until Matt pulled up next to me.

"That was super. What did they say?" I asked.

He shrugged. "The usual crap—who was I, where were you—that sort of thing. I told them I was the repo guy. The whole thing went down so fast none of them had time to get their cameras operating."

Now *this* was my idea of a private investigator. Jim Rockford or Thomas Magnum couldn't have done any better. I loved those old TV shows.

"What now?" I asked. The late afternoon sun beat on the roof of the car, bringing the temperature level up to the roasting category. My shirt stuck to my back, and a rivulet of sweat trickled down my cheek.

"Follow me. I know a motel where you can park out of sight in back. It's nothing fancy, but it'll do."

"As long as it has a bed and a bathroom, I don't care," I replied cheerfully, still happy at how easily he'd rescued my car.

I rolled up my window, turned the air conditioning back on full blast, and followed Matt out of the lot.

It took only fifteen minutes to find the Be Our Guest Motel in a marginal neighborhood on American Way. The old Mall of Memphis had been torn down, and the vacant land stretched behind a twelve-foot-high, chain-link fence in back of the motel.

I waited outside in Matt's car while he went in and registered, then tailed him to a room located on the back side of the place. I got out, grabbed my duffle, and joined him as he unlocked the door.

"Here you go. It's registered in my name. I'll get the rest of your bags."

I stepped into the room and walked past a closet and the bathroom. At least it looked clean. The rest of the room was typical cheap motel: a double bed, a dresser with a mirror, a desk, and a TV bolted to the wall.

I tossed my bag onto the bed and unzipped it. Matt entered with the rest of my things.

"There's a Wonderful Waffles next door for breakfast and lunch. If I were you, I wouldn't drive around town any more than necessary. That reminds me, I'll need your cell phone number. I don't want my calls going through the switchboard."

I pulled out a flip phone and read the number off it to him.

He stopped to stare like I'd grown another head. "What the hell is that?"

"It's my cell phone, and no, I don't know my number because I don't call myself."

"It's ancient. An antique."

"Well, excuse me, but what does it matter? Who the hell would I call? I don't have any friends. I have it for emergencies. I subscribe to a cheap service that only charges me fifteen dollars a month. I use my landline."

He blew out a deep breath as though not believing I lived on the same planet.

"All right. I'll swing by a store and get you a better one. You need reliable service."

"It's a waste of money. I don't need a phone that'll do backflips."

He rolled his eyes. "Take my advice. A smartphone is more reliable."

"You seem to dole out a lot of advice."

"What?"

"While I was in the hospital, you also advised me to get a gun and learn how to use it."

"If your ex was shot with your gun, I'd have to say you took my advice. Did you learn how to use it?"

I nodded and inhaled a shaky breath. Even now I could feel the weight of that little thirty-eight, the pattern on the grip as I held it, and the deafening boom when I pulled the trigger. Unfortunately, I also saw Danny lying on my bedroom floor.

"I know how to use it."

I stared at the phone in my hand. I didn't care how

out-of-date it looked. I still wanted that hot shower and some shuteye.

His eyes softened. "Why don't you rest for a while? I'll pick you up at seven, and we'll go have a decent meal at a real restaurant."

The thought of such a luxury, one I might not see for a long time to come, made me want to cry.

"I'm a simple girl." I named a chain restaurant.

A deep, rumbling laugh burst from his throat. The sound startled me. I gazed at his broad chest, the perfect place for a woman to lay her head. The thought came and then disappeared like smoke on the wind.

"Sounds fine. I'll see you at seven."

He grinned and walked out the door, leaving me with my mouth gaping. For the first time today, I noticed the dimple in his left cheek. A surge of heat I couldn't control rushed through me.

Scruffy or not, Matthew Summers was damned good-looking.

Chapter Three

Matt arrived a few minutes before seven. I cast a sidelong glance at him as I buckled my seatbelt. I rather liked the way his hair curled over his ears and up in the nape of his neck. His clean-shaven face made a world of difference, and the whites of those laser-bright, blue eyes showed only a hint of redness.

The clothes provided the biggest change, however. The wrinkle-free polo shirt went well with the pressed slacks. The shoes remained the same.

He caught me staring and laughed lightly, giving me a lopsided smile, which set that little indentation in his cheek dancing. I tried but couldn't stop the stutter step my heart produced.

"What?" he said. "Surprised I cleaned up so good?"

Heat scorched my face, and I knew I blushed like a schoolgirl. I looked out of the windshield and smoothed my hair to gain composure.

"To be honest—yes."

He pulled away from the motel and into the early evening traffic. I rolled down my window, enjoying the smell of clean, fresh air. I hadn't had that pleasure in the last few days.

"I'm sorry. You caught me at a bad moment this morning. I'll try not to let it happen again."

I wanted to question him further on the subject, but

as he glanced in the rearview mirror, he said, "Our friends from the diner are still with us. The tan car's been traded in on a white one."

I twisted around for a look. "I'd forgotten all about them. I'd have thought they'd lose us in the confusion at my apartment."

"They probably had your place staked out, too, and followed me in your car."

"I suppose they plan on dining with us," I said in a crisp, irritated tone.

"Maybe, but if the restaurant's crowded, they may stay in the car."

A few minutes later, we pulled into the restaurant parking lot, and I noticed with supreme satisfaction the joint was almost full. The other white car had to circle around until finally finding a space toward the back—a country mile from where Matt had parked. The two men inside made no effort to get out.

"Wanna send them a care package?" Matt asked as we walked in the front doors.

"No. Let 'em starve."

We had to wait a few minutes before being seated. When the waitress appeared, both Matt and I ordered iced tea. I wouldn't have minded a glass of wine but decided this would do. I read the menu and tried to decide how to phrase my next question. The waitress brought our drinks. I took a big swallow and then wrapped my hands around the glass, the cool condensation wetting my fingers.

I licked my lips, but Matt beat me to the punch by saying, "I'm an alcoholic. I've been in recovery for two years, but once in a while I backslide. Last night was one of those times."

God, could he read minds? "What happened?"

"I drank to deal with stress. The last few days have been stressful. I left the office last night and instead of going home, walked down to Beale Street. I wanted a drink bad. I should have called my sponsor but didn't. One drink turned into two, two into four, and the next thing I knew, I woke up on the couch in my office reception area."

"You're lucky you weren't mugged or worse. Does this kind of thing happen often?"

"No. It's only happened twice. The first time was shortly after I started going to meetings, and then again last night."

I rubbed my hands up and down the cold, slippery surface of my glass and bit my lip. I needed a sober private investigator—not a...I couldn't even bring myself to think the word.

"Matt, I lived with an alcoholic and substance abuser for nine years. I'm not sure I can sustain even a business relationship with a..." I hesitated.

"A drunk?"

I nodded. Tears welled in my eyes.

Matt placed his hands over mine, stopping their restless movement. His warm fingers breathed life back into my cold ones.

"Theresa, I can't guarantee it won't happen again. It might, but you have my word I'll try my best."

I looked at his hands, strong and sturdy with long fingers and clean, well-cared-for nails, then matched his steady gaze with my eyes.

"I guess that will have to do. Maybe keeping busy with my case will help."

"Having something constructive to focus on is

always better than wallowing in self-pity."

Much to my disappointment, he released my hands as the waitress came to take our order. We both chose grilled salmon, baked potatoes, and a salad.

As our server turned to leave, Matt said, "Bring the lady a glass of Chardonnay, would you?"

I looked up in surprise as she left.

"It's all right. Other people's drinking doesn't bother me, and you look like you could use it."

"I'm not a prig. I don't disapprove of drinking, just…" I couldn't finish.

"Drunks," he said. I nodded. "Let's get off this subject, shall we? Tell me about yourself before your involvement with the Garrett family."

The bus boy brought a basket of warm rolls and some plates. Matt buttered one and handed it to me before doing the same for himself. I bit in and enjoyed the hot, melting butter as I chewed. I swallowed and chased it with a gulp of tea.

"There's not much to tell. I'm thirty-one years old and was born in Jackson, Mississippi. My mother was only seventeen when she had me. I was one of those 'oops' pregnancies. My father's name was Russell Bennett. Never met him and Mom refused to talk about him. I guess he lives in Jackson. We moved to Walls when I was eight."

The waitress arrived with my wine. I took a tiny sip and attacked another roll. I didn't like talking about my childhood. It had been depressing.

"How did you like Walls?"

I shrugged. "It was all right. A trip to the local discount store in Southaven was a big deal. We lived in a grubby trailer park up on a ridge not too far from the highway. I used to sit on the hill and watch the cars, wondering where the people were going in such a hurry."

"What did your mother do?"

"She had a lot of low-paying jobs. Mom may not have graduated from high school, but she did her best to take care of me. I don't ever remember being hungry or going without proper clothing, although I think some of them may have come from a thrift store."

I knew I sounded defensive but couldn't help it. I hadn't known we'd been considered white trash until I was a teenager. The term still hurt.

"No other relatives to help?"

"I think my grandparents threw Mom out when she got pregnant, because I never saw them. Other than my aunt, that's it." I shook my head and sipped some more wine. "When Mom died, I couldn't wait to get out of the trailer park. It's ironic that in most of those nine years I spent with Danny, I wished I'd never left."

"How did your mother die?"

"Car accident. She was coming home from work and lost control of her car on a rain-slicked street. I was twenty."

I wanted to cry but swallowed instead. I hadn't thought about my mother in a long time. We'd had the usual up and down mother-daughter relationship. Her death had carved out a little piece of my heart. I hadn't realized how depressing my childhood had been until I moved to Memphis. The memories choked me. I didn't want to talk anymore.

"Enough about me. Tell me about your work—the real work, not the Hollywood stuff."

He buttered another roll and finished his tea,

rattling the ice cubes in the glass. Someone promptly refilled it.

"There's not much to tell. It's a living—most of the time."

"Did your drinking affect your work?"

"Big time. When my boozing was at its worst, I let things slide, which is why my office is in one of the less desirable parts of town. I lost clients and a large chunk of my business reputation. Both are hard to get back."

"What kind of investigations do you do?" I asked.

"I started out investigating insurance fraud, mostly automobile-accident-related injuries. I used to stake out claimants with a video camera and try to catch them jogging or jumping on a trampoline."

"Good heavens, do people really do that?"

He grinned. "People will do anything to scam an insurance company. One day a friend asked me if I'd help him out. He suspected his wife of cheating on him. I did, she was, and he paid me a cool six hundred dollars for a couple of day's work. He told a friend, and before I knew it, I was making more money moonlighting than at my legitimate job. I quit the insurance company and hung out my sign."

"I'd feel a little creepy spying on people, especially in a motel or something."

"Divorce surveillance is only one aspect of the job."

"Who cheats the most?" I asked, fascinated by this Hollywood glamorized profession.

"Doctors. They work strange hours and have the most money to get away with it. I also do missing persons, deadbeat fathers, and skip traces. I've been a process server on occasion, but the most lucrative and least time consuming is mate-checking."

"What's that?" I'd never heard of it before.

"Men and women hire me to do background checks on their future spouses or the person they're dating."

"I should have known about this nine years ago. I could have saved myself a lot of pain." I tried to laugh, even though it was no joke. "What do you look for?"

He smiled, the action crinkling the corners of his eyes. My heart did that funny little flip-flop again.

"Older clients want to know about health issues. Younger ones are more interested in marital status. And all of them want a glimpse into finances."

"It sounds cold and predatory."

"It can be, but there are a lot of liars out there. Wouldn't you like to know if your most recent boyfriend was married? I might like to know if the woman claiming undying love really had her eye on my bank account. A little bit of information, a few hours on the internet, and I make several hundred dollars."

I sat back, startled when the waitress placed my food in front of me. I'd been so engrossed I hadn't seen her arrive.

The fish smelled delicious, and I ignored cholesterol warnings by dumping both butter and sour cream on my potato. Matt did the same, and when he raised his fork to his mouth, his hand no longer shook. The image of his mouth on mine flashed through my mind.

Girl, don't think along those lines. Ain't gonna happen.

I concentrated on my food. Distractions at a time like this had no business on the schedule. I looked up from my plate occasionally to see Matt's gaze on me.

He had a look in his eyes that said he might be having the same thoughts. Or maybe not. It could have been wishful thinking.

We spoke little during the meal. The longer the silence, the more I became aware of him. I stared at his face, his shoulders, and his chest in between bites, and every once in a while, our glances met, then slid away. The meal took forever and yet ended far too soon.

The waitress cleared away the dishes and brought the check. Matt laid his credit card on top of it, winking. He did a lot of that. It was kind of an endearing habit.

"This one's on me," he said.

I tried to keep my reply light. "Save the receipt."

"I've already started a file."

Our server took the card and returned a couple of minutes later. Matt signed while I polished off the last of my wine and then drained the rest of the tea.

We slid out of the booth. His hand settled in the small of my back as we threaded our way past the diners waiting for tables. I almost yelped when a surge of heat gushed through me. The reaction was unexpected. I bit my lip and took several deep breaths.

Get a grip, Theresa. You're acting like a teenager.

I had enough to deal with and didn't need an unpredicted shot of sexual awareness. Matt opened the car door, and I slipped in. My fingers shook, and it took me three attempts to fasten the seatbelt.

"I see our friends are still waiting," he remarked as he got behind the wheel.

Damn. I'd forgotten about them. "I wonder what they'd do if we peeled out of here and took off at a high rate of speed."

"They'd go back to the motel and wait. We have to return sometime." He laughed lightly. "They know they've been seen. It's all part of the game."

"Well, it's a game I don't like playing." At least this conversation took my mind off other matters. "How long will they do this?"

"Until they're sure you're not about to run off to Hong Kong or another state."

We drove a few blocks where Matt pulled into a strip mall and stopped in front of a chain ice cream parlor.

"Come on. I need to indulge my sweet tooth."

I chuckled when the cops parked in front of a donut shop.

This particular ice cream emporium always rendered me indecisive. All those choices and every one of them sounded good. I finally settled on a scoop each of Mocha Delight and Mint Chocolate Chip in a cup covered with marshmallow sauce. Matt chose three scoops of Chocolate Chip in a waffle cone. We found a table and sat.

I spooned a big glob of Mocha Delight and sauce into my mouth. My taste buds exploded, and my saliva glands warped into overdrive by sending a sharp pain zinging to just below my ears.

I made the mistake of lifting my gaze to Matt as he licked a huge hunk of ice cream off onto his tongue. My heart almost stopped beating, and my mind crashed into wild, lascivious thoughts. I looked into my cup and ate faster, gobbling like a hog, no longer tasting the flavors. Instead, I imagined tasting the flavors of Matt Summers.

Oh, this is not good—not good at all.

I scraped the bottom of the cup, licked the spoon, and then dumped them in the nearest trash receptacle.

Matt shoved the last of his cone into his mouth, smiling at me through the crunches. He licked the remains from his lips, causing me to quiver inside.

"That hit the spot," he said.

"You have no idea how much I enjoyed it."

He wiped a small dribble of ice cream from the corner of my mouth with his finger and popped it onto the tip of his tongue.

"Sure I do."

We both laughed and exited the store. My gaze wandered to the donut shop. The white car had gone.

"What happened to my shadows?"

"Probably waiting back at the motel. Where else would we go?"

The drive back ended too quickly, but I felt better able to deal with my ragged emotions. I guess the sugar helped. Matt walked me to the door.

He didn't touch me but gazed into my eyes with a look that held me spellbound.

We leaned closer to each other, and I closed my eyes, anticipating a kiss, when something whacked the door above my head. The next thing I knew, Matt had thrown me to the pavement by the front bumper of my car, knocking the breath from me.

"Stay down," he barked.

Like I could go anywhere. I couldn't breathe, let alone move. I finally sucked in a lungful of air and raised my head. Matt crouched beside me, a gun in his hand. Where had *that* come from?

"What—what the hell?" I managed to gasp.

"Someone took a shot at us."

"Are you sure?"

"Didn't you hear it? It hit the door less than a foot above your head."

"That was a shot? Why would someone do that?"

He didn't answer but pulled out his cell phone and dialed 9-1-1. He gave the pertinent information to the operator. My mind still refused to believe it. I'd been otherwise occupied and didn't even hear the report.

Matt hung up and grabbed the room key out of my hand. Keeping low, he unlocked the door, dragged me into a stooped position, and then shoved me through it.

"Stay inside."

"Get in here. They could shoot again," I shouted.

"They're probably gone, but do as I say until the cops get here."

He closed the door, leaving me sitting on the floor, wondering what kind of a maniac lurked in the darkness outside.

Chapter Four

The cops arrived, but their take on the shooting didn't fill me with confidence. "Yeah, we've had trouble ever since the mall was bulldozed. It's popular with drug dealers. Sounds like a business transaction gone bad."

"In that case, wouldn't there have been more than just one shot?" Matt demanded.

"Who knows? We'll go take a look, but I wouldn't hold my breath. Probably long gone by now. We've been busy lately. There's been a rash of carjackings on the east side in the last couple of weeks. We got pulled off one to come here."

Matt turned and looked at me. "Go pack. I have no intention of leaving you here alone tonight. We'll come back in the morning, get your car, and check out. Hurry. I don't want to give them another target once the cruisers have gone."

I didn't want to be alone in this cheesy motel after a shooting either.

The police investigated but found nothing. Matt spoke with the officers a few more minutes and then climbed in the car.

I sat in the passenger's seat, my arms hugging my chest, trying to stop the nervous tremors rippling through me. I hadn't counted on this turn of events.

"Where are you taking me?"

"My place."

Matt's home. I couldn't say the prospect made me unhappy.

"Where do you live?"

"Germantown. I bought a nice four-two about ten years ago when I was flush. It needed work, so I got it for a song. Its best features are a pool and a raised deck."

"Sounds wonderful. You must love it."

"I do. I recently put a lot of sweat equity into it."

I didn't need to ask why. It was his form of therapy. I cleaned after a minor beating. I shivered, remembering those frenzied hours dusting and vacuuming. A dirty coffee cup in the sink would often be the excuse for Danny to take out his fury and frustrations on me.

"Are you all right?" he asked. "There's a jacket in the back seat."

I shook my head. "No, I'm fine. I guess the last few days haven't been the best of my life. Do you think this was just a drug deal gone bad?"

We stopped at a red light. Matt ran his hand through his hair and then sighed.

"I don't know. Maybe I've got an overactive imagination. Either way, I feel better about you staying with me. It's a quiet neighborhood, and any strangers lurking around will be noticed."

"Including cops in white cars?"

The light changed, and he stepped on the accelerator. "Including cops in any color car. If you stay inside or in the backyard, they won't be able to see you."

"It sounds like I'm a prisoner again." He didn't

answer, and a little dart of anger pulsated through me. "I'm not, am I?"

"Not what?"

"A prisoner. I want to be able to come and go. I may not have that privilege much longer."

"This shooting has me spooked. I'd rather you'd not go gallivanting off."

"But I have to see my lawyer and go to school."

"No school." His voice was sharp.

"But there's only another few weeks left in the semester. I have to take finals, or I'll fail. I've worked too hard to do that."

"Then go there tomorrow and ask for a leave of absence. Explain the situation. See if they'll give you an opportunity to make it up later."

"You mean from my prison cell?" I enjoyed those classes, even math. "And what about my job at the university bookstore? I need the money. I have rent and bills to pay, especially now. I've just given birth to a private investigator."

Matt turned into a quiet residential area. The wide streets and mature trees spelled stability and a firm anchor for raising families. We turned right again into a cove. Matt pulled up in the second drive on the left. I got out and did a quick survey in the glow of the lone streetlight in the rear of the cul-de-sac.

The house was a traditional red brick and white clapboard two-story with low maintenance shrubbery under the windows.

He grabbed a couple of bags, and I followed him up the walk to the small front stoop.

"This is lovely," I said.

"Thanks. I like it."

He opened the door, and we entered a white marble foyer. Matt dropped the bags and said, "Would you like something to drink? Water or iced tea?"

"I guess iced tea." I followed him to the back of the house. Suddenly nervous and uncomfortable, I gazed around the kitchen. "Nice layout." My voice sounded stiff, unnatural.

"The kitchen might be a little small, but I have no problems with it," Matt replied in a relaxed tone.

"Do you cook?"

"Only if I can nuke it, scoop it out of a can, or throw it on the grill."

My nervousness fled, and I had to laugh. It was so male. He laughed with me. It had a comforting sound. Weariness crept over me.

"Please don't think me rude, but it's been quite a day. I think I'll skip the tea and go to bed. I didn't get much sleep in jail."

"Sure. Follow me."

We picked up my bags and climbed the stairs. He led me into a room and flipped on the light.

"This is quiet. It overlooks the backyard." He opened the closet door. "Make yourself at home. Bath's next to you. If you need anything, I'm just across the hall. I'll see you in the morning."

"Goodnight, and thank you."

He smiled, walked across the hall into the master bedroom, and closed the door. I retreated and did the same.

A queen-sized bed with an old-fashioned quilt and lots of pillows called my name.

I found my toothbrush, scurried into the bathroom, then returned to shed my clothes and pull my nightgown over my head. I slipped between the covers, sighing. The clean, fresh scent of recently washed linen tickled my nose. I breathed in and slowly released my breath.

For the first time in days, I felt safe and tossed in a little hope for good measure. Matt slept only a few feet away. I drifted off to sleep only to awake suddenly.

I shivered. Another bad dream. I'd had several since Danny's death. I guess the shock of seeing my ex dead brought them on. The nightmare had been so vivid, so real. Danny stood at the foot of my bed, that evil gleam in his eyes telling me I didn't have long to live. And then, suddenly, the gun was in my hand. I have no clue how it got there, but dreams have a habit of not making sense. Then I shot him. A look of total astonishment and shock spread across his face as he muttered, "Bitch," before collapsing onto the floor.

I got out of bed and walked softly to the bathroom, rummaging in my cosmetics bag until finding the bottle of sleeping pills my therapist had prescribed.

Just one. That's all I need. Just one.

****

I slept the rest of the night, not awakening until after nine. I poked my head out of the door. The inviting aroma of coffee wafted up the stairs.

I showered and then donned a pair of jeans and a T-shirt. All I wanted was that coffee.

The kitchen was empty. I poured a mug, then added cream and sugar. Through the eating area picture window, I spied Matt sitting at a table on the covered, raised deck, nursing his own mug. I pushed the door open and joined him.

He looked up, smiling. "Good morning. How did

you sleep? Any nightmares?"

"Better than expected and not a nightmare in sight," I lied, pulling out a chair, and sat, taking a sip of coffee.

"Good. I've been thinking the cops were right. The shooting was probably the result of a bad drug deal."

"At least it gave those cops following me something constructive to do."

"I'd have thought they would have shown their faces once the cruisers arrived."

"You mean they didn't?"

"Nope. Not a plainclothes cop in sight—all uniforms."

"Bastards. I can't believe they just sat there during all the commotion."

"When we left, they were gone."

He resumed staring at the pool, its blue water sparkling in the morning sun. I didn't like the frown.

"Is something wrong—besides, the obvious, I mean?"

"Those cops *should* have been there. I'm trying to figure out why they weren't." Matt paused for a moment, fished in his pocket, and placed a new cell phone next to my mug. "Here. In all the excitement last night, I forgot to give this to you. I've already entered my home, office, and cell numbers on speed dial. You can add in your lawyer and anybody else. It's prepaid. You've got five hundred minutes for the next couple of months. After that you can subscribe to a plan if you want."

I picked it up and wondered how long it would take me to learn how to use a smartphone.

"I can't imagine who I'd call other than you or

Warshovsky, which reminds me, I guess I should tell him what happened."

"Might not be a bad idea." Matt drained his mug and stood. "How about some breakfast? I'm a whiz at breakfast."

I had to laugh at the earnest tone of his voice. "What's on the menu?"

"What do you want?"

"Something at least as good as Wonderful Waffles."

He grinned. "Pancakes with sausage or bacon?"

"Add a couple of eggs along with some fruit—strawberries and whipped cream if you have it."

He gave me a sardonic look. "I'm sorry, ma'am, but there's been a run on strawberries and whipped cream this morning."

"What's happening to this restaurant? It used to be so customer friendly."

"It's hard to get good help." He laughed and entered the kitchen.

I gazed around the backyard and sipped my coffee while he whipped up the meal.

The deck overlooked a patio and the elliptical-shaped pool. Blooming shrubs grew along the privacy fence. Two giant oak trees shaded the area to my right. I wondered how much had been planted by Matt.

I could get used to this.

I stretched and yawned, eyeing the lounge chairs on the patio. I'd love to spend the day sunbathing and swimming, but the real world intruded. I needed to call my lawyer.

I reentered the house and sniffed. Ah—bacon. My stomach grumbled, and I hurried upstairs to retrieve the card Warshovsky had given me, finally finding it in the bottom of my backpack.

Back in the kitchen, Matt looked up from the stove while I poured another cup of coffee.

"Breakfast will be ready in a couple of minutes."

"No hurry. I have to call my lawyer anyway."

I wandered outside, picked up my new phone, and dialed.

"Public defender's office, how may I help you?"

"Is Ben Warshovsky in? This is Theresa Lennox."

"Are you a client?"

"Yes."

"Please hold."

I listened to classical music as background noise before he came on the line.

"Miss Lennox?"

"Yes. I'd like to come in today, if you have time. There are a few things you should know."

He sighed, and I heard the sound of pages being ruffled as though he searched through an appointment book.

"I have an appointment at one and am due in court at two. I suppose I can squeeze you in around eleven thirty."

Don't rupture yourself. It's only a murder charge.

I wanted to say it but didn't need to piss him off. After all, idiot or not, he was defending me.

"That's fine." The clown hung up without another word.

Matt brought out two plates laden with pancakes, eggs, bacon, and sausage. I spread a generous amount of butter on the pancakes and then covered them with syrup. I crammed a forkful into my mouth and closed my eyes in bliss. I didn't need to chew—they melted on their own.

Two link sausages and a slice of bacon followed. I alternated among pancakes, eggs, and meat, occasionally washing it all down with the coffee.

Matt grinned. "You pack away more food than any woman I've ever known. If you're not careful, your scale will soon beg for mercy or go on strike."

I stuck my tongue out and replied, "You try jailhouse food. It sucks. I'm going to enjoy the real McCoy as long and as often as I can."

"Did you get a hold of your lawyer?"

"I have an appointment at eleven thirty. I'll tell him what happened last night and that I've hired you. I'll also give him the names of Danny's friends."

"Can the man at the shooting range verify you were there the night before the murder?"

"I said hello when I entered and had to sign in before they let me on the range, so I'd hope he'd remember me."

"Good. What are you going to do after your meeting?"

"Go to school, see how I did on my test, ask if I can have special dispensation regarding finals, and then go see my boss. Maybe he'll give me some extra hours. I need to keep busy. What's on your agenda?"

I stared hard, daring him to object to the job thing. He must have gotten the hint, for he nodded and ate another slice of bacon.

"As soon as we're done here, we'll pick up your car. I'll go into the office, begin tracing Danny's buddies, and work on locating your ex's possible drug supplier, The Juice. You can meet me there if you'd like."

I polished off the breakfast and insisted on helping clean up. When we finished, he left to shower and dress. I needed to change clothes, too, but being female was unable to curb my curiosity and took a quick tour of the downstairs.

The den was done in neutral shades of beige, the only colors being the chocolate brown and orange throw pillows on the sofa and matching chairs. The colors looked masculine, but the furniture style didn't seem like Matt's personality. I visualized him with leather and clean lines, not this soft plushiness. The living and dining rooms also had a feminine touch.

I climbed the stairs and poked my head into the master bedroom, half expecting Matt to walk out of the bath with raised eyebrows. The shower still ran, so I had a brief moment to peek at where he slept.

Now this is a man's room. A cobalt-blue comforter covered the king-sized bed. Matching draperies contrasted with the cream-colored walls and off-white carpet. The dark, sleek furniture had modern lines. I knew he wasn't married but wondered if a woman had done the decorating downstairs.

He had set up one of the other bedrooms as an office, and the last one had the usual bed, dresser, and nightstand. It didn't look as if it received much use.

I glanced at my watch. I needed to hustle and chose a pair of conservative, navy-blue slacks and a long-sleeved, yellow blouse. The latter might be warm for May, but it looked classy, and I wanted to look classy today.

I grabbed my purse, smoothed my hair, and then joined Matt in the foyer, ready to confront my lawyer who believed me guilty of murder.

****

I gazed across the parking lot to the old mall property. In the bright sunlight, I saw acres of weed-choked land with the occasional glimpse of concrete or asphalt peeking through to show the remains of roadways and parking spaces. The ground was flatter than this morning's pancakes.

I shivered, remembering the loud whack of the bullet drilling the door above my head. I glanced toward my room. The solitary crater stood out, a black hole in an otherwise ordinary, if dirty, white door. Given the circumstances, the Be Our Guest hadn't charged us for the room.

"Are you all right?" Matt asked from his car as he waited for me to get in.

"Yeah, I'm fine," I muttered, sliding into the driver's seat. I silently cursed my trembling fingers as they fumbled to insert the key. The shooting, impersonal or not, gave me the jitters now that I had returned to the scene.

The car started, and I backed out of the space, waving as Matt turned one way headed for his office and me the other toward Warshovsky's.

I took the elevator to the public defender's office on the sixth floor and, when the doors opened, thought I'd gone straight to hell.

The waiting area was packed with people, some of whom needed a close encounter with soap and water. The babble of voices, most of them swearing and demanding to see an attorney, hammered against my eardrums.

I battled my way to the reception desk, weaving around frustrated people filling out forms. I shouldered two arguing women planted in front of the desk out of the way, ignoring their hostile glares.

"My name is Theresa Lennox. I have an eleven-thirty appointment with Ben Warshovsky."

The receptionist checked her appointment book. "I'll tell him you're here. Have a seat."

"Where?" I gazed around the crowded arena.

"Hey, how come she gets in and we don't?" one of the women I'd pushed aside yelled.

"Yeah, we've been waiting over two hours. She just walks in, and you're letting her go ahead of us?" the other one snapped.

The receptionist rolled her eyes and gave them a go-to-hell stare, pointing to the open book.

"Ah…point…ment," she said in a snotty voice. "She had the intelligence to call for one. You just waltzed in unannounced. I told you. Your lawyer is in court this morning and may not be back until late afternoon. Now you can either make an appointment or wait. It's up to you."

"It ain't fair. We've got just as much right…"

I tuned out the bitching and finding no place to sit, stood over near the stairwell, trying not to breathe in the noxious smell of body odor.

Luckily, I didn't wait long. A petite, dark-haired woman pushed her way through the crowd. "Theresa Lennox?"

"Here." I raised my hand and stepped forward.

"Follow me."

I trailed after her until we rounded a corner and

strode down a blessedly empty corridor.

"This place is a madhouse," I said.

"Are you kidding? This is a *good* day." She paused in front of a door and then opened it. "Ben, Miss Lennox is here."

I stepped around her and saw my lawyer seated at his desk inside a cramped cubicle. Three other attorneys occupied similar space in the room. Two jabbered on their phones, and the other had a client. It didn't look as though privacy was of much importance.

"Have a seat. I'll be with you in a moment. Let me finish my lunch." Short and skinny, he reminded me of that TV character, Barney Fife, from the old *Andy Griffith Show*.

I sat in a hard, plastic chair and watched him finish a Big Mac and fries, then slurp the last of his Coke. He tossed the containers into a wastepaper basket and belched, not offering an apology.

"Now, Miss Lennox, what is it you need to see me about?"

I took a deep breath and told him what had occurred since my release the day before.

"Good move. Hire a PI, and it looks like you're not guilty. That could help, but I still think your best bet is to plead to the lesser charge."

I couldn't believe it. "I didn't do it. How many times do I have to tell you?"

"Miss Lennox, I'm your lawyer. Anything you tell me is in confidence. I can appreciate your anxiety, but just tell me the truth of how you killed your ex, and we can work from there."

I resisted the urge to wrap my fingers around his scrawny throat and squeeze until his eyeballs popped out.

"I *am* telling you the truth. I came home and found Danny dead on my bedroom floor."

"You know, as a battered woman, we could claim self-defense or battered wife syndrome. It's gotten more than one wife or girlfriend off the hook."

"Mr. Warshovsky, you are not listening to me. I am innocent!"

He jotted notes on a legal pad. "Okay, tell me again how you spent the morning of the murder and make it quick. I have another client due in twenty minutes."

"Oh, well, don't let me hold you up. Have you ever won a case?"

"Of course. It's my job to get my clients off just as it's the DA's job to put them behind bars. Why?"

"Because you don't seem to give a rat's ass about me or my case. You have an honest to God victim of the justice system here, and you don't seem to care."

He pointed to the files overflowing his tiny world. Manila folders sat on the desk, the shelves, the floors, and every other horizontal surface in sight.

"Lady, take a look. You are one of over fifty cases pending. I don't have time to care about your guilt or innocence one way or the other. All I want is a fair shot at getting you off or having you accept a plea bargain so I can call one more case closed. Now let me hear your alibi story again."

I'd had enough. My stomach churned, and I trembled with temper. I wanted to cry. Hopeless. This was hopeless. I stood and clenched my fists at my side.

"Mr. Warshovsky, I'm done talking. You're fired."

I turned, stomped out of his office, ran down the hallway, and back through the crowd in the waiting area. Not bothering with the elevator, I pushed open the door to the stairwell, stumbling and clutching the handrail as tears flowed down my cheeks.

God Almighty, what was I going to do now?

****

I spent several minutes in my car wondering if I had been impulsive in firing Warshovsky. The sorry son of a bitch might have been a jerk, but he was better than no lawyer at all. A different public defender would be just as busy and perhaps as uncaring, and the money to hire a private attorney didn't exist. On the other hand, if he wasn't prepared to believe me, then I wanted no part of him.

I slammed my fists on the steering wheel and shouted, "Dammit!" Discouragement settled on my shoulders like an overcoat in July.

I inhaled a deep breath, refusing to give in to the negative. I'd go to the university and then to Matt's office. Maybe he could help find a new attorney.

Noontime traffic was heavy. I maneuvered my way east from downtown and out Central to the University of Memphis campus. I finally found a parking spot and headed to the math building. The grades for the math test I'd taken should be posted by now.

I entered the building and walked upstairs to the bulletin board outside my professor's office. I found the results and winced when I saw the fifty-six next to my registration number. I wanted to apply for a scholarship next year and couldn't afford a *D* or even a *C*. My spirits tumbled. *Damn, can't anything go right for me?*

I hurried across campus to the administration building and the dean's office to request a leave of absence until my legal troubles ended. I explained the situation to his secretary and then sat down to wait. Fifteen minutes later, I entered Dean Wilmont's lair.

"Please be seated, Miss Lennox. I'll be with you in a moment." His voice was ice cold, and he didn't look up from what he was doing.

I sat and tried to steady my trembling hands, not liking the feel of this.

He finished signing several papers, leaned back, and frowned. His fingers fiddled with a pen, and he declined to meet my gaze, further increasing my anxiety.

"You wished to see me about a leave of absence? Finals begin in a few weeks."

"Yes, I know, but I am involved in a situation—"

"The murder of your ex-husband," he interrupted.

I launched into explanations when he held up his hand and stopped me. "I'm glad you dropped by, Miss Lennox. I was going to call you this evening. The university has a certain image to uphold, and I'm afraid having an accused murderess on campus is not the sort of image we wish to convey."

I rubbed a hand across my forehead. "I'm not sure I understand, sir. Aren't I innocent until proven guilty?"

"That is not the point. There have been complaints. Miss Lennox, I'm afraid that for the good of the school, I'm suspending you until a jury decides your fate."

My breath stopped somewhere in my chest. The room receded and darkened. I swallowed hard and fought the nausea clawing at me. I refused to faint. I also refused to accept his words.

"Dean Wilmont, this is *not fair*. I've worked hard and have excellent grades. You can't toss me out like this."

"I'm sorry, Miss Lennox, but the decision is not mine alone. Other parties are involved. If you are found not guilty, then you can reapply."

Other parties? What the hell was he talking about? Then I understood.

The University of Memphis was the last university Danny attended. He'd managed to either flunk out or get thrown out of Ole Miss, Tennessee, and Alabama. Memphis had been his last shot, and the Garretts had pumped beaucoup bucks into the institution to ensure his graduation. They still contributed heavily to the school.

"My in-laws are behind this, aren't they?"

"Mr. and Mrs. Garrett had nothing to do with this decision in spite of their generosity." His voice took on a pompous tone.

I wanted to kick him. The son of a bitch lied. I saw Diana's fine hand in this. Hamilton would never have thought of it.

I rose. "Dean Wilmont, you tell my ex-witch-in-law I will not take this lying down. I'll sue her and the university if I'm not allowed to continue my education."

"Good day, Miss Lennox," he replied in a clipped, hard voice.

I whirled and strode from the room. Tears once again formed in my eyes, but I held them in check. Diana Garrett was *not* going to make me cry.

Outside, I slipped my sunglasses on and walked to my place of employment, The Campus Notes Bookstore. An entire semester was down the drain, and while I doubted I'd ever win a lawsuit against my former in-laws, I could certainly put them on notice I would not stand for this kind of treatment. And as soon as I found another lawyer, I'd do it, too.

I lifted my chin. *I won't let a Garrett beat me again, in any way.*

The hot sun pounded on my head as I walked the four blocks to the bookstore. Sweat trickled down my back, and I regretted trying to look classy in a long-sleeved shirt. What good had it done?

I pushed open the doors to The Campus Notes and wound my way past students lined up, buying those last-minute study aids. I turned the corner into the break room. Two of the clerks stopped their conversation to stare at me. I grabbed a soda out of the fridge and chugged it.

"God, I needed that."

"Uh, we'd better get back to work," one said, rising.

"Yeah, I guess so." They skittered out of the room, giving me a wide berth.

Get used to it. A murder charge doesn't invite casual chit-chat, even among co-workers.

I wet a paper towel and daubed my face. The air conditioning and the water helped cool my overheated skin. My boss, Harry Nobles, came in.

"Uh, hi, Theresa. Could you come into my office for a moment?"

"Sure. I need to get my schedule and wondered if you could give me some extra hours?"

He shifted his weight from foot to foot and jerked his head down the hallway. "Let's talk in private."

I followed him. Dread, like in Dean Wilmont's office, crept over me. I knew what he was going to say but pretended I didn't.

"Close the door, Theresa." He sat down and looked everywhere except my eyes. "Um, Theresa, please understand that this isn't my idea, but the bookstore is on campus property and owned by the university. I've been instructed to—that is, I have to…"

I felt sorry for him. It wasn't his fault. "I'm fired, right?"

He nodded. "I'm sorry, Theresa. The word came from the dean's office this morning. I argued, but they wouldn't listen. They aren't being fair, and I told them so, but…" He shrugged.

I took a shaky breath. "It's all right, Harry. I don't blame you."

"Maybe when this is all over, you can come back."

"Yeah, maybe." I turned and opened the door with a trembling hand.

"Theresa. For what it's worth, I don't think you did it."

If I looked at him, I'd burst into tears, so I stared straight ahead and said, "Thank you, Harry," then walked out.

I retraced my footsteps to the parking lot. I wanted to scream at the injustice of it all but couldn't whip up the energy to do so. I remembered nothing of my trip from the bookstore to the parking lot. I got behind the wheel and sobbed.

I should have realized this might be a consequence of Danny's death. There are always consequences.

Yet in spite of my past, I was an optimist. I just believe everything will work out for the best and am always surprised when it doesn't. Danny was scum, and I had no problem with him being dead. He deserved it. But most of all, I hoped he was burning in Hell.

In a few short hours, I'd been emotionally stripped naked and left standing in life's center ring with nothing to shield me.

Chapter Five

For the second time in two days, Matt shoved the box of tissues across the desk toward me. I pulled one out and mopped my tears. I thought I'd had myself under control by the time I reached his office, but the minute I opened the door, the water works had turned on again. Between sobs, I told him how my afternoon had gone.

"You *have* been shit on today, haven't you?"

"I can't imagine what else could happen," I wailed. "Can they revoke my bail?"

"Only if you break the law, your bond agreement, or they find new evidence. Come on, honey. Stop crying and let's get you a new lawyer."

He was right. I needed to focus on the important things. Tears never solved problems. I blotted my cheeks and blew my nose.

"I guess I'll have to get another public defender. I can't afford a good attorney, especially now. I'm not even sure I can afford you," I said between sniffles.

"Don't worry about me. There must be a women's advocate lawyer out there willing to work pro bono or at a reduced fee for the privilege of humiliating the Garretts. Rich and powerful can make a lot of enemies." He paused, his brow wrinkled. "I wonder…" he murmured.

"Wonder what?"

"I had a lawyer client several years ago. He loved tweaking the establishment and fighting for the underdog."

"Who?"

"Jerricus Monroe."

"Jerricus Monroe? Are you kidding? I see him on TV all the time. He probably charges an arm and a leg. He'd never take me on."

There likely wasn't anyone who *hadn't* heard of Jerricus Monroe. His money was older than the Worthington's, and his law firm the most prestigious in Memphis. A publicity hound, his face often appeared in front of the cameras as he defended both high society criminals along with the lowest of the low. Slick and eloquent, he had a high acquittal rate, and his services were much in demand. He chose cases guaranteed to give him maximum exposure. Prosecutors hated his guts.

"If a case is really juicy, Jerricus has been known to work pro bono," Matt replied.

"I don't think I like being called juicy," I said, bristling.

"Honey, you're as juicy as they come. This is right up his alley—high society scandal, wife beating, murder, and a possible gubernatorial candidate thrown in for good measure. God, he won't be able to resist."

Matt pulled up a contact list on his computer and then dialed a number.

"Hello, my name is Matthew Summers. I'm a private investigator who did some work for Mr. Monroe a few years ago. I'd like speak with him if he's available…Matthew Summers…yes, I'll hold."

He grinned at me, looking confident.

My spirits lifted. "Do you think he'll remember you?"

"He'd better. The work I did saved him a bundle on his last two divorces." He tapped a pencil on his desk while he waited, then ceased the action and gave his attention back to the phone. "No, I don't mind waiting. You might tell him I have a case with his name written all over it."

"Do you really think he'll take the case? I can't pay him a dime," I said.

"Pro bono means he'll do it for free, and if he's in the mood to present a helping-the-little-guy image to the press, he will."

Several minutes ticked by. I got a couple of sodas out of the fridge in the reception area and tried to quell my racing heart.

God, let him say yes. I couldn't take another disappointment today.

Matt sat up straight. "Jerricus, Matt Summers here. How're you doing…? Good to hear it. I know you're busy, so I'll cut to the chase. I have a client who just lost her public defender and needs an attorney…At the moment, murder two…Theresa Lennox, formerly Mrs. Daniel Garrett."

Matt laughed and winked at me. That sounded and looked encouraging.

"Yeah, that one. The evidence is circumstantial. He beat the crap out of her on a regular basis. Mommy and Daddy always managed to keep it under wraps."

I cringed inwardly. I sounded pathetic.

"I do, too, and they aren't even subtle about it. There's a small problem. Miss Lennox just got fired, courtesy of her in-laws. She has next to nothing." Matt smiled and nodded. "I understand. Two o'clock on Monday sounds fine. She'll be there—and Jerricus, thanks."

Hope surged through me. I could use some good news for a change.

"Oh, and one more thing. The press is camped outside Miss Lennox's door. Can you do anything…? An apartment complex called the Quince Gardens. It's on Quince Avenue in East Memphis…Thanks." Matt listened for a few more seconds. "Be glad to help out. What's her name? I'll check on it and get right back to you. Give me a few hours. I should have an answer…Hey, no problem."

He hung up and scribbled something on a pad of paper.

"He'll meet you at his office on Monday at two. Be on time. The only person allowed to keep others waiting is Jerricus Monroe."

"He's agreed to represent me?" I couldn't believe my luck.

"No, he's agreed to talk to you. He'll make his decision then, but I could almost hear him smacking his lips at the possibilities. Tell him your story. He'll jump on it. Besides, he owes me, and Jerricus always pays his debts."

"How does he owe you?"

"A few years ago one of his friends recommended me for some personal work. Jerricus, never the most discreet of people, had a liaison with a woman in Nashville during a convention and was being blackmailed. He knew he'd been set up and hired me to find out who'd done it."

"Let me guess. The woman had a boyfriend."

Matt grinned. "Nope, a girlfriend—Mrs. Jerricus Monroe."

"You're kidding. She set up her own husband?"

"Mrs. Monroe's little friend had expensive tastes, so the two of them thought they'd fleece Jerricus out of as much as they could, then she'd divorce him, pocket her settlement as per the prenup, and live happily ever after with her lover."

"Holy shit. What was his reaction?"

"I went with him to his house, produced the evidence, and watched him toss wife number three out the door." Matt chuckled. "She got nothing. The prenup was one of the best, but then Jerricus wrote it. He learned fast. A couple of years later, he hired me again when he suspected wife number four was fooling around."

"Was she?"

"You betcha. He wasted no time divorcing her, too. And just now he's being proactive and asked me to check out his newest lady."

"Mate-checking?"

Matt smiled and nodded. "He's also going to get rid of those reporters at your place. Knowing Jerricus, he'll have a restraining order waving under their noses in less than an hour."

"Thank God. I want to get home. You've been a great host, but I can't stay with you forever."

"I know."

His answer irritated me because quite honestly, I didn't see any reason not to stay with him.

He got up, walked to the file cabinets in the corner, and opened a lower drawer. He bent over to flip through the folders, giving me a good view of his derriere. I'd managed to turn off my overactive imagination most of the day, but now the heat switch flipped to high.

I had spent a great deal of time staring at his face and hands in the past twenty-four hours but had to admit he also had one damned fine ass. The fabric of his slacks stretched across his rear end, and my fingers itched to grab and squeeze.

Since I was in the territory, I let my eyes wander down the backs of his legs. As befitted his six-foot frame, they were long and, I suspected, lean. He wasn't overly muscular, although the broad chest gave him that appearance. Trim described him best.

I knew he was strong. He'd proved that last night when throwing me to the ground after the shot. His reflexes had been panther quick.

He straightened, closed the file drawer, and sat down to work on the computer. I sighed. *Okay, show's over—it's time to get back on track. I don't need a relationship anyway.*

"Matt?"

"Hm-m."

"I have to do something to keep busy. Maybe I could help with the investigation."

"No. Let me handle things. I think it's best if you stay out of sight."

"But I'll go nuts with nothing to do. I'm used to working or studying."

He turned and stared. "Look, Carleen isn't here today. Why don't you go file some of the stuff left on her desk from yesterday? Trust me, as soon as we went to lunch, she was out of here. I've got a couple of hour's worth of investigating to do online. When I'm done, we'll go check out your place. If the press is gone, you can move back in. Okay?" His voice had taken on an impatient tone.

"I suppose so."

I rose and walked into the reception area. He'd sounded as though he couldn't wait to get rid of—or pacify—me, like a troublesome child. I glanced through the door. He was busy and paid no attention to me.

I stuck my tongue out at his back and picked up a file. At least, I'd be doing something.

****

I passed two news vans parked across the street from my apartment complex. Jerricus Monroe had some serious juice. The two vans were a damn sight better than the five of the day before. I was yesterday's news. I slid my Jeep into my usual parking spot. *Home at last.*

I got out and glanced toward the complex entrance. Matt was nowhere in sight and must have gotten hung up in traffic. We'd gone to pick up my things and had driven here separately.

I dropped my suitcase, duffle, and backpack on the small stoop in front of my door and slipped the key into the lock. A honking horn interrupted me as I reached for the door knob. Matt pulled into the spot next to mine.

"Let me go first," he said, exiting the Ford.

"Oh, for Pete's sake, do you think the boogeyman's going to jump out and get me?" I asked tartly, still smarting that he'd allowed me to leave so easily.

I ignored him, opened the door, and stepped through.

A tornado might have done more damage, but not

by much. Someone had trashed the place. The cushions on the sofa and chairs had been slashed, the stuffing pulled out. It covered the floor ankle deep like dirty snow. My coffee and end tables had been rendered into kindling. Every lamp was smashed to smithereens. My TV and stereo resembled gutted junk.

"Oh, my God," I whispered, unable to come to terms with what I saw. "This can't be happening."

Matt shouldered his way past me, gun drawn.

"Get out of here. Call the cops," he ordered.

I heard him but couldn't bring myself to obey.

The dining room furniture had been overturned, the seats of the chairs kicked out. A small secretary had had the doors ripped off, its contents scattered on the carpet.

I shook and had trouble breathing. My ears buzzed. Like an accident on the turnpike, I was unable to look away.

Matt moved quickly through the apartment. He shoved his gun into his slacks' pocket. "We're alone. Jesus, what a mess. I didn't expect to find this."

I took a step toward the bedroom when he laid his hand on my arm.

"I wouldn't. There's nothing left. They even slashed your clothes."

"But—but who? Why? I—I don't…" I couldn't find the words. I was too shocked to cry.

"Did you call the police?"

"Oh. No. I didn't—I will." I sidestepped the remains of my laptop and entered the kitchen, also a mess, to grab the landline. The answering machine lay on the floor. I picked it up. The message received light flashed.

I have no idea why I jabbed the "play" button.

Force of habit, maybe. The first six messages were from newspapers and TV stations, followed by several hang-ups, and a couple of obscene calls.

Matt didn't wait for me to come out of my daze. I heard him on his cell demanding the police come immediately. He joined me as the last message played.

"Like my decorating? Your time's running out, bitch. I want what's mine, and you know what I'm talking about."

The whispering voice sent chills up my spine, and my knees, already shaky, buckled. Matt grabbed and held me upright.

"Come on. Let's get out of here. We'll wait in the car."

I didn't protest and allowed him to guide me through what remained of my life. He kicked the bags I'd left on the stoop out of the way and lowered me into the front seat of his car. I sat numb, barely cognizant of my surroundings, not rousing until the cops arrived. We told them what happened and about the threatening phone call.

"Any idea what the caller was talking about, Miss Lennox?" one of the officers asked.

"None. How did they get in?"

"Patio door. Not even subtle about it. Just smashed it. Do you have a place to stay?"

"She'll be staying with me," Matt said. He gave the policeman his address. "Did the neighbors hear anything?"

"Haven't found anyone who can give us answers yet. We'll do the best we can, but I have to tell you that without an eyewitness, it's going to be hard."

The cop closed his notebook, nodded to me, and

then joined another man who snapped photographs through the front door. I watched the yellow crime scene tape being strung across my stoop—again.

My shock wore off, replaced with sheer blazing anger. It burned in my stomach, worked its way to my lungs, and finally my brain. I catapulted out of the car and screamed at the man's back.

"So what if it's hard? Get your ass out there and find these sonsabitches!"

He turned to stare. Someone tapped me on the shoulder. I whirled and stood eyeball to eyeball with a man. He shoved a microphone under my nose.

"Miss Lennox, what happened? Is it related to the death of your husband? Is it true you'll be using the battered wife syndrome as a defense?"

I doubled up my fist and punched him in the nose. He dropped the mike and staggered back, his hand clapped over his face. Blood dribbled between his fingers.

"Leave me alone!" I raised my fist again.

"Theresa, no!" Matt pulled me away from the gasping reporter.

Diana's actions the night of my arrest flashed through my mind, making me angrier to think I had mimicked them.

"I'll sue!" he hollered, holding a handkerchief to his dripping nose.

By now the officers had run up.

"I don't think so, mister," Matt said. "Officer, all reporters are under a court order to stay one hundred feet away from Miss Lennox. It was issued earlier this afternoon."

"Come on, buddy. You're not dying. It's just a

bloody nose. This is private property. Go back across the street where you belong."

Matt shoved me back into the car while the cops escorted the reporter away.

"Calm down."

"I have a right to be angry, damn it."

"I know, but when the cops are done, we'll talk to your neighbors. They'll be more likely to answer *our* questions."

Matt walked away. My breath hissed in and out between my teeth, and my chin trembled. Smacking that reporter had felt good, and I wanted to hit something else. I settled for kicking the floorboards of Matt's car instead. It helped.

Most of the cops left when forensics arrived. In spite of the mess, I didn't expect them to find much. Not even fingerprints. Whoever had done this likely wore gloves.

"Are you all right?" Matt asked.

"Yeah, I guess so. This has been one hell of a day."

"Amen." He helped me out of the car. "Are you ready to talk to your neighbors?"

I nodded. We approached my next-door neighbor's front door. He opened immediately, and for the first time in several hours, I saw a friendly face.

"Theresa, my dear, please come in. I'm so sorry about your apartment. The police said there was a lot of damage."

"Thank you, Mr. Spencer. I'm afraid it's a total loss." My neighbor stepped aside, and we entered his neat-as-a-pin apartment. "Matt, this is Thaddeus Spencer. Mr. Spencer, I'd like you to meet Matt Summers. He's a private investigator I've hired to find out who killed my ex-husband."

Matt's hand shot out. "A pleasure, sir."

"No, the pleasure is all mine. The idea of Theresa doing something like that is ludicrous. I told both the cops and those nasty reporters so in plain language. Do you have any leads?"

"Not yet, but it's still early," Matt replied.

"Please, sit down. Could I get you a drink? Coffee? Iced tea? Bourbon?"

"Uh, no thanks, Mr. Spencer," I said hurriedly. We perched on the edge of the sofa. "What we'd really like to know is if you saw anyone hanging around my place either last night or on the day of the murder."

He shook his head and sat in a chair. "No, unfortunately, I wish I had, but I was at work."

"Mr. Spencer works in the mornings at the grocery store where we stopped yesterday," I told Matt.

"That's right. I work part time from nine until noon Monday through Friday."

"What about last night or early this morning? Did you hear sounds of things breaking over at Miss Lennox's?"

"I wasn't home last night." He turned to smile at me. "Casino night."

"Oh, of course. I forgot."

Matt raised his eyebrows. "Casino night?"

"Every Thursday evening a bunch of us from the American Legion charter a bus and head down to Tunica. We go to a different casino each week. Last night was the River's Bend. They have an excellent buffet and aren't stingy about handing out comps. I pulled a few one-armed bandits and played some blackjack. Won fifty bucks."

"What time did you get home?" Matt inquired.

"I'd say somewhere around two o'clock, maybe two thirty. I went straight to bed and didn't wake up until after eight. Then I left for work. I didn't hear or see anything out of the ordinary. Sorry."

Matt and I rose. "That's all right, Mr. Spencer. Maybe somebody else will have heard or seen something."

I pushed down the disappointment as the two men shook hands again. "Are you ready, Matt?"

We waved goodbye to Mr. Spencer.

"He seemed nice," Matt commented.

"He is. He's a retired school teacher and the one who helped me apply at the university. I was hoping he'd give us some information."

"Who's next?"

"Mr. Ferriday, I guess. He's next in line." We knocked on the door but received no answer. "What time is it?"

"Almost four thirty. Why?" Matt asked.

"Golf. Mr. Ferriday plays golf Mondays, Wednesdays, and Fridays with three of his buddies. They start at one, finish around four, hoist a few cold ones, and then have dinner. He doesn't get home until late."

"Okay, skip Ferriday. Who else?"

"Mr. Brockman? He saw me pull into my parking space on the day of the murder."

Mr. Brockman confirmed what I'd said and told us he'd informed the police of the same. "They're idiots to think you could have done something like that. I'm sorry I didn't hear anything last night."

The stairs to the second floor were in the middle of

the units. The apartment above Mr. Brockman was empty, so we stopped at June Dayton's next. She worked graveyard at a Tunica casino and hadn't been home at the time of the murder or during the probable hour of the vandalizing.

We knocked on the door of another neighbor before I remembered they had gone out of town the previous weekend for an extended vacation.

That left Myrtle Pendergast. We heard the TV blaring through the closed door. Matt turned questioning eyes in my direction.

"She's eighty, at least fifty percent deaf, and refuses to wear a hearing aid."

"So why are we bothering?"

"Because she'll find out we talked to everyone else and feel left out if we don't."

Matt groaned but knocked loudly anyway—twice. The door opened, and a wizened little gnome of a woman gazed at us through the gap of the chain lock.

"Theresa! Oh, I am glad to see you. Thank goodness those stupid cops had the sense to let you go. Just a minute." She closed the door. The chain rattled, and then Mrs. Pendergast opened up, waving us inside. "And now I hear someone vandalized your apartment. I've already called the manager and complained about the lack of security. It seems nobody's safe anymore. I can't imagine what this world is coming to. Have a seat. Can I get you anything?"

My neighbor patted a stray strand of gray hair back into the bun on the crown of her head and hitched her sagging slacks higher around her waist.

"No thanks, Mrs. Pendergast," I almost shouted. "This is Matt Summers. He's helping me find out who did it."

"It's a pleasure to meet you, ma'am," Matt said, raising his voice over the TV.

"Nice to meet you, too, Nat."

"It's Matt."

I smothered a laugh behind my hand. The elderly woman settled into a corner of the sofa. The end table held a lamp, her reading glasses, and a novel whose cover featured a half-naked man with muscles on his muscles and a swooning young woman.

I did a double take. The suggestive title stood out in clear, bold print and the publisher, *Sexamania*, had a firm grip on the hot and spicy market. *Mrs. Pendergast reads erotic romance?* I didn't want to go there.

"Now, dear, how can I help you?"

Matt glanced at the TV, but she didn't take the hint, so he had to shout, "Were you home last Monday morning?"

"I'm always home, except when I go to the grocery store, of course. My daughter comes by every Saturday to take me."

"Did you see or hear anything—like a gunshot?"

"Oh, no. I would have remembered. I had the TV on. Oprah comes on at nine—I never miss Oprah. *The Price Is Right* follows at ten. I should go on that show. I'm closer to the actual retail price than any of those goofy contestants."

"What about last night?" I asked.

"That oldies TV station all night. *Bonanza* followed by an *Andy Griffith Show* marathon. They just don't make decent TV shows anymore. I took my pills, went to bed, and slept like baby."

Of course she did. One of her pills was Valium.

She wouldn't have been able to hear the glass breaking in her apartment, let alone mine. This was useless.

"Thank you, Mrs. Pendergast. I appreciate your time."

The old lady smiled. "You know, dear, if you're short of money, I have a little stashed away for a rainy day. You're welcome to it."

I swallowed the lump in my throat. "Thank you, but I'm all right for the time being. It's sweet of you to offer."

"Nonsense. You've been a good neighbor, sometimes running me around to do little errands, and I told the cops the same earlier."

We thanked her again and then left. Matt tossed my bags into his car.

"It looks like you're going to remain my houseguest. Let's head for home. We'll go out for dinner. My treat."

"If I take time to think, I'll get the blues. How about a home-cooked meal? I'll stop at the store on the way home. Fried chicken, mashed potatoes and gravy, country green beans, and rolls sound good to you?"

"My mouth is already watering. Want me to come with you?"

"No. It'll only take a couple of minutes. I'll meet you at the house."

"Okay. Keep your chin up. Your neighbors love you." He leaned down and brushed his lips across my cheek. "I think you're pretty special, too."

His action made my heart gallop, stop, then gallop some more. A queer melting feeling stole over my muscles. At least one thing had gone right today. I'd still be living in his house.

"Thanks. Things can only look up from here."

****

I wheeled around the parking lot at the local supermarket, trying to find a spot close to the door. It was getting late, and every harassed working mother did the same. I gave up and parked about two-thirds of the way down a lane from the store.

I undid my seat belt, slipped the strap of my purse over my shoulder, and sat for a moment, mentally making a list of things I needed, when the door suddenly jerked open. Startled, I whipped my head around and stared down the barrel of a gun.

"Get outta the car, bitch!" a voice demanded.

I couldn't move. My breath stopped, and I think my heart had ceased operations, too. I peered into that black hole. Lightheadedness made my head swim and my vision blur. A cold chill swept over me even though the temperature hovered in the high eighties.

"He said *out*. Now! Or we blow your fuckin' head off," a second man snarled.

I still couldn't move. The two of them took matters into their own hands by yanking me out and violently flinging me from the Jeep. I landed in the vacant space next to where I'd parked, skidding along the asphalt, tearing open the knees of my slacks and the elbows of the yellow blouse. A searing burn scorched the skin on those now-exposed body parts and my palms. The pain brought me out of my shocked numbness.

I sat up and screamed, but the punks moved fast. They already had the car in gear and backed out. I scrambled to my feet and yelled again.

"Help! Help!"

I heard the rush of footsteps. Shoppers abandoned

their carts and ran toward me.

"Lady, are you hurt?" one man asked.

"Another carjacking!"

"Oh, my God. You're bleeding. Somebody call the cops and an ambulance," a woman's voice echoed.

"What happened?"

"They—they stole my car." I pointed at my Grand Cherokee disappearing down the pavement.

The thieves wasted no time. They floored the gas pedal, laying rubber, and squealed away. Rather than use the exit, they headed straight for the median strip between the parking lot and the road. Traveling a good thirty miles an hour, the Jeep's wheels hit the curb, sending the front end three feet in the air before slamming back down into the grass.

A brilliant flash dazzled my eyes a second before the deafening explosion. A fireball erupted from my car. Everybody screamed and ducked for cover. I threw myself flat and covered my head. Smoldering debris rained down. Bits and pieces of metal and fiberglass clattered on the pavement, stinging my flesh.

I raised my head and stared in horror. What was left of my car burned intensely, and through the flames, I had no trouble seeing two human torches.

Chapter Six

I lay clamped to the asphalt, embracing it like a lover, my ears reverberating from the sound of the explosion. I was vaguely aware of people shouting. Someone lifted and then carried me to the curb where I sat transfixed by the scene in front of me, unable to move. Gradually, the numbness wore off. I cringed as a tire popped, sending another ripple of screams through the crowd.

I passively listened to what went on around me—sirens for the most part. They came from every direction to converge on the smoldering remains of my Jeep. Stunned, I counted four fire trucks, three meat wagons, and no fewer than six cop cars. All the 9-1-1 calls had produced results.

"Honey, are you all right?"

I looked up to meet the concerned gaze of an elderly woman. The shock lessened, and reaction set in. I shook and gasped for air. No, damn it, I wasn't all right. I'd just had the piss scared out of me and watched two men get incinerated along with my Jeep, the best freaking car I'd ever owned.

"Get a paramedic over here, now," the lady shouted. "She's going to pass out."

Damned if she wasn't right. Black dots danced before my eyes, and darkness crept into my peripheral vision. A loud buzzing rang in my ears. My body pitched forward an instant before my world turned black.

When I opened my eyes, I was lying on the narrow strip of grass between the parking lanes. I couldn't have been out long because the paramedics had just arrived. A rock embedded in the soil angrily jabbed my shoulder blade. I struggled to sit up.

"No, no, dear. Lie down. You've had an awful shock," the woman's voice said.

"I'm—I'm okay. Just shaken." My head swam, and my heart still hadn't reached normal beats per minute.

The lady retreated when the paramedics knelt beside me. They checked all the usual medical things—blood pressure, high; heart rate, high; temperature, on the low side. This I could believe—I shivered like the middle of January at the North Pole. Convinced I wouldn't pass out again, they rolled up my pant legs and the sleeves of my blouse and then tended my scrapes.

They flushed the wounds with some kind of solution. It stung. "Ouch!"

The pain cleared my head. I thought rationally for the first time since I'd parked the car. Matt. Oh, my God. I had to call Matt. I looked around for my purse, finally spying it in the hands of the elderly lady.

"Ma'am? Could I please have my purse? I need to call my—my husband."

She rushed over. "Of course, here you go. Is there anything else I can do to help?"

"No, thank you. You've been wonderful. I appreciate you looking after me."

"I was glad to do it. I've never seen anything like this before in my life. It was divine retribution if you ask me. They stole your car, and God punished them."

I nodded weakly and fished through my purse for my cell with trembling hands. "Well, thank you again."

I found the phone as the woman turned to talk to a policeman. I hit Matt's speed dial and waited impatiently for him to pick up.

If I get voice mail…

"Theresa? What's taking so long?"

"Uh, I've had a little car problem," I said, unwilling to say too much in front of the paramedics who now worked on my other knee.

"What? It won't start? Or do you have a flat?"

"Ah, both…kinda." More police cars swept into the parking lot.

"What do you mean—both? Theresa, what's going on? Are you all right? I hear sirens. Have you had an accident?"

"Not exactly."

"Theresa!"

I didn't want to even think about what had happened, let alone put it into words, but Matt's frustrated shout told me I had no choice.

"I'll be right there." He hung up without saying goodbye.

I winced as the paramedics dabbed more of that stinging solution on my left hand and elbow. Wrinkling my nose at the pungent odor, I realized a more obnoxious smell drifted my way on the wind. The smell of burning rubber, hot metal, and gasoline stank, but I rather suspected what turned my stomach was the rankness of cremated flesh.

I swallowed and turned my head away. I preferred watching blood being wiped from my arms and legs. At least mine still flowed.

"Which hospital would you like to go to?" one of the paramedics asked.

"I don't need to go to the hospital for a few scrapes and bruises."

"You passed out. You should have a few tests just to be on the safe side."

"I don't have insurance. I'll be all right. Someone's coming to take me home and stay with me. If I feel dizzy again, I'll go to a clinic. I promise."

They made me sign a waiver but insisted I sit on a gurney until my ride showed up. With the medical help finished, a cop quit interviewing the witnesses and headed for me.

"Hello again, Miss Lennox. I was at your place less than two hours ago. You're keeping us busy tonight."

"Not by choice, I can tell you."

"Okay, what happened?"

I gave him the story in excruciating detail. All the while my gaze scanned the parking lot, now encased in miles of yellow tape, watching for Matt's white car. I needed him desperately. A couple of news helicopters circled overhead.

"Sounds to me like the curb-jumping must have loosened your fuel line. When the gas hit the hot engine—bam," the cop said.

I looked over his shoulder at my car again. The bodies had been removed, and a flatbed arrived to tow the burned-out hulk to the scrap pile or the impound lot where forensics would go over it. I wanted to cry. I loved that damned Jeep. I'd used part of my divorce settlement to buy it. It had represented my first step toward independence and healing after nine years of hell.

Out of the corner of my eye, I saw a flash of white and turned to look. Matt parked in a space not cordoned off and got out. I breathed a sigh of relief. He stared at my car. His hands clenched into fists, and his lips moved. I couldn't hear the words but assumed them to be profane. He hurried toward me.

I slid off the gurney and took two steps. His arms closed around me. I clung to him, and for the first time since the incident happened, cried. He held me, crooning and saying soft words of comfort until the storm passed. He pushed a handkerchief into my hand. I wiped the tears from my face and blew my nose.

"Are you sure you're all right?" he asked in a low voice.

I nodded. "I'm fine. Just scared and glad to see you. I can't believe this has happened."

"What do the cops have to say?"

Before I could answer, another cop from earlier in the day sauntered up.

"Well, Miss Lennox, we meet again. We seem to be spending a lot of time with you lately."

I didn't like his snarky, sarcastic tone, and neither did Matt.

"The last time I looked, that's why the people of Memphis pay taxes—so you can do your job," Matt said.

The policeman ignored Matt and spoke in a bored voice, "Tell me what happened."

"I just told that officer over there," I replied, pointing at the first cop, now talking to another witness.

"Well, tell me."

I went through it all again, exhausted by the time I

finished.

"You know, you've got to be real careful in parking lots. It's always a good idea to look around before you get out. I thought everyone knew that."

"Are you saying I'm stupid? Of all the nerve! I didn't have a chance to look around. I'd barely stopped when they yanked my door open."

"Always keep your doors locked. Can you give us a description? What's left isn't real identifiable."

I heard Matt's breath hiss between his teeth and felt him tense. I didn't blame him. I wanted to hit the son of a bitch, too.

"Yeah, I can. The barrel of the gun was big, black, and aimed at my nose."

"The men, Miss Lennox. I don't have time for smart-ass answers."

"And she doesn't have time for smart-ass cops," Matt snarled.

I waved him quiet. "Sorry. I was focused on staring down the black hole of the barrel. Prior to becoming crispy critters, they were a couple of homeys with tarantulas on their heads and jeans belted south of the border," I answered back.

He snapped his notebook shut and glared at me. "This has been an interesting week for you, hasn't it? You're arrested for murder, duck a wild shot at a cheap motel, have your apartment trashed, and now this. Maybe I should arrest you again for obstructing an officer and put you back in jail where you belong."

"What the hell is that supposed to mean?" Matt yelled.

"It means I've been a staunch supporter of Hamilton Garrett for years. He's cop friendly, and the fact she made a ridiculously low bail turns my stomach."

The cop curled his lip and strode away. Matt shoved me aside and took a step after him, his eyes narrowed and his fists balled. I grabbed his arm.

"No, Matt. Let it be. He's an asshole, not worth fighting over."

"He's an obnoxious piece of shit. He had no right to say that to you. I'm going to get his badge number and lodge a formal complaint."

He shook off my hand, but I clutched at him again.

"Forget it. The Garretts have long tentacles into the police department and the court system. I'm lucky I got arraigned in front of one of the few judges unimpressed by wealth and power. Let it go, Matt. Please? For my sake. I'm tired, I'm scared, and I've had about as much as I can take today."

I laid my hand on his cheek and gazed into his eyes. He relaxed, running a hand through his hair.

"The son of a bitch. I still think I oughtta report him. Make sure you mention this to Jerricus when you see him on Monday. He'll love the David and Goliath aspect."

"I will. I promise."

A younger policeman walked up to us. "Miss Lennox, do you have a ride home?"

"Yes, thank you."

"Are you finished with her?" Matt asked, his voice still hard.

"Yes, for now. She'll have to come down to the station for a formal statement. The sooner, the better. Do we have your number in case we need to get in touch with you?"

I nodded, and Matt gave him his address. The policeman touched his cap, smiled, and then walked away.

I winced as Matt cupped my elbow and led me toward his car.

"Sorry," he muttered. "I didn't even ask if you were hurt. I was so relieved to see you breathing I forgot."

"I scraped my knees and elbows when I was thrown from the car, but it's nothing permanent. I'll be fine in a couple of days."

He opened the car door and helped me in, fussing over me like a mother hen with her wayward chick. I enjoyed it. We drove back to Germantown through the thinning Friday night traffic.

"Are you sure you never saw either of those guys before? Could they have been friends of Danny's?"

"No, I doubt it. What I told Officer Jerk-off was true. I didn't have time to really look. The whole thing flashed in front of my eyes like a video in fast forward. All I saw were generalities."

"I don't suppose they have any theories for the explosion, do they?"

"One of the cops said something about the fuel line breaking when the car jumped the curb."

"Fuel lines don't just come loose over a bump in the road."

"They were haulin' ass and hit the curb pretty hard," I replied. I glanced over at him.

The muscles of his jaw clenched and then relaxed. "Doesn't matter. Did you smell gas anytime during the last couple of days?"

"No."

"Are you sure?"

"I've been distracted, but not *that* distracted. I'd have noticed. Did you smell anything odd when you rescued it from my apartment?"

He shook his head. "Then that leaves only one other possibility."

"What's that?"

We stopped at a red light. Matt turned his head and looked at me with a grim expression. His eyes held worry and fear. My breath caught in my throat, and my heart suddenly thudded in my chest. I didn't want to hear the answer.

"A bomb."

The light turned green, and we sped away. I stared straight ahead out of the windshield and bit my lip. Yeah, the thought had crossed my mind, too.

****

Oscar's Bar and Grill sat in the middle of Germantown on a wedge of land between three streets and the railroad tracks. The parking lot was almost full, and Matt had to settle for a spot quite a way from the front door. I noticed a white car with two men in it enter and park nearby. My police surveillance was back. I didn't know whether to feel comforted or not.

Conversation in the car had lagged after Matt's comment. What could I say? It had been the first thought to go through my mind, too, although why I couldn't imagine. As I had lain kissing the asphalt of the parking lot, the bomb idea had sprung to mind. In my terror, I had connected it to the men who carjacked me. That was nonsense, of course. No one put a bomb in the car *after* the carjacking. Had they been carrying it? But why?

I'd also visualized something like a grenade being launched by a rival gang. Crooks had all kinds of weaponry. That, too, was silly. I'd seen nothing streaking through the air, and no one had come close enough to the Jeep to toss one.

The hostess greeted and then led us to a cozy booth next to the window facing the old Germantown Railway Station, now a museum. Within seconds a waiter appeared.

"May I get you something from the bar?"

I didn't care if Matt was a recovering alcoholic. I needed a drink—and something a hell of a lot stronger than wine.

"The biggest frozen margarita you've got."

"And you, sir?"

Matt raised his eyebrows, shrugged, and then smiled. "I'd love to have a belt right now, but I'd never be able to stop at one. Make it iced tea."

The waiter left, and I looked Matt straight in the eye.

"Why a bomb?"

"I don't know."

"Okay, then who?"

"I don't know the answer to that either."

"You're just full of cheerful news, aren't you?"

"Someone had to plant it last night when you stayed with me," he said, the worry in his eyes intense.

"Or at the university. Maybe they did it while I was at my lawyer's."

"It would have taken brass balls to install it in broad daylight. No, my bet is last night. Your car was parked on the backside of the motel. They'd use the cover of darkness. Trust me, that place doesn't have cameras around the parking lot." He sat and thought for a moment. "I can't remember whether or not I locked your car. Did you beep it open this morning?"

"I don't know. I had other things on my mind." I thought hard but for the life of me couldn't recall even pressing the alarm button. "But why detonate it after the carjacking? I wasn't in the car. They must have seen that."

The waiter brought our drinks, and I gulped, the mellow mixture of tequila, triple sec, and lime instantly giving me a brain freeze. I licked the salt from my lips and waited for the pain in my head to subside.

"Are you folks ready to order?"

Matt also guzzled half his iced tea. "Not right now. Give us ten minutes or so."

The man nodded and left. I repeated my last question.

"Not all bombs are remote controlled. Someone extra careful, who didn't want to be on surveillance cameras or remembered by witnesses sitting in his car and taking off immediately afterward, wouldn't use one. He'd be off establishing an alibi. My guess is it was a contact bomb."

"What's that?"

"It's simple to rig—some dynamite, a battery, a spring-loaded detonator with something between the spring and the contact point. You go over a bump, the barrier is dislodged, the connection made, and boom."

The simplicity of it made me sick. And to think I'd been driving around all day with the damned thing. I drained my margarita and shivered, this time not from the drink.

"Any ideas on who'd do this?" he asked.

"God, no. I don't have any enemies—except for Danny and he's dead." A horrible thought slashed across my brain. "Matt, you don't suppose Danny really *did* owe a lot of money to someone, do you?"

"You mean like a drug dealer? It's possible, but why go after you?"

"Maybe they thought Danny had left money or drugs with me. Maybe that's who trashed my place. And don't forget the message on my machine. Maybe that's what the caller meant."

"The police took the tape. Let's hope they're trying to find the person, or persons, who did it. And speaking of the police, we should go downtown to the station as soon as we're done here. You can make your statement and then go home to bed."

"That sounds fine."

"Could Danny have gotten into your place prior to the day he was killed?"

"And hidden something?"

"It's a possibility and something the cops should investigate."

"I guess I could amend my statement and say I *thought* someone had been in my apartment a few days earlier. Would that help?"

"I don't know, but it's something to think about. Theresa, could Danny have had other debts? Any failed business ventures. Did he borrow money? Did he gamble?"

"Yeah, but not for a long time."

"What do you mean?"

The waiter came by, and I ordered another drink. When he left, I continued.

"Danny used to go down to Tunica a lot with his

friends. They'd gamble, drink, and try to pick up girls. A couple of drinks made Danny feel invincible. He'd bet heavily, generally losing."

"Any particular casino?"

"All of them, except for the Fantasy. He didn't care as long as the drinks kept coming and the girls were pretty."

I couldn't keep the bitterness out of my voice. When I'd complained about his behavior, he'd backhanded me, saying if I were more of a woman, he wouldn't have to go searching.

"You never mentioned Danny's gambling before. Why not the Fantasy?" Matt asked with an intent look.

"He lost a bundle in there. I guess he signed marker after marker, and when the time came to pay up, he couldn't. Hamilton had to cover the loss. I didn't mention it because until now didn't think it mattered."

The waiter brought my drink. We ordered burgers and fries even though I wasn't sure I could choke anything down. Alone again, I went on.

"I remember we were summoned to the house one night. Diana wasn't there. Hamilton told me to stay in the den. He took Danny into the study. Almost immediately I heard shouting. I tiptoed down the hall and listened at the door. The wood was thick, but I heard some of what was being said. Hamilton was furious."

I sipped the margarita and remembered that night. I had still sported a bruise on my cheek courtesy of Danny. Hamilton had seen but ignored it.

"He said 'never again,' 'under control,' and a couple of other things along that line. It was the first time I'd ever heard Hamilton lose his temper. It scared the hell out of me. I scurried back to the den and waited. A few minutes later, Danny came out madder than hell, and we left. He took it out on me later that night."

Matt frowned. "Why didn't you tell me any of this before?"

"To the best of my knowledge, it never happened again."

"Yeah, but you've been divorced for a year and a half. He could have drifted back into old habits. I'll check it out tomorrow."

I was about to ask another question when the sudden dinging of a loud bell pulled my attention out of the window. The crossing arm had lowered. A few seconds later a freight train, its horn screaming, roared past, making conversation impossible. I watched in fascination as the cars click-clacked on the rails not a hundred feet away. Since I was in a morbid frame of mind, I visualized the train jumping the tracks and landing in my lap.

When it passed, I noticed the two men from the white car seated at a table five feet away.

"Why did they wait so long to come in?" I whispered.

Now we wouldn't be able to continue our discussion. And what did they expect to hear? Matt and I congratulating each other on a bombing well done?

"They probably asked for a table near us and had to wait. It's Friday night. The restaurant's crowded. Shall we request our food to go and see how fast they can move?"

I sat back. I didn't want to talk about Danny anymore anyway. I floundered for a topic of conversation, but Matt beat me to it.

"So, Theresa, what sent you to the University of Memphis? What's your major?"

I relaxed my posture and took another sip of my margarita. "I haven't declared one yet, but I'm thinking I'd like to be a psychologist and counsel battered women."

"That's understandable. You mentioned your neighbor helped you?"

"Mr. Spencer encouraged me and helped fill out the paperwork. I received a good-sized settlement from Danny and decided to use some of it for my education. Mom would have been proud."

The waiter brought our burgers, and we dug in. I'd forgotten about Dumb and Dumber sitting next to us. Matt had the neatest way of calming and making me refocus. I looked at him as he chomped into his sandwich. He winked.

A gush of warmth rolled over me. Suddenly, I wanted to feel the strength of his arms holding me again.

"Do you like higher education?" he asked.

I nodded. "It's opened my mind, allowing me to see things I never noticed before."

We ate in silence for a few minutes. Then I asked, "How did your search for Mr. Monroe go?"

He crammed a french fry in his mouth. "Great. He's finally hooked up with a good one. Most of what she's told him is true."

"Most?"

"She lied about her age. She's forty-seven, not thirty-seven. God bless the wonders of plastic surgery and Botox." He chuckled.

"What was his reaction?" I was curious about my possible attorney's view on little white lies.

"He laughed, said thanks, and promised the check would hit my desk on Monday."

He'd laughed? I couldn't wait to meet this guy.

We finished our meal. The waiter brought the bill, and I slapped my credit card down on the table first.

"My turn," I said.

The waiter returned. I added a tip and signed the slip. We got up to leave when I heard a voice from next to me call out, "Waiter, check please." I wondered how fast my surveillance could pay and if they would follow us. We took our time walking back to the car.

****

We entered the house, and I gazed out of the sidelight window just as a white car swept around the cove, hovered for a second at the end of the driveway, then left. Their day was done now. Matt and I were home, and not likely to stray during the night. They had even followed us to the station, waiting patiently for the two hours it took to make my statement.

I followed Matt into the den. My body was drop-dead tired, but I couldn't shut off my mind. It whirled and dipped with unanswered questions and theories. I had to relax, or there would be no sleeping tonight. I glanced at Matt. He paced into the kitchen, picked up a couple of items on the counter, and then set them down again.

"Can't turn off your mind?" I asked.

"That and I want a drink—bad."

"I'm sorry. I shouldn't have had those margaritas."

He waved a hand and shook his head. "Not your fault. It's my problem. I find exercise helps. How about a swim?"

A swim sounded great—except…"I don't have a suit."

"We'll use our underwear. A bra and panties cover more than most swimsuits anyway. I'll turn the lights off once you get down the steps, if you like."

He talked me into it. A few vigorous laps and maybe my mind would slow to my body's pace.

I trotted down the steps of the deck to the patio and slipped out of my tattered slacks and blouse. Both items were bloodstained candidates for the garbage. And to think I'd had dinner while wearing them. I wondered if anyone at the restaurant had noticed.

The lights flashed out, and I slid into the shallow end of the pool. The cool water soaked through my bandages. I ripped them off and left them on the coping to retrieve later. They could join my clothes in the trash.

A splash from the deep end told me Matt had dived in. The stars and the glow from the street light in front sent enough light into the back to see. Matt surfaced and swam to the side of the pool.

I pushed off and stroked. I swam two, three, five laps up and down, digging hard with my arms and kicking my legs furiously. It had been a long time since I'd done this. I finally stopped and floated on my back, gulping in huge draughts of air. Matt appeared at my side.

"Take it easy. Don't go having a heart attack on me."

I tried to laugh. "Don't worry, I won't. I'd hate to bring the cops down on me for the fourth time in twenty-four hours."

He laughed, too, and swam the length of the pool.

When I recaptured my breath, I made my way to the side, resting my outstretched arms on the coping to watch.

His lithe body cut through the water without effort, barely causing a ripple. The water gleamed silver on his skin, and for a moment, my mind envisioned us naked and making love, here and now, wrapped in the embrace of liquid sheets.

My body throbbed in spite of the cool water. I swallowed hard, resisting the temptation to start something. I wanted him as badly as he wanted that drink. I abandoned my resting place, matching him stroke for stroke up and down the pool. I don't know how long we swam side by side before stopping.

"Feeling better?" he asked.

"Much. I think I'll sleep now." I didn't lie. While I still tingled and throbbed, the gush of desire had lessened. I grasped the handrail, slowly climbing the steps in the shallow end, and made my way back to where I'd left my clothes.

"Oh, I don't have a towel."

"Bottom of the chaise next to you. I got a couple out of the laundry room."

He swam another lap or two while I toweled off, before joining me. I wrapped the oversized strip of terry cloth around my shoulders and then gathered the discarded bandages along with the remnants of my clothes. I tried not to look as he dried his body and secured the towel around his hips.

He followed me up the steps. I wondered fleetingly if he riveted his gaze on my rear end the way I had mine on his earlier in the day.

We entered the house. He took the torn, filthy

clothing and bandages from me.

"I'd say these things have had it."

He ducked into the laundry room and opened the door to the garage. I heard a side door open and the clang of a trash can lid. He returned within a few seconds, and walking past the hutch in the eating area, looked at his answering machine. The message light blinked. Matt punched the button.

"Tell the bitch I want what's mine, and I want it now. If I don't get it soon, you'll both regret it."

Chapter Seven

I shoved another file into the drawer and sighed. Exactly, how boring could this get? Matt sat in the other office, busy tracking down some of Danny's old cronies. Occasionally, he'd make a few phone calls and then go back online. Meanwhile, I was unemployed and unhappy.

The weekend had been less than stellar. Matt had called the police about the threatening message on his machine. Their reaction didn't fill either of us with confidence.

"They can't or won't do anything about it," Matt had said.

We went to the grocery store on Saturday morning. I held my breath over every bump in the road, half expecting to be blown to kingdom come.

Matt rented me a car—a coffin on wheels. If I had a collision with a large dog, I'd lose. I wanted my Jeep, damn it.

Since the vandals destroyed most of my clothing, Matt drove me to the mall. I kept a close eye on the price tags. Jobless and with no prospects, I pawed through every sale rack and stuck to the basics. I did, however, invest in a bikini. I needed something to boost my spirits. Matt approved.

I spent the rest of the weekend lazing around the pool. Matt worked. Finding Danny's ex-partners in crime had taken longer than expected. Bored beyond belief by Sunday evening, I demanded to accompany him to the office the next day. I couldn't face being alone, and while Matt wouldn't admit it, I suspected he didn't want me by myself either.

The office door opening jerked me out of my thoughts. Carleen stood in the doorway, hands on hips, looking surprised and not too happy.

"What the hell are you doing?"

"Filing."

"That's my job." Her pencil-thin eyebrows drew together in a scowl, and her lips formed into a line.

I tossed a folder at her. She snared it one-handed in mid-air.

"Then why don't you do it?" I snapped. I was in a lousy mood and didn't care what the woman thought of me.

Today she dressed like a refugee from Whore's-R-Us. A white, lace, see-through blouse, plunging almost to her navel, allowed me to see more than I wanted of a hot-pink bra. Her turquoise and lime zebra-striped, spandex miniskirt barely covered the necessities. White fishnet stockings encased her legs, and she wore lime-green, snake-skin ankle boots—with stiletto heels, of course.

Carleen glared and then stormed into Matt's office. I followed, needing the entertainment.

"Hey, what the hell's going on here? Why is a client doing my work?" she shouted.

Matt didn't bother to turn around. "Maybe because Thursday was the last time I saw you. You left early and never finished. Remember?"

"I have a life. I had things to do."

"Yes, but I pay you to file."

"Yeah, and you don't do that too often. Which reminds me—you owe me fifty bucks."

Matt swiveled his chair to face her, rose, and glared at the receptionist. He reached into his back pocket, withdrew his wallet, and slapped two twenties and a ten on the desk.

"Here. Fifty bucks. Happy now?"

Carleen snatched the money, shoved it into her bra, and then gave Matt the finger.

More money hit the desk. "Here. This is for the work you didn't do. Beat it," he said.

Not bothering to count the bills, she joined them with the fifty already hidden.

"Does this mean I'm fired?"

"Yes."

"You can't fire me. I quit!"

She whirled and flung the file back in my direction. I made a wild grab and missed. It hit the floor with a splat. Papers flew everywhere. I bent to retrieve them. Carleen stalked across the scattered pages, her high heels punching holes as she passed.

"You'll play hell finding anyone willing to come into this shitty part of town for the shitty money you sometimes pay," she shouted. "Let Little Miss Husband Killer here do it, since she's so eager."

A second later the door slammed followed by the sound of angry stiletto footsteps clattering down the stairs.

"I'm sorry, Matt. I *was* kind of nasty to her," I said, picking up the last of the perforated papers.

"Don't worry about it. She's kind of nasty herself. I won't really miss her—although she did make a hell of a cup of coffee."

I laid the file on his desk and sat down. "I make pretty good coffee. I can even answer a phone. Let me help. I don't have anything else to do, and I won't demand fifty bucks."

Matt laughed. "I love cheap labor."

"How did you ever hook up with her anyway?"

"I was putting up the sign on the street door when she stopped and asked if I was looking to hire."

"What was she doing in this neighborhood?"

"At the time, she lived in a cheap apartment on Vance. She'd just gotten off work when she saw me. She needed the extra money, and I needed someone to file, so I hired her."

"Where did she work?"

"Carleen's a dancer at the Kitchee-Koo Klub on Brooks."

"Dancer? You mean stripper?"

"Yeah. She also works after-hours private parties in the back of the club."

"Lap dances and other things a specialty?" I asked.

Matt shrugged. "I never asked and didn't care."

He swung back to his computer. I strolled out to the reception area and glanced round. Drab and uninspired, the place needed help.

The receptionist's desk, strictly utilitarian and unremarkable, nestled in a corner. I wondered if Carleen had ever run the computer sitting on it. The rest of the waiting room furniture had been shoved along the walls with little thought.

Some rearrangement and pillows would work wonders. And the walls could use a picture or two. Cushions for the chairs would be nice. And plants to make the place look less dreary.

I spent the next half an hour switching a battered leather sofa, a scarred coffee table, and two wooden chairs to other positions, then stepped back to view the results. Much better.

Matt came out of his office and asked, "How about an early lunch?" He did a double take. "What are you doing?"

"Keeping busy. Besides, this arrangement works better. You don't mind, do you?"

"Just don't go putting lace and girly stuff all over, okay? Want to go to the Starlight before it gets too crowded? Jerricus's office is in East Memphis. You don't want to be late."

"I just hope he takes me on," I said, slinging my purse over my shoulder.

"Honey, you'll have him eating out of your hand."

****

I sat on the plush leather sofa in Jerricus Monroe's waiting room, crossing, then uncrossing my legs. The receptionist took calls, worked on her computer, and ignored me. It was after two thirty, and I'd been here over forty-five minutes. Important lawyer or not, I considered it rude to keep a client, even one who couldn't pay squat, waiting without a word of explanation. I clenched my teeth, jiggled my foot, and glanced at my watch again.

Two minutes later the door to the magic kingdom opened. A perfectly groomed and clothed woman paused, looking at me with arched eyebrows.

"Miss Lennox?"

Who else would be waiting? I wanted to snap the words out but refrained. Why piss her off? For all I knew she might be on my side.

"Yes, I'm Theresa Lennox."

"Mr. Monroe will see you now."

She offered no apology and turned. I followed her through the doorway. Her office was huge and richly appointed. Even the file cabinets matched and blended in. Burgundy velvet draperies hung at the windows, and expensive paintings adorned the walls. And this was the secretary's domain! A name plate on her desk read Doris Singleton.

She opened the door to the inner sanctum and said, "Miss Lennox to see you, sir."

Doris moved aside to let me pass and smiled. Too nervous to smile back, I entered the sacred hall.

"Miss Lennox, I'm Jerricus Monroe. It's a pleasure to meet you."

The best-known attorney in the tri-state area rose and walked around his desk to shake my hand. I'd seen him on TV, of course, but Jerricus Monroe in the flesh was overwhelming.

He stood six feet, five inches and tipped the scales at close to three hundred pounds, give or take. He bore the weight well with only a hint of middle-aged bulge. His mane of white hair was on the longish side, and his craggy face made him look like a benevolent Olympian god, or the Devil incarnate depending on his mood and the image he wished to project, I supposed. Sharp brown eyes stared at me from under shaggy brows. When he smiled, the lines in his face deepened into grooves. His hand engulfed mine.

Matt's advice rang through my mind. *Tell him everything right down to the smallest detail. Don't leave anything out.*

I swallowed. "Thank you, Mr. Monroe. I appreciate you taking the time to see me."

He held my hand for a moment and looked into my eyes before replying with a smile, "Don't be nervous. I won't eat you. I've already had lunch. Have a seat and tell me about your case. I only know what I read in the papers."

I settled into a cushy armchair. He resumed his seat behind the desk, reached into a drawer, and pulled out a tape recorder the size of a credit card, then arranged a yellow legal pad in front of him. From the inside pocket of his navy-blue suit coat, he produced a slim, very expensive looking pen.

"Now before we begin, Miss Lennox, I have to warn you that I want the truth and only the truth from you. As your attorney, I am bound by the law never to divulge our conversations. That holds true even if I don't take the case. Okay?"

"I know. Even if you're no longer my lawyer, you can't tell anybody anything unless I release you to make a statement, or I die."

"I see you've done your homework. Excellent. I like an intelligent client. I'm sure you plan to tell me everything. No bullshit. I cut through manure like a plow through topsoil. I don't lose many cases. The ones I have lost were because my client lied or omitted telling me things. I don't like being surprised during discovery or in court. Now are you ready to begin?"

He tapped the top of the recorder, leaned back in his chair, crossed his legs, and balanced the pad of paper on his knee. His eyes skewered me, slicing and dicing all the way into my soul.

I stared back, held under his hypnotic gaze. I

couldn't have lied even if I wanted to.

I visualized wildflowers and streams, sucked in a deep breath, and then told him everything from the day I first met Danny to the car bomb and the messages. My revelations took over an hour and when I finished, I sat back, exhausted—like I'd run a marathon.

My efforts did not appear to impress Jerricus Monroe.

"Uh-huh. Now tell me about your relationship with the Garretts." He turned another page on the pad and wrote.

"There's not much to tell. I didn't have to deal with Hamilton very often. Diana never liked me but was too well-bred to show it overtly."

"No, she wouldn't. What was their reaction to your husband beating you?"

"Hamilton never said anything. I dealt with my mother-in-law. She talked and twisted my words so badly that in the end I said whatever she wanted me to say. It wasn't until after the divorce that I refused to drop the charges on a savage beating, and Danny did jail time. Even then the Garrett money bought a lighter sentence than the son of a bitch deserved."

The serene meadow scene faded from my mind to be replaced with the last beating Danny had inflicted four months after our divorce. A wave of nausea rolled through my stomach, and I shook. Biting my lip, I tried, but failed, to keep the tears in my eyes from overflowing. Jerricus picked up the phone on his desk.

"Miss Singleton, would you please bring in a glass of Chardonnay and a box of tissues?"

Less than a minute later, the secretary appeared with both. She set the glass in front of me on the desk and handed me the tissues. I could tell she'd done this before.

I dried my tears and mumbled, "Thank you. I'm sorry."

"No need to be. You had a horrific marriage and every right to cry. Go ahead—be angry."

I raised the glass to my lips with a shaking hand and took a sip. It was delicious and had probably cost a small fortune.

Jerricus placed the legal pad on the desk, covered it with his crossed arms, and leaned forward. By sitting back while I'd given my story, he'd distanced himself from me. Now the atmosphere became more intimate— like two old friends talking—putting me at ease. God, this guy was good.

"Why did you fire your public defender?"

"Because he wanted to cut a deal, and I wouldn't do it. I was just another statistic to him, another case to close and be done with. I didn't have confidence that he would even try to get me off."

"I don't plea bargain very often, Miss Lennox. Now tell me again about the morning of the murder with the times as close as you can recall."

I gave him the details again. When I finished, he pursed his lips, nodded, and then smiled.

"Did you know I grew up with Diana Worthington? We went to the Memphis Academy together—a very exclusive prep school. I had a crush on her when I was thirteen. Luckily, I outgrew it. I've watched her manipulate others to get what she wants for years."

I tried to visualize a teenaged Diana but failed.

"Everyone was surprised when she married

Hamilton Garrett. His money talked, and believe me, Diana listened.

"I run in the same social circles. I don't think Diana cares much about old Ham one way or the other. The only thing Diana ever loved was her son, and he was a mean, vicious SOB." Jerricus frowned. "Hamilton is the consummate politician, straddling the fence and making everyone think he's on their side."

I'd calmed down some and took another sip of the excellent wine. "He always seemed to look right past me—like I was invisible or an annoyance he sometimes couldn't ignore."

"That's the way he views most of his constituents. Diana takes care of the unsavory aspects of their lives and is vindictive as hell. I remember when Ham's head was turned by a good-looking campaign worker. Diana saw to it the poor woman, who did nothing to encourage the attention, had to leave town. She was a paralegal, and after her dismissal from the campaign, no one would hire her."

I believed it, remembering how my former mother-in-law pressured the university and cost me my job.

Jerricus continued. "I never liked Hamilton, and after the age of fourteen, I didn't much care for Diana either. They're both users who've browbeat people into doing what they want, including getting their son off when he should have been in jail. I hate it when people use their money, power, and influence to manipulate the system."

Under the circumstances I thought mentioning that Jerricus Monroe didn't do half bad at manipulating the system either was a bit undiplomatic.

I took more than a sip of my wine and relaxed, a

mellow glow embracing me. Jerricus leaned back, his intertwined fingers behind his head.

"I'll take your case, Miss Lennox."

I almost fainted with relief. "Oh, Mr. Monroe, how can I thank you? I have no money. I told you that, didn't I?"

He waved his hand. "I don't care. I'll work pro bono for the chance to take the starch out of Hamilton and Diana. We have to bring the whole story in front of the public. Give me a few days to gather fodder for the cannon, and then we'll announce I'm your new attorney at a press conference." He frowned and shook his shaggy head. "I don't like these things happening to you, especially the car bomb. We'll incorporate everything into the statement. Within twenty-four hours the cops will have a new respect and scramble to find out who tried to kill you."

Already my spirits lifted. His enthusiasm was infectious.

"The reporters, God love 'em, will dig into your ex-husband's past with a scalpel. They'll also slice into yours. Are you sure you've told me everything?"

"I swear I've told you all of it. After the other day, I'm not fond of reporters."

"Them nosing around will put the Garretts on alert that you refuse to be a victim again. And a no-nonsense letter to the university threatening a lawsuit is also in order. Now go home and stay out of sight as much as possible."

"I'm staying with Matt in Germantown."

"Good. Germantown cops don't put up with any bullshit. Matt'll come up with what you need. He saved my ass twice." He rose. "Make sure you leave your

117

address and any phone numbers with Doris on your way out. I'll be in touch in a couple of days."

"Thank you, Mr. Monroe."

"Call me Jerricus. Oh, and go buy a good conservative suit for the press conference. Have your hair styled. I want you to look genteel and meek."

Genteel? Meek? Me? "My money's a little short at the moment, and I'm not sure…"

He reached into the inside pocket of his suit coat, extracting a thin, alligator wallet, then laid five one-hundred-dollar bills in front of me.

I gasped. "I can't take this."

"Sure you can. You need to look your best. Use whatever is left over to pay any bills you have. I want you as free from debt as possible. Those reporters will rake you over the coals if they find anything."

"But—but—"

"Go on. I'm your attorney. From now on, you'll play the game according to my rules."

I put the money in my purse. I was new at this attorney-client thing. I'd met my divorce attorney exactly three times. So if that's what Jerricus Monroe wanted—that's what he got. I murmured another thank you and left, stopping to give Miss Singleton the information he requested.

The best attorney in the city had just agreed to take my case. My feet barely touched the floor. For the first time, I had confidence in the outcome.

****

I burst through the door of Matt's office, yelling in jubilation. "He took the case! He took the case!"

Matt rose from the desk, picked me up, and twirled me around, then kissed each cheek.

"I knew he would. Jerricus knows a publicity-laden case when he sees it."

I sank into a chair, fanning myself with my hand.

"I feel like the weight of the world has been lifted from my shoulders. And he's doing it pro bono, too."

"Knowing Jerricus, he'll write the entire fee off to advertising with the press coverage he'll be getting." Matt grinned and sat back behind the desk. "Now tell me everything."

I gave him a full description of my interview, including Jerricus's comments regarding my former in-laws.

"Your lawyer is one of the few people in the city unimpressed with the Garrett influence or wealth." Matt chuckled but quickly sobered. "A press conference could force the cops to seriously investigate the threats and admit the explosion was a car bomb meant for you. Instead of hearing all about how the son of a prominent family was murdered by his ex-wife, the newspapers will have to give you a fair shake or look like they're under the thumb of your former in-laws."

"I don't think the media cares much about that. I can't figure out why the papers haven't jumped all over the battered wife syndrome."

"I wonder," he said, turning to his computer. He typed for a few seconds and waited until the information flashed onscreen. "Ah-ha! The owner of the local rag is an alumnus of the Memphis Academy." He typed some more. "According to this, he graduated two years ahead of Diana and Jerricus."

"Do you think Diana is influencing what is printed?"

"Of course she is. Socially, he's one of them. She's

not a politician's wife for nothing. 'Spin' is her middle name," he replied while typing some more. He was silent for a couple of minutes until the information he sought came up. "Interesting. Hamilton and Diana Garrett contributed heavily to District Attorney Robert Lee Jefferson's election campaign and hosted several fundraisers."

The news surprised me, but I didn't know why. Politicians always feed off one another, like cannibals.

"And the chief of police is Bobby Lee's wife's cousin. And she is a cousin twice removed to Diana."

Swell. Blood is thicker than water. The deck was stacked against me.

"I can't find any direct connection between the Garretts and the TV stations in the city, but I'll dig deeper. There has to be something. A crusading station like Channel 22 wouldn't pass up this opportunity without a reason." He swung back to face me, a grin on his face. "I have some good news, too. I found Richard Bartlett."

"Danny's friend? Really? Where is he?"

"Mr. Bartlett lives—oddly enough—in Bartlett. I called, and he's willing to talk."

"Great. When do we leave?"

"We don't. I do. I think it's better if you stay at the house. Lock the doors and pull the drapes."

I sat back in the chair and crossed my arms. "Don't patronize me. I'm not a child. I knew Rich when he used to come to the house. I want to be there."

"Theresa, it's not like he's going to confess."

"I don't care. I'm coming."

"God save me from a determined woman. All right, you can come but keep quiet. Let me do the talking."

He gave me a stern look.

I nodded my understanding. All I wanted was to be in on the interrogation. I'd remained silent when Danny and his friends hatched their schemes, but had listened—and remembered.

****

Matt had scheduled the meeting for seven o'clock at a sports bar called the Locker Room in a strip mall off Stage Road. Traffic had been heavier than anticipated, so we arrived a few minutes late.

The crowded bar buzzed with activity. The NBA playoffs were on TV, and the Memphis Grizzlies would play later in the evening. I looked around and spotted Rich sitting at a table in the far corner of the room. I touched Matt's elbow and led the way.

Rich hadn't changed much over the last few years. Of medium height, his stocky build had added several pounds, and his ruddy complexion told me he probably had high blood pressure. A half-empty pitcher of beer sat in front of him.

"Hello, Rich," I said.

He nodded. "Theresa. It's been a long time. You look well, considering. Have a seat."

We sat down, and a waitress appeared.

"Diet Coke for me," I requested quickly.

"The same," Matt echoed.

"Rich, this is Matt Summers. He's a private investigator I hired to find Danny's killer."

Matt held out his hand. Rich hesitated before shaking it. "Nice to meet you, Mr. Bartlett. I appreciate your time."

"I was surprised to get your call. I don't know what I can tell you. I haven't seen or heard from Danny in over five years. That was one of the conditions of my parole—no contact with former associates." His gaze shifted to me. "No offense, Theresa, but I thought you did it. I was going to call and offer my congratulations."

"I take it there was no love lost between you and the late Mr. Garrett," Matt said, bringing out his notebook.

"I'd known Danny for close to ten years. During the entire time he was full of bullshit, only I never recognized it."

"How did you know him? I know you weren't in the same social set."

Rich snorted and poured beer in his mug as the waitress arrived with our diet Cokes.

"I was a caddy at the Memphis Country Club. I caddied for him one time, gave him some good club choices, and he had the best round of his life. After that, he requested me whenever he came in. One night he invited me out for a drink with some of his buddies. We started hanging together."

"How did you end up in jail?"

"Through my own stupidity. I was flattered someone with Danny's background and money would choose me for a friend, but then all of his friends were like me—not quite poor, but always in need of ready cash. We'd meet at his place and make super plans to get easy money." Rich looked at me, a shamed expression on his face. "I knew Danny pounded on you. I wasn't blind, but because he bought us booze and drugs, we all kept our mouths shut."

Matt's hands tightened on his pencil, and his lips thinned. I spoke quickly before he could say anything.

"It's all in the past now."

"What kind of schemes did Danny come up with?" Matt's voice showed none of the anger I knew he felt.

"He loved the thought of cheating the casinos. He'd bankroll us for the high-stakes tables. We'd play a few hands, and then he'd create a distraction at another table nearby. When everyone's attention was diverted, we'd swipe chips from other players' stacks."

"But the cameras don't follow the distraction. They stayed trained on the tables," Matt said.

"He convinced us the 'eye in the sky' would never notice. Within a few minutes, security guards tapped us on the shoulder. They hauled our asses into a back room, showed us the tape, took our pictures, and then threw us out."

"Danny, too?" I asked.

"Hell, no. He'd play for a couple of hours while the rest of us sat in the car. He'd act all disappointed it didn't work on the way home."

"What landed you in jail?" Matt asked.

"Mail fraud. Danny had us send letters to people, telling them they'd won some nonexistent lottery. All they had to do to claim the million-dollar jackpot was send in two hundred dollars for a processing fee. I can't believe how many people fell for that. The feds got wind of it, staked out my apartment, and picked us up one afternoon after I got back from the post office with the latest batch of checks."

"I remember that one. Danny stayed too long and got caught up in the arrests," I said.

"Yeah, he'd done a couple of lines of coke, drank a six pack or two, and then fell asleep. He and his lawyer claimed he had nothing to do with the scam—that he'd just dropped by to visit me. The prosecutor bought it and dropped the charges."

"Let me guess, nothing connected with the fraud was in his name, so you took the fall," Matt stated.

Rich nodded. "The son of a bitch took most of the money, too. Said he needed it for operating expenses. Like a moron, I believed him." He drained his beer. "Every day I was in jail, I hoped someone would take him down. Cheered when I heard he finally got popped."

"Speaking of which," Matt said. "Where were you when Danny bit the big one?"

"At work. C & J Construction. I was up in Millington the entire day."

Matt snapped his notebook shut and stood. I followed.

"One other thing, Mr. Bartlett—did you ever hear of a guy, a drug connection of Danny's, called The Juice?"

"I remember him calling a guy for scores. I think that was the name he used. I didn't do much other than a joint now and then. Try Lester Meeks. He and Danny did the most coke. Les usually made the drug runs."

"Did Danny owe his connection money?"

"Show me a time he didn't."

"Okay, thanks for your help."

"Goodbye, Rich, and good luck," I said.

We left the Locker Room and drove back to Germantown. In my opinion it had been a good interview. The cops *had* to pick up on the drug connection now.

At the house, I went into the kitchen to make some iced tea while Matt opened his mail.

"Uh-oh," he said.

"What?"

He placed a piece of paper on the table. Constructed out of letters snipped from newspapers and magazines, the message read: *TELL THE BITCH SHE'S DEAD!!*

Chapter Eight

"Oh, my God," I said in a hushed tone. "I had no idea things would turn out like this. Matt, about the shooting…"

"I think it's wise not to speak of the crime at all, even in private when we think we're alone."

"Why?" I asked.

"Just being cautious. The cops know you're here, but obviously some of Danny's associates also know. Anyone could have come in while we were gone and bugged the place. Same with my office. The landlines could be tainted. I'm not even sure about my car."

My shoulders slumped. "There's just no end, is there? We can't talk anywhere. I can't unburden myself about, well, anything regarding the case."

Matt picked up my hand and raised it to his lips. "I know, but you're strong. You've proved that. You'll come out of this on top. I promise."

Finding the rest of Danny's old friends proved elusive. Lester Meeks, the coke-head Rich suggested we interview, had dropped off the face of the earth, or at least out of Memphis. Matt hadn't been able to find anything on him. Carl Wexford, another buddy, still lived in the area but had no landline phone and moved every few months. We were always two apartments or rooming houses behind him.

Matt had turned the threatening note over to the

Germantown police, but none of us held out much hope of finding anything other than Matt's fingerprints on it.

On Tuesday morning, I actually had to answer the office phone. The woman on the other end turned out to be a new client from East Memphis requesting a meeting out that way, and Matt, not wanting me to stay alone in the office, insisted I return home.

Seeing boredom on the horizon, I killed the rest of the morning poking around in the upscale Germantown stores and treating myself to lunch at Oscar's. I hoped no one recognized me as the bloodstained lady of the other night.

I had just arrived back at the house when a black Lexus glided to a stop at the foot of the driveway. Given the events of the past few days, my heart pumped a few teeth-rattling thumps in my chest, but the young man getting out was well dressed and smiled as he approached.

"Miss Lennox?"

"Yes," I said in a wary voice.

"I'm from Mr. Monroe's office. He asked me to give you this." He handed me a large manila envelope. "If you have any questions, call Doris. Have a nice day."

"Thank you," I murmured.

Curious, I ripped it open on the front stoop and read. Jerricus hadn't let any grass grow under his feet. He'd called a press conference for Wednesday afternoon at three o'clock.

Good grief. That's tomorrow. I held what amounted to a script. I sat at the kitchen table, trying to memorize everything, when Matt walked in.

"What's up?" he asked.

I waved the paper under his nose. "This. Jerricus has scheduled a press conference at three tomorrow. Matt, I'm not sure I can say any of this. It's not true."

Matt read the letter, then the script, and laughed. "Good old Jerricus missed his calling. He should have been a screenwriter or an actor. Just go with the flow. He'll do most of the talking and answer any questions. All you have to do is look confused and pathetic—in good clothing, of course. Did you buy a suit yet?"

"No. I'll go to Penney's tomorrow morning."

"Why go there? Jerricus gave you five hundred dollars. Get something extravagant."

"If the image I'm to convey is one of a lowly victim, then a simple, inexpensive outfit works. No one is going to sympathize if I'm dressed in designer duds. I don't understand why he needs to hold a press conference in the first place. All they'll do is ask embarrassing questions."

"Because your attorney is a master at manipulation."

"Of the press?"

"Of everybody. Look at how many high-profile cases have been tried in the media over the years. O. J., the guy out in California who killed his pregnant wife, the disappearing student on that Caribbean island, numerous rap artists, athletes, even the woman accused of killing her toddler—all of them. The press had a field day, and the public ate it up. No one could find an untainted jury pool anywhere."

"In that case, I guess I'd better work on my pathetic act," I said in a dry tone. I thought the whole thing distasteful, but not half as distasteful as spending the rest of my life in prison. "How was your interview with the new client?"

"Fine. She's a wealthy widow who's been dating a younger man for the last several months. He's just asked for a substantial amount of money to invest in a real estate deal. She wants me to check him out before she calls her lawyer and draws up a loan agreement complete with interest. The lady is very savvy when it comes to money. I'll take a couple of days to check him out and get us some much-needed cash."

I caught my lower lip between my teeth in guilt. So far, I hadn't crossed his palm with anything silver. Even with my attorney working pro bono, I hesitated to cash in another CD. I might need that money later—like for a fresh start when I got out of prison.

"I'm sorry, Matt. You can have what's left over from Jerricus's advance."

"Don't be silly."

"I'm not. I'm living in your house and eating your food. It's your name on the rental car receipt, and now you're getting threatening phone calls and mail. Maybe I should just hole up at a cheap motel somewhere."

"And pay with what? Your credit card? If anyone wanted to find you, credit card transactions would be the first place they'd look. Just stay cool. After tomorrow, you'll be better off staying out of sight here than coming into the office with me anyway."

My eyes welled, and I sniffed when a tear trickled down my cheek. "What's going to happen to me? If we don't come up with a killer soon, I'll go to jail."

"Quit thinking about Danny's death."

"Matt, I've tried, but it's always there. I know we agreed not to think or speak about it, but it's in my mind all the time. It's an image I can't erase. I'm not even sure what's real and what isn't anymore."

"It's too easy to let those thoughts and images take root. Once they do, it's tough to separate fact from fiction. Even innocent people get confused, make mistakes, and before they know it, they're in prison."

Matt was right. I needed to push what I'd seen, what I thought I'd seen, and what I said I'd seen to the back of my mind and stick to what I had told the police.

"I'm innocent. I didn't do it. I have no idea who did. The list of suspects is long," I chanted like a mantra.

He hugged me. "That's my girl. Keep saying that, and you'll be fine."

"Oh, God, what if it doesn't work out the way we want?"

"Hey, don't think that way. You have the best lawyer in the city, and I'm working on the case. You'll be set free. I promise."

I took a deep breath. He promised a lot, and I trusted him, but in the end it was my ass on the line.

He held me closer. I liked being in his arms. They conveyed strength, comfort, and a sense of security I'd not experienced in years. I swallowed my tears, sliding my arms around his waist. His hands stroked my back and hair, sending my heart rate up.

I wanted to kiss him in the worst way—and not some little peck on the cheek. I needed it hot, wet, and demanding. I realized that need involved a hell of a lot more than a kiss. I imagined us naked and sweating up the sheets on his king-sized bed.

He pushed away and smiled. "I do have some news."

"Oh? What?" I dried my tear tracks with the back

of my hand, disappointed at the loss of physical contact.

"I know why we can't find Lester Meeks."

"Why?"

"He's dead."

"Dead? What happened?" My voice rose in consternation. He had topped our list of suspects.

Matt opened the fridge and poured two glasses of iced tea, then handed me one.

"He moved to LA three years ago. That's why I couldn't find him. I was only searching in the tri-state area and then decided to check for Lester on a national basis."

"How did he die? Something gross, I hope. He was slime."

"He was found shot to death in a vacant lot last year. He had a long rap sheet with the LA cops for burglary, assault, drugs, and armed robbery. He also had a crack habit he couldn't keep up with financially. He bought two in the back of the head, execution style. If you don't pay up, your supplier gets you in the end," Matt explained, taking a long swallow of his tea.

I did the same. A live Lester Meeks would have suited our purpose well, but I was glad he'd met a gruesome end. An idea occurred to me.

"Matt, if a supplier killed Lester, then why couldn't one have killed Danny?"

"My thoughts exactly." Matt smiled. "I emailed the information to Jerricus. He'll put it to good use. I have some other good news, too. I finally found Carl Wexford."

I shuddered. I loathed the man. Calling him pond scum was an insult to algae. "Where?"

"He's staying with a girlfriend down in Southaven.

131

He was arrested two days ago on a DUI and is presently in the Desoto County jail. The girlfriend is trying to arrange bail. I'll help her out in exchange for a face-to-face."

"When?" I wasn't eager to meet up with Carl again, but if it produced results, I'd go for it.

"This afternoon. This evening I have an appointment with Joey Wheeler. Do you remember him?"

That wasn't one of the names I'd supplied. I thought for a moment and then gave up. No picture came to mind.

"Not really. Danny's peripheral friends changed frequently."

"Peripheral? What do you mean?"

"Those were the guys on the fringes. Danny only associated with them when he wanted something or needed to feel important. They were like Rich—easily impressed and flattery prone. Who is he?"

"I discovered him from an old arrest file, and he might not be peripheral. His apartment was the last known address of Lester Meeks before he took off to California."

"You've talked to him?"

Matt nodded and finished his tea. "A little while ago. He sounded willing to help. I won't know until we set up a time and place. But first, I have to get Wexford out of jail and meet with him."

"We," I said in a calm voice. "I'm going with you."

"I never thought otherwise. I'll be in the upstairs office if you need me."

He finally understood that I was determined to help. I went back to memorizing my script. I finally took a break and wandered out onto the deck. The sunshine of earlier had given way to dark clouds. Thunder rumbled, and as I sat at the small dining table, the rain began, first as a gentle patter, then increasing.

It drummed on the roof of the covered porch. I stared at the drops pounding into the pool. A flash of lightning followed by a cracking boom of thunder a second later made me jump, causing me to knock over my glass of iced tea. My mind immediately transported from Matt's porch to the firing range and the flash of my gun firing with the reverberation of the gunshot ringing in my ears. Then just as quickly, my eyes no longer saw the pool but Danny in my bedroom.

I leaped to my feet and ran inside. *Stop it, stop it, stop it! Don't think like this, or you'll crack up!*

Breathing heavily, I forced myself to visualize a meadow and a tranquil stream. Within a couple of minutes, my heart rate had slowed, and my nerves had calmed.

If I didn't get a grip on my emotions, I'd end up either in jail or a looney bin. Neither prospect was appealing.

****

Carl Wexford glared from across the table. He sneered and poured another mug of beer from the pitcher in front of him. I remembered how he'd laugh whenever Danny ordered me around or backhanded me. I'd hated him then, and I saw no reason to change my mind now.

His greasy, blond hair styled in a mullet hung down his neck in dirty, limp strands. He scratched at the stubble on his face with filthy fingers and hadn't bathed in a while—he stank to high heaven. He must have come directly from jail to the Stateline Bar where he'd agreed to meet us.

"If I'd a knowed it was you bailin' me out, I'd a stayed put," he declared, venom dripping from his voice.

"Miss Lennox didn't bail you out. I did," Matt said in calm, even tones.

"You mean Mrs. Garrett, dontcha? You never did have no respect for Danny. You dissed him all the time, but he showed you who was boss." Carl drained his mug and poured more. "Enjoy your freedom while you can, because a judge is gonna slap your ass back in stir."

I wanted to punch the little weasel right in his nasty mouth but resisted the urge. Besides, with my luck, I'd probably break the skin of my knuckles on his yellow, unbrushed teeth and get the deadly creeping crud. His breath could kill a moose at ten paces.

I glanced at his girlfriend. She sat back in her chair, a sullen look on her heavily made-up face. In spite of the concealer and powder, the remnant of a purplish bruise was visible on her jaw. It explained the surly expression. No wonder she had taken her time trying to bail Carl out.

"Miss Lennox didn't kill her ex-husband. We think it was someone with a score to settle."

"Yeah, right." He shot me a hate-filled look.

"When did you last see Danny Garrett?" Matt asked.

"I ain't seen Danny in a coupla years." He swigged more beer.

"That's right," Matt said in a conversational tone. "You were busy serving a twelve-month sentence for domestic battery on your former girlfriend, weren't you?" He smiled and shot a glance at the girl while Carl glared. "Tell me about Danny Garrett."

"He was my best friend. He looked out for me. If you think I'm going to say something bad about him, you're fuckin' nuts."

"Some friend. Didn't he leave you holding the bag, literally, on a marijuana bust?"

"Hey, we'd a never got caught if that idiot Les hadn't led the cops right back to my apartment."

"Yeah, but Danny got off. You did six months for possession—your fourth offense."

"Danny was my buddy, and he did his fair share of time thanks to this bitch here." Carl threw me a filthy look and curled his lip in a snarl.

Matt's fingers clenched around his pencil for a moment and then relaxed. "Where were you last Thursday night, say around nine o'clock?"

I saw where Matt was going with this. Could Carl have fired the shot at the motel?

"I was at home with Katie. Right, babe?" He skewered his girlfriend with a hard look.

Katie gulped and nodded. "Yeah, right. We were watching TV."

"What about later, after midnight?"

"In bed."

Katie nodded to confirm Carl's words.

"How about the morning of the murder?"

Carl drained his mug and poured another. "Sleepin' one off. Didn't wake up until afternoon. Tell him, Katie." His words slurred.

"I was at work from ten in the morning till six that day," she said. Carl glared at her, and she quickly amended, "But he was sleepin' real sound when I left."

I didn't believe a word of it. This whole meeting had been a waste of time. We'd get nothing useful.

"Did you ever meet a guy called The Juice?" Matt asked.

"Once or twice."

"Danny owe him money?"

"Danny always owed The Juice, but The Juice was cool with it. He knew Danny'd pay sooner or later."

Matt's eyebrows rose. "A drug dealer running a tab? That sounds a little far-fetched."

"Hey, Danny knew how to treat his friends. He was damned generous. I once heard Les say The Juice was like one of those discount clubs."

"Know where I can find The Juice?"

Carl finished his beer, poured yet another, missing the mug and slopping a good portion of it on the table.

"Nope."

Matt handed the man a business card. "If you get any sudden visions, give me a call. Come on, Theresa."

We rose, but before I left, I leaned over and addressed Katie.

"This is advice from a person who's been there. You don't have to take it. He's not going to change, and the beatings will only get worse. Walk away now while you can."

I cast a glance at Carl and curled my lip. He bared his teeth, looking ready to explode. Poor Katie just looked scared. I hoped I hadn't made things worse for her.

"I—I'm all right. Leave us alone," she said in a shaky voice with downcast eyes.

I turned and left, saying a silent prayer for her.

****

"That was a bust." I fastened my seat belt as Matt blended in with the evening rush hour traffic. "We didn't get anything out of him except nastiness."

"Actually, we did," Matt replied, steering around an eighteen wheeler and heading north on I-55.

"We did?"

"We can eliminate Carl as the shooter last Thursday. He'd have had no idea when you'd make bail. And I don't peg him for trashing your place either. He isn't smart enough to have found, let alone staked out, your apartment. Carl strikes me as too lazy to do any more than mentally plot revenge. He doesn't think beyond his next drink or snort."

"Could he be the one leaving the threatening messages?"

"Possibly, that's more his style."

"And the car bomb?"

Matt paused for a moment. "I can't see it."

"You said it would be simple to rig."

"Not simple enough for Carl."

"Too bad you didn't use the tape recorder. We could have sent the tapes in to see if the voices matched."

"Who says I didn't tape?" Matt flashed me a cocky grin. He reached into his shirt pocket and pulled out a device similar to the one Jerricus had used. "Be prepared—Boy Scouts. My new toy. I also had it running when we talked to Bartlett. I'll drop it off at a friend's tomorrow morning. He'll analyze it. Carl made a comment I found intriguing."

"What?"

"Did you hear that crack he made about Les

referring to The Juice as a discount club?"

"Yeah, but it didn't make any sense."

"Think about it. What is a discount club?"

"A wholesale distributor. You pay a fee and shop in bulk for…less." I paused, astonishment ripping through me. "Buy in bulk—for less. Oh, my God. You think Danny was dealing?"

"Why not? Like you said, he had a lot of peripheral friends for potential customers. Did your ex carry large wads of cash?"

"Not really. Maybe three or four hundred."

The prospect of Danny dealing drugs staggered me, although now that I thought about it, the idea didn't sound so surprising.

"So he was a small-time dealer. Maybe he upgraded after your divorce. You took him to the cleaners. Maybe Hamilton made him sign an IOU. Your ex was always looking for ways to make easy money. Wonder what would have happened if he'd tried skimming from his supplier."

"I'd say the supplier might be angry enough to kill." Excitement buzzed through me. Oh, God, maybe this was the answer.

"I'll check it out."

"I knew throwing in with you was a good move. So where are we going now?" I asked.

"A little restaurant called the Town and Country up in Cordova. We'll meet with Joey Wheeler, have dinner, and then go home. You have an important day tomorrow."

My first press conference—and I hoped my last. The thought of facing all those reporters and the glare of TV lights made me want to cower in a corner. While

Matt negotiated the traffic, I leaned my head back, concentrating on what I was supposed to say, and how to act as Jerricus had instructed.

The Town and Country was a small buffet style restaurant, standing alone in the parking lot of a strip mall on Germantown Parkway in Cordova. We walked in the front door and found a seat. I looked around but didn't see any single men. The place was popular with the older crowd and young families.

A few minutes later a tall, lanky man entered. I remembered him now. He'd been around for several months during the middle years of my marriage. I waved my hand. Joey nodded and then joined us.

"Joey Wheeler? I'm Matt Summers. This is Theresa Lennox, Danny Garrett's ex-wife."

"Miss Lennox, I'm glad to see you again, although you probably don't remember me."

"I remember you were around, but that's all."

"Joey, Miss Lennox and I are looking for Danny Garrett's killer. We've already talked to Rich Bartlett and Carl Wexford. What can you tell us about Danny that might shed some light on his murder?"

"Not much, Mr. Summers. It was a long time ago, and I didn't run with that crowd too long. I was barely eighteen and wanted to taste life on the wild side before I left for college."

"We're going on the theory Danny's murder may have been drug related. Can you tell us anything?"

A waitress came by to take drink orders. We all requested iced tea. She left, and Joey sat back, his brow knit as he thought.

"There were drugs around, of course. I used to blow a little pot with them, but mostly I just drank

---

beer."

"Who paid for the drugs?"

"Danny. He'd make a phone call, and then Les Meeks would go get it. Now there was one scary dude—street wise and mean as a snake. He always carried a gun or two, and after he got high would take one out and flash it around, warning us not to mess with him. Carl was another badass only dumber. He looked up to Les like some kind of hero."

"How'd you get hooked up with Garrett?" Matt asked as the waitress brought our drinks.

"The Memphis Country Club—I was a caddie. Rich introduced us."

"How come you only hung around for a few months?"

Joey shrugged. "College. I went to the University of Kentucky that fall and lost contact with everyone. Rich was always the quiet one, although he did have a blazing temper. I remember him and Danny brawling on the floor of Rich's apartment one night. How did you get my name?"

"It popped up on an old arrest record. You had the bad luck to be in a car with Carl Wexford one night when he got pulled over. I read the arrest report."

Joey's head snapped up. "That was a misdemeanor drug charge—my one and only. I did six months probation. It should have been expunged."

"If I were you, I'd contact a lawyer and straighten it out. Something like that could look bad to an employer."

"I work for an accounting firm. I'm supposed to take my CPA exam next month. I can't have them find out about this. I have a wife, a two-year-old daughter, and one on the way. Damn."

"How come Lester Meeks listed your apartment as his last known address in Memphis?"

"I was a newlywed. My wife wanted a larger place in a better area. We rented here in Cordova. I still had two months to run on my lease with the old digs. When Lester showed up needing a bed, I let him stay. He was supposed to pay me rent. He never did and left the joint in a mess."

"You said you hadn't seen any of the old crowd since before college. How did you meet up with him again?"

"Damnedest luck. I was having a drink with a friend at a bar near the University of Memphis campus when in walked Lester. He bugged me for over a week. To get rid of him, I let him use the apartment." Joey drained his iced tea in several gulps. "Is there anything else? I've got to get home. My wife's making dinner."

"Did you ever hear anyone refer to a guy called The Juice?"

"The Juice? No, not that I can remember."

Joey said goodbye and left. The waitress returned to refill our glasses. We hit the buffet and sat down again.

"I guess this one was pretty much a bust, too," I said.

"Not necessarily. Peripheral friends notice things because they aren't as involved."

"Like what?"

"Like the bit about Richard Bartlett's temper and he and Danny fighting."

"But Rich said he'd been at work in Millington the day of the murder."

"But was he? Danny Garrett let him take the fall for mail fraud. Could be those five years in prison gave Rich the time to perfect a plan. He may have learned patience. I'll check that out, too."

"We take one step forward and ten back," I complained, my voice rising. "We haven't found this Juice person, and everyone else seems to have an airtight alibi. This is my life here. I don't want to spend the rest of it in prison." Several people at nearby tables turned their heads to stare.

Matt grasped my hand in his. "Calm down, Theresa. I said I'd help get you off, and I will. You've also got Jerricus on your side, and don't forget your neighbors. If this actually goes to trial, they'll make great character witnesses. Now is not the time to run scared."

"Trial? I don't want this to go to trial. I don't want to hear a guilty verdict from a jury made up of a bunch of unemployed people who don't have anything better to do."

Before I could help it, a sob escaped from my throat. Conversation around us stopped.

"Honey, tomorrow is your press conference. Jerricus will broadside the Garretts and the prosecution. He always does. By this time tomorrow night, the DA may drop the case. If so, you're home free. Buck up. You're made of strong stuff. I'll find The Juice—if necessary." Matt spoke in a quiet, soothing voice, then frowned, letting go of my hand to stare into space. "I know I've heard that name before. Tomorrow, I'll go through my old files. I'll also look into the dealing angle."

I closed my eyes and conjured up a meadow and

stream in my turbulent mind. I hadn't thought this whole thing would be so hard. I'd envisioned finding evidence of someone else's guilt, presenting it to the police who would then apologize and let me go. *Still naïve after all these years.*

Matt had warned me from the start not to be too optimistic, but then, in spite of my past, I always saw the glass as half full. That basic optimism had been what kept me alive through the Danny years.

We finished dinner in silence, paid our bill, and then headed home.

Matt scanned the messages on his machine while I flipped through the mail. There was nothing of a threatening nature except a past due notice from the cable company.

Chapter Nine

In a downtown park Jerricus Monroe leaned against a podium bristling with microphones on a makeshift stage. I stood beside him under the improvised awning. My attorney looked at ease and in control. On the other hand, I was a wreck. My stomach churned, and I trembled right down to my toes.

I smoothed the lapels of my new navy-blue suit, tweaking the bow at my throat of the powder blue blouse I wore under it. A quick trip this morning to a local discount store had paid dividends. A stray breeze lifted a few strands of my newly styled hair. The waves had been tamed with a generous application of mousse, a blow dryer, and a straightening iron. I didn't look like me.

Several bright lights blazed for the TV cameras. The reporters stood in front of us, resembling a pack of hungry jackals poised and ready to jump. My stomach clenched with nerves, and I couldn't quell my shaking hands. My fingers twisted the soft folds of the handkerchief I held. I wanted this whole thing over.

Jerricus turned to me and smiled before addressing the assemblage. "If y'all are ready, we can begin. Ah imagine we'd all like to call it a day and go have a cold one, eh?"

The reporters laughed politely and settled in. My attorney's Southern accent had deepened into a good-ole-boy drawl, relegating Harvard to the background.

"I'd like to announce I am the attorney for Miss Theresa Lennox who has been wrongfully charged with the murder of her ex-husband, Daniel Garrett. My client will issue a brief statement. I will then further enlighten you to the facts of this case and take questions. Theresa?"

I took a deep breath and approached the podium. Showtime! I licked my lips and cleared my throat.

"Good afternoon. Please forgive me, but I'm a little nervous. I wanted everyone to have a chance to meet me. My name is Theresa Lennox. The police think I killed my ex-husband. I'm here to tell you I didn't."

So far, so good. My voice had just the right amount of earnest confidence and quavering tones to sound believable. I'd been ordered into the office two hours prior to this so I could practice in front of Jerricus and Doris as they schooled me in Acting 101.

"I'd like to give you a bit of background. My father died when I was a baby, so it was just Mom and me. We didn't have a lot of money, but my mother worked long hours to put food on the table. She was my best friend and confidant. I grew up knowing hard work and love."

Only part of that was true. Mom did work long hours, and she was my friend and confidant, but the rest made me sound like the little girl selling matchsticks in the snow. I thought it was hokey.

"My mother was a good, Christian woman who gave me solid values. I know the difference between right and wrong. Sunday church services were very important to us."

I waited for the lightning to strike. Mom had

declared Sunday a day for sleeping in and resting. Our church attendance had been nil.

"Her death ten years ago left a gaping hole in my heart. Unfortunately, I thought Danny Garrett could fill that hole. I was wrong. He drank heavily, took drugs, beat, and threatened to kill me for most of our married life. I had no one to turn to for help. I tried to leave him on several occasions but always returned because I like to think there is good in everybody—even Danny. I kept remembering the good times."

Now I wanted to puke. I remembered no good times. They never existed, and Danny had no redeeming social qualities.

A slight cough from behind reminded me to daub my eyes with the hanky. I did. My eyes immediately stung and watered. They should have. Jerricus had planted a tiny sliver of soap in its folds to insure tears. I sniffled and wiped the tears away with the knuckles of my free hand. I felt like a fraud, which I was. Jerricus, however, had insisted, saying it would strike a sympathetic chord with viewers of the six o'clock news.

"My optimism has been used against me by people with money and power. I have neither. I approached my husband's family for help, but they believed Danny when he told them I was clumsy. I was alone and friendless."

God, were they buying this crap? I sounded like a pathetic wimp, and it made me angry, because at that time in my life, I had been.

Jerricus stepped forward, placing his arm around my shoulders. "You have me, Theresa. I'm your friend, and by the time this nightmare is over, you'll have plenty of friends."

He squeezed my shoulder, which was my cue to once again produce soap-induced tears. I stuck to the script, even though I wanted to shout, "Danny Garrett was a son of a bitch, and I'm glad he's dead." Naturally, I didn't.

"Thank you, Mr. Monroe," I said with another sniffle. "You don't know what that means to me. I don't expect the members of the press to be my friends, but I hope I'll get a fair shake. Thank you all very much."

I stepped back and took up my previous position beside and a step behind Jerricus. Thank God that was over. If my attorney wanted to do this again, it would be without me.

Jerricus draped his large frame over the podium. The reporters shouted questions.

"Why did you fire your public defender?"

"How can you afford Mr. Monroe's fees?"

"How did you make bail?"

"Are you saying Mr. and Mrs. Hamilton Garrett are accomplices in your domestic violence?"

"Is it true you've hired a private investigator?"

I cringed at the bombardment, but Jerricus took it in stride.

"Ladies and gentlemen, please direct your questions to me. I'll make a brief statement and then answer what I can."

The crowd quieted, a miracle brought about by my lawyer's deep, booming voice and commanding presence. He was worth every dime I couldn't afford and wasn't paying.

"The police and the district attorney have drawn a line in the sand, declaring my client a cold-blooded killer. This is a rush to judgment. They have no eyewitnesses to the crime, and even less evidence. Her alibi is solid. The scenario they are suggesting is unrealistic.

"Attempts have been made on her life, which tells me someone thinks she has either information as to the real killer or is in possession of something that killer wants but didn't get from her ex-husband before his death. The police should be looking for this person or people."

I let my mind wander. Earlier, Jerricus had given me news regarding the police investigation. For starters, the cops had traced two phone calls made to Danny's cell. One had come from an untraceable number at eight twenty-two the morning of the murder. Another had come from a pay phone outside a convenience store three blocks from the university at eleven-oh-five.

The police ignored the first call, preferring to concentrate on the second, suggesting I had stopped and called, luring Danny to the apartment. Jerricus had said it was all part of the game and to ignore the accusations. If they believed that, and had any evidence to support it, they would have charged me with murder one.

The good news was no one at the store remembered having seen me, but they did remember a man—no description—using the phone sometime that morning. More good news had followed. Jerricus had found several people who could put me in the university cafeteria at one o'clock. I licked my lips and refocused my attention on my attorney.

"Take a good look at my client. Does she look dumb enough to use her own gun to kill a man and then leave it lying on the floor beside him? And if she wanted to kill her ex-husband, why wait eighteen months to do it? Miss Lennox is being railroaded.

"She has been trying to put her life in order after almost a decade of torture. She wants to make a difference and enrolled in the University of Memphis to achieve that goal. But now even the dream of helping the children of abuse has been crushed."

He turned and cast a sad look in my direction. Oops, that was my cue. I screwed up my face, daubed my eyes, and sobbed. It would take hours to wash out the soap. I'd argued about the child abuse thing, but Jerricus insisted that while counseling battered women was noble, assisting children was even more so.

I listened as he droned on about my job loss and how I was being persecuted by rich and powerful forces. He brought up several biblical analogies I thought a little over the top, but what the hell? He was Jerricus Monroe, and no one in the crowd of reporters looked surprised. They'd probably heard it a dozen times before.

"And I am putting the University of Memphis and the Campus Notes Bookstore on notice that if Miss Lennox is not reinstated immediately, they will be sued. All right, now I'll take a few questions."

"Why did Miss Lennox fire her public defender?" a man in front asked.

"Because he didn't believe her innocent. I do. Next? Mr. Holcombe."

"What other suspects do the police have?"

"Daniel Garrett was a multi-layered individual, addicted to cocaine. Whenever you have an addict murdered, then the drug angle *must* be considered. Yes, the lady in the red blouse. What's your question?"

"Mr. Monroe, you've used the phrase 'rich and powerful' several times. Are you insinuating Mr. and Mrs. Hamilton Garrett are involved in covering up domestic violence and are trying to influence the district attorney's office?"

"I have no proof of that, nor did I say it. Mr. and Mrs. Garrett are the parents of a slain son. We can understand their frustration and grief."

Great answer. Of course that's what he insinuated, but his reply made it sound compassionate. My ex-in-laws still came off looking rich, powerful, and manipulative. I loved it.

"The man in the back with the tan shirt. Your question, please."

The reporter held a microphone, but from this distance I couldn't read the TV station's call letters. The soap blurred my vision.

"I understand your client attacked a TV reporter the other day. Any comment?"

"Miss Lennox was distraught. Her home had been vandalized so badly she had to seek shelter elsewhere. The man was in violation of a court order to stay a hundred feet away from my client. She turned and found a microphone shoved in her face. She regrets the incident, but I'm sure you can understand her momentary lapse."

"Is it true Miss Lennox has hired a private investigator, and where is your client staying?"

"Yes, that's true, and she's staying somewhere safe and secluded. Thank you, ladies and gentlemen."

Jerricus turned away from the reporters, draped his arm over my shoulders, and led me to a waiting limo.

He slid in after me and slammed the door, cutting

off the questions still being shouted. He gave me a hug and planted a big smacker on my cheek.

"You were wonderful. You tore their hearts out."

"How can you tell? Their questions sounded damned ornery to me."

"Yeah, but their eyes were sympathetic. They'll ask questions of the cops and DA now. Expect a damage-control press conference in a few days."

"I was worried they'd see through the bullshit."

"They didn't buy all of it, but you sold it, especially with the tears."

"How could I not? What kind of industrial strength soap did you use? I may go blind."

He laughed. "Never underestimate the power of a little deception. I stole the idea from a movie."

"So what happens next?"

"The TV stations will have it on the six o'clock news. I saw four Memphis reporters and one from Nashville—he was probably here because Ham is thinking of running for governor. We'll be page one in the morning papers.

"Go home and keep a low profile. It won't be long before reporters sniff out Matt, so be prepared. Let me know the minute you see one. The restraining order only mentions your apartment. I'll have it amended to include Matt's home and office."

His phone rang, and while he conferred with another client, I gazed out the limo's tinted window to watch the traffic on Poplar Avenue. We arrived back at Jerricus's office where he escorted me to my car with one last warning.

"Remember, stay out of sight as much as possible and don't talk to anybody about the case."

"I won't."

I drove away with confidence. Today had gone well. It was about time.

****

It was after five by the time I pulled into the driveway. My heart did a little flip-flop when I saw a strange car parked out front. God, could a reporter have found me this fast? Then I noticed the car was a late model Mercedes, and the man sitting in it was my former father-in-law. Shit. Just what I needed.

I hurried toward the front door, keys in hand, pretending I didn't see him. Matt's car was gone.

"Theresa. I want to talk to you."

I glanced over my shoulder as Hamilton cut across the lawn to join me on the stoop.

"I don't think I should be talking to you. My lawyer wouldn't like it."

"Let's go inside. I don't conduct business on the front porch."

"How did you know where to find me?" I asked, unlocking the door. I wanted to slam it in his face, but curiosity got the better of me.

"I make it my business to know things." He closed the door behind him.

I wasn't scared of Hamilton but swallowed a lump of nerves in my throat anyway.

"What do you want, Hamilton, and please be brief. It's been a long day." I wondered if he'd already heard about the press conference and had come to confront me. If so, he moved fast. The whole thing had ended less than ninety minutes ago.

"I have some advice for you. Take the plea bargain you were offered. Don't let this go to trial. Why put yourself through a messy court room scene?"

"What you really mean is I should take the deal so a trial doesn't coincide with your run for governor. A lot of unsavory things will come out about your son. Things I'm sure you'd rather your constituents didn't know."

His lips thinned, and his nostrils flared. Anger blazed in his eyes. I, an insignificant former cocktail waitress, was daring to defy the mighty Garrett. My spirits rose.

"I don't think you've considered how this is affecting Diana. She's been a wreck ever since Danny's death. A trial would be hell for her."

"Phfft. Like I care. She never gave a rat's ass when her precious son beat the crap out of me. Why should I do anything to make life easier for her—or you?"

"Theresa, may I remind you I have resources you can't begin to comprehend?" he said in a supercilious tone. "The prosecutor is going to make mincemeat out of that overworked lawyer you were assigned."

That answered my question about the press conference. He'd probably have a coronary when he got the news about Jerricus. The idea further cheered me.

"Maybe I have a few surprises up my sleeve, too. You've said your piece. I have no objection to you leaving."

"If you won't listen to reason, then perhaps cold hard cash will change your mind. It has in the past."

A car door slammed in the driveway, and through the sidelight I saw Matt walking up the sidewalk.

"Drop dead, Hamilton."

"I will deposit one hundred thousand dollars in an account of your choosing anywhere in the world. All you have to do is admit killing my son. I swear you'll only spend a few years in prison. You'll get out still a young woman and able to start over. I suggest you take it. I won't offer again."

"You cheap-assed son of a bitch. Do you really think I'd sell my soul for a paltry hundred grand?" I laughed. His face flushed a deep red.

The front door opened. Hamilton turned to glare at the intrusion. Matt glared back, his brows drawing together.

"What are you doing here, Garrett?"

"None of your business." Hamilton turned back to me. "I'll give you until noon tomorrow to say yes."

"Yes to what?" Matt asked.

"My former father-in-law has suggested I take the plea bargain. When I refused, he sweetened the pot with a hundred-thousand-dollar bribe."

"Get out," Matt said between clenched teeth. "Get the hell out of my house. If you ever show up again, I'll have you arrested for trespassing."

"I suggest you stay out of this, Summers."

"Out!" Matt grabbed Hamilton's arm, twisted it behind his back, and shoved him through the door.

"You can't treat me like this! Who do you think you are? I'll sue," he sputtered.

Matt ignored him and slammed the door, then took me in his arms. "How did he find out where you were?"

"I have no idea, but I guess it had to happen sooner or later," I replied, loving the warmth and strength of his arms holding me close. My tense muscles relaxed. I could stay this way forever.

"How did the press conference go?"

"According to Jerricus—very well. I guess he

should know." Much to my disappointment, Matt dropped his arms. "He says it'll be on the six o'clock news."

"Why don't you change into something less formal while I order in?"

I ran upstairs, shed the suit, and slipped into a pair of cutoffs and a tank top. I felt like me again.

Thirty minutes later we sat in front of the TV eating kung pao chicken and watching my performance.

"When do I break out the violins?" Matt asked with a dry chuckle. "Jerricus is a genius. You'll have a lot of people pissed off you were arrested and furious about your treatment. The DA and the Garretts will have to do some serious damage control."

"That's what he said. I wish I could see Hamilton's and Diana's faces when they find out he's representing me."

Matt flipped off the TV. I looked around the room and remembered my curiosity about his decorator.

"Matt, did you decorate the house?"

"Only my bedroom. My money decorated the rest."

"Is it indelicate of me to ask who spent your hard-earned cash?"

"No. I have two ex-wives and a sister. It's kind of a mix of all three."

I couldn't help it. I had to ask. "Do you ever see yourself taking the plunge a third time? Do you want a family?"

"If the right woman tempted me, I'd consider it."

I wanted to explore the possibilities along that line a little further, but Matt's cell rang. He answered, then sat up straight and lowered his plate to the coffee table.

"It's good to hear from you…Yes, I'd like to meet,

too…I need information about Danny Garrett."

I put my plate down and leaned closer. "Who is it?" I whispered.

Matt ignored me. "I understand. I don't want to know that much. I'm working for his ex-wife. She's been accused…I'm sure you *have* heard. The point is she didn't do it. I need information that could help her…An hour? Fine. How about a bar on the east side called Newton's…? You do? Good…I swear, no recorder."

Matt hung up and grinned at me.

"So who was it?"

"That was The Juice. Guess one of the words I put out on the street got through."

My heart gave a mighty thump, lurching in my chest. I jumped to my feet and grabbed the dirty dishes while Matt put the leftovers in the fridge.

"Do you think he can help? Will he tell us if Danny owed him money? I mean, won't that be like incriminating himself?"

"We'll know when we get there."

I shoved the dishes into the dishwasher. My hands shook.

Oh, God, please let him be the one.

****

Newton's was located in an older section of East Memphis. Its clientele was varied, making for an interesting mix of college students, the well-to-do, and everyone in between.

I'd enjoyed working there. My co-workers had been friendly, and if I had listened to their advice, would have never married Danny. But that was then. With any luck, tonight my problems would be solved.

We arrived a few minutes after seven thirty. Mike Harper, bartender and friend, greeted me.

"Theresa? Is that you? Damn, girl, it's been a long time. How are you holding up?"

Mike was of medium height and build with a wicked sense of humor. His eyes could crinkle with laughter or shoot sparks when angered. Most of the time, he smiled.

"Mike, it's good to see you." I rushed to the bar and leaned over it to kiss his cheek.

He kissed me back. "The minute I heard about that son of a bitch's death, I cheered. Thank God, you got out of jail. The cops were nuts to arrest you in the first place."

"Thanks, Mike. I'd forgotten I once had friends. Mike, this is Matt Summers. Matt, Mike Harper."

The two men shook hands, sized each other up, and then smiled. I felt better.

"We're here to meet a man. I don't know his name, but if you have no objections, we'll sit over there where we can be seen," Matt told him.

"No problem. What can I get you to drink?"

"I'll have a club soda and Theresa…?" he looked at me with raised eyebrows.

"A glass of Chardonnay, Mike."

We seated ourselves. A few minutes later a waitress brought our drinks.

"Do you think he's going to show?" I asked.

"Maybe, maybe not. We'll give him an hour."

I spent the next twenty minutes fiddling with my wine glass, taking tiny sips. In spite of my dry mouth and throat, I had trouble choking down the excellent beverage. Matt sat across from me, drumming his fingers on the tabletop.

Another thirty minutes passed. Matt worked on his second club soda. I emptied my wine glass and gave up.

"He's not coming." Tears filled my eyes. "I'd hoped so hard…"

Matt sighed. "So did I. We still have a few minutes left. Would you like another glass of wine?"

I shook my head. It was over. The Juice wouldn't show. I should have known better. A shadow fell across the table. A lithe, young black man stood next to us.

"You must be The Juice," Matt said. "You're late."

"No, you were. I was sitting over there in the corner when you came in." He turned dark-brown, almost black eyes onto me. His gaze was a curious mixture of menace and raw sexuality. "Whew-eee. You Danny's squeeze?"

"No, I was Danny's wife."

He grabbed a chair, turned it around, and straddled it. The waitress appeared immediately. I ordered another glass of wine. The Juice ordered Crown, neat.

"So you want to talk to me about Danny."

"Miss Lennox is accused of having murdered him. She didn't. We're looking for the man who did."

"If you expect me to confess and solve your problems, I'm afraid I can't help." He leaned forward and flashed what I assumed passed for a sexy smile. A gold tooth gleamed. "I didn't do it either. You sure you didn't pop him, sweet-cheeks?"

"Absolutely," I replied as our drinks arrived.

"But I have the feeling you know who did," Matt told him in an even voice.

"Not this time around." The Juice took a sip of his whiskey, leering at me again. "If you ever need work, I know a guy who can oblige."

I'll just bet he did—someone with a street name like Big Daddy who'd take ninety-nine percent of what I earned on my back for himself. I kept my silence.

"Did Danny owe you money?" Matt asked.

"Danny always owed money, but I never worried. He was good for it one way or another."

"How?"

"His mommy paid. I didn't care where it came from as long as I got it."

"Did he check out owing a lot?"

The Juice took another sip and focused his attention on Matt. "Yeah. Over ten grand. Now why would I snuff him before I got my money?"

"Was Danny into dealing?"

"He'd do little favors now and then."

"He ever hold out on you?"

"Danny wasn't that stupid."

"How was his gambling?"

"He used to go the casino route, but not for a while."

"Any idea who might want him dead?"

The Juice turned to stare at me and laughed. "Yeah. His ex-wife. There was no love lost there. She nailed his ass a few months after the divorce. He spent a big chunk of time in jail. He didn't like it. Talked about revenge."

"Danny always talked big," I said. "If that was the case, I'd be the dead one."

The Juice slammed down the rest of his drink. "Not if you got to him first. What do the doctors call it? Preventative medicine?"

I didn't answer but instead raised my glass with

trembling hands and drank deeply. This guy was dangerous. My heart lurched and pounded.

Matt countered. "Maybe you were tired of Danny always owing. Maybe you found out exactly how stupid he *could* be. Maybe he snagged a few extra bucks from your account, and you decided to do something about it."

Rising, The Juice stared down at us. "Maybe, but I didn't. See ya around."

He turned and left. The dealer had scared the crap out of me. I drained the remaining wine in a single gulp.

"Come on. Let's get out of here," Matt said.

I slid into the car and buckled my seat belt, giving myself a couple of minutes to calm down, and then asked, "So is he the one?"

"Possibly, but I don't think so." His cell phone rang. "Summers here…Hi, Andy. Got any news…? Uh-huh, are you sure…? That's what I thought, too. Okay, thanks. Do me a favor and email the report to me." He hung up and tossed the phone into a cup holder in the console. "That was Andy at the crime lab. He's got news about the bomb."

"*Was* it a bomb?"

"Yep. Simple and easy to make, just like we thought. They used dynamite, flashlight batteries, and a marble between the frame of the seat and the spring. Unfortunately, the spring was stronger than they thought, and the Jeep had one good suspension system. It took the heavy jolt of going over the curb to set it off—thank God."

"I'd be burned to a crisp if they hadn't goofed," I replied shakily.

We were silent the rest of the way home. I didn't know which was worse, knowing someone wanted me dead, being used by my lawyer, or having my hopes of exoneration evaporate. Matt had warned me not to get too excited, but I'd wanted this whole thing over so badly I didn't listen.

The story of my life.

I could understand Jerricus's manipulations. It got results over time. I didn't feel I had a lot of time.

I also saw The Juice's point of view. Why would he confess? There was nothing in it for him, except jail. So if we couldn't pin the murder on him—then who?

I had no idea who wanted me dead.

****

I shoved my hands into my pockets and paced the floor of the den, antsy as hell. I needed to release this strange energy building inside me. It wasn't anxiety but a different kind of tension. I wanted someone to soothe me, to tell me everything would be all right, to reassure me my life wouldn't be a waste.

Matt came out of the kitchen with a glass of ginger ale and handed it to me.

"Here, drink this."

I swallowed. The tart, cold fizz sliding down my parched throat helped settle my nerves.

"Did you recognize The Juice?" I asked.

"I've seen him before, but I can't place where."

"Well, please hurry it up. Time's running out. I can't take much more of this." My voice sharpened. How could he be so calm?

"Theresa, relax. Everything's going to be fine."

"Yeah, that's easy for you to say—you're not looking at life in prison."

"You're not either. Jerricus will do his job, and I'll do mine."

His soothing voice should have had an effect, but instead tears filled my eyes. I slammed my glass down on the coffee table and sat heavily on the sofa. Gripping my head in my hands, I cried.

"Theresa, don't. It's been a long day. Why don't you go to bed? Tomorrow things will look brighter." He sat next to me, patting me on the back.

I jumped to my feet and stared down at him. "Damn it, don't patronize me!"

He rose, grasped my shoulders, and gave me a shake. "You're letting emotion cloud your logic. I swear to you—this will work out."

I gazed into his concerned face, wanting to believe. Then his expression changed. Concern vanished, and desire blossomed in his eyes. His hands tightened, and the next thing I knew, his lips crushed mine.

Chapter Ten

Oh, my God. This was what I had wanted all evening, all day, all week. I'd wanted him from the first day I'd met him.

His lips demanded a response. With a whimpering moan in the back of my throat, I slid my arms around his neck and glued my body to his. My heart pounded, my nerves throbbed, and the blood roared in my ears. Heat scalded my body from the inside out.

Matt groaned and then pushed me away. I fisted my fingers in the front of his shirt and tried to pull him closer.

"No, Theresa. We can't." He stepped back and pried my hands off him.

"Why not?" I said with a gasp.

"Because the timing's not right."

How many disappointments could I take in a day? I moved away, breathing heavily, ready to cry again, and then said the first thing that popped into my mind.

"You—you don't want me?" The instant the words left my mouth, I knew they sounded ridiculous.

"Of course I do." Matt gestured below his waistband. "I look like I'm smuggling a banana in my shorts. But we can't mix business with pleasure. It's not a good idea. It clouds judgment. We have to keep this professional—until it's over."

My nerves hummed, and his apology made me

want to smack him in the mouth. Professional? Business? Couldn't he see I needed him in a more fundamental way? And whether he realized it or not, he needed me, too. The stress had built all week, and Matt dealt with stress by drinking. I kept him focused.

"Yeah, well, things aren't going according to plan, are they?" Miffed, I turned and flounced out of the room, snapping over my shoulder, "Stick your apology where the sun don't shine, but I'll take your advice and go to bed."

I ran up the stairs and into my bedroom, slamming the door behind me. I pounded my clenched fists against my thighs.

Goddamnit! Didn't anything ever work out the way I wanted?

****

Cold water shocked me awake. I gasped and sucked in a lungful of the stuff, then realized I was totally immersed. Disoriented, I fought to hold my breath and kicked my legs until my head broke the surface. Coughing, I flailed my arms in an attempt to clutch something—anything—as a support. Then my feet touched bottom. I struggled forward until the water leveled out waist high, stopped, and coughed again, expelling more water from my lungs. I had fallen into the pool.

I staggered toward the steps and hauled myself out, somehow making it to the chaise lounge where I collapsed, panting. My heart drummed a million miles an hour, and I couldn't stop shivering even in the warm night air.

Where's Danny?

Danny? I shook my head to clear it. Danny was

dead. I shuddered. A nightmare—a lousy, stinking nightmare. Not the first, but definitely the scariest.

The dream had been so vivid, so real, I lifted my head to scan the bushes seeking my late husband's hiding spot. It was foolish, of course. I closed my eyes and leaned back on the chaise, still coughing up the remnants of my plunge.

I'd dreamed Danny chased me up the stairs into my bedroom. He carried a dead cat, a noose tightly drawn about the poor creature's throat. Cornered, I cowered and wept while Danny smiled and swung the cat in front of my face.

"You're next, precious."

A sob choked my throat. Precious—Danny's favorite endearment just prior to a beating.

Dream anger had coursed through my veins. I opened the drawer of the nightstand and extracted a gun, then shot him twice in the chest. He fell, staring at the ceiling with sightless eyes. Leaping over the body, I reeled toward the door, and then paused to look back.

Danny sat up and laughed. "You can't kill me, precious. I'll always be with you—day and night, night and day, forever."

I'd screamed and raced for the stairs with Danny just inches behind me.

I opened my eyes and shivered again. Already the dream images had faded around the edges. My nightgown clung to my body in limp, wet folds. I needed to get inside. Swinging my legs off the chaise, I glanced at the darkened house. Matt's bedroom faced the front. He wouldn't have heard the splash. I must have sleepwalked down the stairs quietly in spite of my dream panic.

I twisted my fingers in my hair and wrung out some of the wetness. It was just as well he hadn't seen me. I didn't want to explain the sleepwalking or the nightmare at the moment. My stress levels had spiked at an all-time high. Given my day, it wasn't surprising.

I made it back into the house without undue noise. Pausing at the top of the stairs, I listened. Silence. Matt's door remained closed. I resisted the urge to open it and fling myself next to his body, begging to be held and cuddled.

Instead, I entered the bathroom and pulled off my sodden nightie, draping it over the shower rod, and then rummaged through my cosmetics bag until finding the bottle of sleeping pills. I hesitated, not liking how I turned to them so often since Danny's death.

Gulping one of the capsules, I towel dried my hair and slipped back into bed. I cried while waiting for the drug to take effect. My nerves were frayed, like an unraveling rope with only a few strands left to support a heavy load. I was losing control.

****

I sat at the breakfast table and spooned cereal into my mouth, trying to act as though nothing unusual had happened the night before. The pill had worked. I'd slept the rest of the night. Outside, the weather matched my gloomy mood. The rain alternated between a gentle patter on the roof to the drumming of a downpour.

I chewed and swallowed, not tasting what I ate. An inspection in the mirror this morning had reflected a haggard face, and the scale informed me I'd lost close to five pounds in the last few days. I couldn't recommend my weight loss for any diet plan.

Matt sat at the other end of the table, his face

hidden behind the newspaper, with a cup of coffee and a plate of toast in front of him. Every once in a while, his hand appeared to grasp the cup. It would disappear behind the newsprint screen for a few seconds before returning.

He turned a page, chuckled, then folded and tossed it over to me.

"Page eight," he said.

I picked it up and read the two-column report of yesterday's press conference. It was fair, and I couldn't help noticing the accompanying photo showed more of Jerricus than me.

"Not page one? Oh well, it's a start," I replied, laying the paper down and continuing my breakfast.

"I'm sure Jerricus wanted something better than page eight, but this'll do. Toast?" he asked, shoving the plate in my direction.

"No, thanks." My voice sounded stiff.

"Theresa, about last night…"

"I don't want to talk about last night. Let's just chalk it up to an emotional day and forget it."

"All right." He sipped his coffee and bit off a chunk of toast. "What's on your agenda for today?"

"I haven't really thought about it—go into the office with you, I suppose."

He shook his head. "I'm working from home."

"I thought you needed files."

"Most of my files are on the computer. I keep hard copy at the office for back up."

I glanced out at the rain, now in the downpour stage.

"I'll go nuts with nothing to do."

Before he could answer, my cell phone rang. Caller

ID identified Jerricus. I answered immediately.

"Good morning, Theresa," his voice boomed in my ear. "Did you see the newscasts last night and the paper this morning?"

"Yes. Everything went well."

"You bet it did. I've been getting calls from reporters wanting more information on the attempt to kill you. I'll see to it they know the score. By the end of the week, you'll be the most sympathetic murder suspect in the state. Count on it."

"Uh, thanks, Jerricus." I wasn't sure if that was a good thing or not.

"I also got an irate call from Diana Garrett. She ranted and raved for ten minutes about how evil you are, and how I'm going to regret defending you. Even threatened to sue for slander. She shut up when I asked if she really wanted to get into a pissing contest with me. She sounded like a woman on the edge."

"According to Hamilton, she's been like that since the murder. He came out here yesterday."

"The devil he did. What did he want?"

I told Jerricus about the threat and attempted bribe.

"A hundred thousand dollars? He must be nuts. I'll slap him with a restraining order to cease his harassment and then let the media hear about it. He'll be furious. Not good press for a potential gubernatorial candidate."

I held the phone away from my ear as he bellowed with laughter, then I laughed with him. Diana would probably have a stroke. One could only hope.

"Have you heard from the DA's office yet?" I asked.

"No, but I will soon. They'll deal if they think their

case is going down the toilet. Until then, take it easy, and don't do anything stupid like talking to the press. If you do get cornered by one of them, just say 'no comment.'"

"Do you think that's likely to happen?"

"I've amended the court order against the media to include Matt's house and office, but knowing those vultures, they could jump you at the grocery store."

I didn't tell him I had developed a phobia regarding parking lots and grocery stores.

"I'll be careful, Jerricus. I promise."

"I've got to go. Keep your chin up. It's only going to get better from now on." He hung up without a goodbye.

"What did Jerricus say?" Matt asked, polishing off the toast and coffee.

I gave him the details as I finished my breakfast.

Matt grinned. "I'd love to be there when Hamilton Garrett gets served with those papers. I'm sure Jerricus will pick the most public place in the tri-state area to do it, too."

I laughed. "I read in the paper Hamilton has a rally scheduled for Swanson Park at noon."

Matt laughed, too. "X marks the spot. It's almost worth the price of admission to see it first hand."

"I'd better not be seen anywhere near a Garrett." I stared into my empty bowl for a moment. I wanted to tell him about the dream and its result but decided to apologize instead. "Matt, I'm sorry about last night. You were—are—right. Business comes first. I—I…" My voice cracked, and I fought for control.

He reached across the table and took my hand in his.

169

"Lady, when this is all over…"

He didn't have to say anything else. I understood, and my spirits rose. I extricated my hand and carried my dish to the sink to regain some composure.

"How long is this rain supposed to last?" I asked.

"It should be done by noon. Why?"

"I think today is a mall day."

"The mall? Are you sure? It's so soon after the press conference. Maybe you should wait a few more days."

"I feel much better, and it's time. Things are progressing well, and I'm not likely to be recognized yet. It might be hard to pull off later."

Matt rose with a frown on his face. "Jerricus told you to stay put."

"I know, but I don't have to do everything my lawyer tells me." I knew my attorney would not approve a trip to the mall. I laid my hand along Matt's cheek. "I'll be fine. Everything will be all right."

He inhaled and blew out a deep breath. "When are you going?"

"Noon. The rain will be over, and the place packed. I'll be just another face in the crowd."

"Lunch time," he said, nodding. "People will be hurrying to eat and do a little shopping before returning to work. They'll be intent on their own business and not notice you, unless you fall off the second-story balcony."

"Which I have no intention of doing." I stood on tiptoe to kiss his cheek.

"I should go with you."

"Sorry, that's not in the plans. I have to be alone."

"All right. In that case, I'll be upstairs. I have a

couple of calls to make. Let me know before you leave. And be careful."

He left the room, and I shook my head as I loaded the dishwasher. He was a worrywart, but I enjoyed it.

****

The Galleria Mall was tucked into the northeast corner of the county at the junction of two major roads. Once small, two-lane byways, they had been widened, then widened again, and still couldn't handle the traffic. Though the mall was a mere ten miles from Matt's house, it had taken me close to thirty minutes to get there. As expected, the parking lot was jammed.

I strolled unrecognized past the stores, stopping to stare into the windows, and had seen most of the shops on the lower level. No shopping bags encumbered me. I didn't need to buy anything. Just being able to window shop was enough.

I crossed the mall, heading for the escalator. The second level awaited. Dodging through the crowd, I caught a flash of color in one of the windows.

Changing course, I sidestepped shoppers and then stopped to stare at a bright turquoise sundress with yellow, pink, and green flowers around the hem. I resisted the urge to try it on.

Someone stopped next to me. My nerves hummed, and my scalp prickled. I sensed danger. An instant later, a hard object jammed into my ribs.

"Nice and easy, baby. Don't make any sudden moves and don't scream. If you do, you're dead," a voice growled in my ear.

I swung my head around and stared into a pair of hard brown eyes. I gasped and took a step backward. The man grabbed my arm and stepped close. Tall and wiry, he wore jeans, a black T-shirt, and sneakers. His light brown hair was pulled into a tight ponytail, and his lips compressed in a thin line.

Wave after wave of cold rushed through me, and I couldn't stop the tremors rippling up and down my legs.

"Who—who are you? What—what do you—you want? I don't have much money," I stammered. The trembling had reached my arms, and he narrowed his eyes in what I interpreted as a warning.

I tried jerking away, but he tightened his grip and ground the object harder into my side. I shifted my gaze and saw the barrel of a gun.

"Shut up and don't struggle. Just come with me."

I was too scared to move. He yanked me away from the window. My legs refused to cooperate, and I stumbled.

"Walk, bitch," he snarled.

"Where—where are you taking me?" My voice quavered, and my heart slammed in my chest so hard I was afraid I'd pass out. My breathing wasn't so hot either.

"Don't ask questions. Just enjoy the ride."

"Why?" In moments of panic we all ask stupid questions.

"You'll find out. Now shut the fuck up and walk."

The anonymity of being a face in the crowd worked against me. No one paid any attention to us. Couldn't they see the gun?

I glanced down and realized they couldn't. My kidnapper held the pistol in his right hand with a lightweight windbreaker draped over it. His left arm clutched my shoulders tightly, and we walked side by side as though glued together.

We made our way down the length of the mall, and with every step I cast frantic glances at passersby, hoping someone would see the desperation in my eyes.

"Quit moving your head," he ordered, digging his fingers painfully into my upper arm.

Tears filled my eyes.

"And don't cry."

I choked down my tears and tried to marshal my thoughts. I needed to make a run for it.

Now the crowds helped. As a twosome, we had to slow and step around knots of people. The mall exit loomed ahead. I glanced down at the windbreaker and tried to think rationally.

One of the shops had a sidewalk sale going on with racks of clothing in front of the display windows. The crowd was thick, and as he pushed me through, I jerked hard. He lost his grip on my shoulders. Free, I turned to run.

A large woman stepped in front of me, impeding my progress. Before I could dart around her, a hand grabbed my arm.

"Don't do that again, you bitch," he said in a loud voice.

A couple of women turned to look. The ball bounced in my court.

I jerked away again and yelled, "Help! He's trying to kidnap me!"

"Shut up, you stupid cow!"

More people ceased sliding hangers of merchandise along the racks and directed their gazes toward us.

We'd drawn the attention of other shoppers, but instead of a path opening to allow escape, the crowd increased with people coming to see what all the excitement was about. I dodged away. He followed, cursing and calling me names. It must have sounded like a lover's spat, for no one came to my aid. He caught me and grabbed my arm.

I jerked free, pulled the windbreaker from over his hand, and dropped it on the floor, exposing the gun to view. Several people screamed. Jamming the gun into the waistband of his jeans, the man snatched at my hair and missed.

My kidnapper shot panicked glances at the surrounding throng, which grew by leaps and bounds. He lunged, his hands grasping my shoulders, and then hurled me through the air.

I landed hard against the door jamb of the shop, momentarily knocked breathless, then careened off and into the store as two portly women exited. I slammed into them like a bowling ball. We all hit the floor in a tangled heap. Everybody screamed and shouted at the same time.

"Are you all right?"

"Help! She's trying to kill me."

"What the hell is going on?"

"Get off me!"

I tried to oblige the last demand, but two hundred and fifty pounds of flab lying on top of me made it difficult. Finally, Moby Dick rolled over, and I staggered to my feet.

I clutched at a woman standing immobile just inside the door. In my shock, it took me a moment to realize I had grasped a mannequin. My momentum carried both it and me back to the floor with a crash. I fought my way out from under the heavy plastic model and pushed through the clogged entryway.

I searched the crowd but saw no sign of my abductor. He had disappeared.

Chapter Eleven

I ran a few steps, hoping to catch a glimpse of the man, but he was gone. Someone grabbed my arm. Given what had just happened, I balled my fist, ready to strike, and whirled to face an irate woman.

"Hey, what the hell do you think you're doing? You broke my mannequin, and I have a good customer down on the floor claiming she's having a heart attack."

"I'm—I'm sorry, but—"

"Back off, lady. She just had a nasty quarrel with her boyfriend," a man said.

"He was not my boyfriend."

"Yeah, he was calling her names, and he had a gun," a woman chimed in.

"It wasn't real. It was just a toy," another voice answered.

"It was real," I declared.

"What about my mannequin?"

Everyone stared. Two security guards pushed their way through the mob.

"Okay, lady, what's all the fuss about?"

"A man tried to kidnap me." Before I could explain further, everyone around me put in their two cents worth.

"It was her boyfriend."

"He had a big, black gun—a revolver. I saw it."

"No, it was a silver semi-automatic."

"He tossed her through a plate glass window."

"He tried to snatch her purse."

"He grabbed his jacket and headed for the doors. Go get him!"

"Quiet!" one of the guards shouted. The crowd settled down, and he turned to me. "Now what's this all about?"

I drew in a shaky breath and gave him the details. While I talked, the other guard called the police. Another police report with my name on it. Jerricus would be furious, because I'd done exactly what he'd told me not to do.

"Why would this guy want to kidnap you? Does your family have money?"

Oh, brother. What could I tell them?

"I have no family, and I can't imagine why anyone would want to kidnap me. I'm nobody. Maybe it was a case of mistaken identity." This wasn't the time to bring up the Garrett name.

"Are you sure he wanted to abduct you and not just steal your purse?"

"No. He never made a move for my purse."

The mall paramedics arrived to attend the woman I'd fallen on in the store. She now sat, loudly declaring someone had tried to kill her. The woman who had tumbled onto me stood with her spine braced against the door jamb, fanning herself with her hand and moaning her back had been seriously dislocated. Somebody would get sued from all this. I had no money, so it wouldn't be me.

The security guard handed me a clipboard with several sheets of paper attached and a pen.

"You need to fill this out."

I took everything over to a bench and sat down. But before I did anything, I pulled out my cell and called Matt. He answered on the first ring.

"How's everything going?"

"I've had better days," I replied and then told him what had happened.

"I'll be right there. Have they called the cops?"

"Yeah, they should be here any minute."

"I'm leaving now. Don't forget to call Jerricus and inform him."

I called my attorney. Miss Singleton informed me Jerricus was in court but due back in the office before the end of the day. She'd pass along the information and have him call me later.

The cops arrived as I finished filling out the incident report. I breathed a sigh of relief. I'd never seen any of them before.

"Miss Lennox, please tell me what happened," one of the many officers asked.

Now a pro at answering cop questions, I launched into my story, including a detailed description of the man, while the other deputies took statements from witnesses. When I finished, the officer skewered me with a sharp gaze.

"Lennox? Didn't I see you on TV yesterday? You're out on bail for the murder of your ex-husband, right?"

I ground my teeth and nodded. Damn. The cop didn't look any happier than I did.

"Please, have a seat, Miss Lennox. Don't go anywhere. We may have some more questions for you later."

Of course they would. I sat down when an elderly

woman carrying two shopping bags from Macy's tugged at the officer's sleeve. She was tiny with concerned blue eyes and wore a funny-looking felt hat crammed over her white hair.

"Yes, ma'am, what can I do for you?"

She threw a timid smile in my direction and said, "I saw it all."

"Yes, ma'am, I'm sure you did. Leave your name and number with that man over there. If we need anything, we'll be in touch." He touched the brim of his hat respectfully and resumed writing in his notebook.

"You don't understand. I saw it from start to finish. I saw him approach this lady, shove something into her side, and make her walk away."

The cop shot her an annoyed glance and then flipped a page over. "Your name?"

"Louise Rathport. I live at 1064 Breezeway Lane in Memphis."

"Okay, let's have it. Take it from the top in chronological order—that's from beginning to end."

"Young man, I know what chronological means."

I wanted to smile while he fidgeted like a reprimanded schoolboy.

"I was seated on one of the benches near the escalator. I'm seventy-three and sometimes need to take a little rest while shopping, especially after lunch." She turned to me. "You know how it is. These bags get heavy after a while, and my dogs were barking."

I nodded at the old-fashioned phrase for sore feet. "Of course, I understand."

"At any rate, I was sitting there when I saw this young lady looking into a window. Were you eyeing that pretty little blue dress? It would look lovely on you, my dear. I can't wear that style anymore—too much flab under the arms and I hate it when that stuff flaps around when you move. Kinda like a turkey's neck, you know?"

"Uh, ma'am, can we get back to the alleged kidnapping?" the policeman asked.

"Oh, yes, of course. Sorry. And there was nothing alleged about it. Now where was I?"

"Miss Lennox was looking in a window," he prompted.

"I saw this scruffy man sidle up next to her. I could tell he was up to no good. He stood much too close. He had evil on his mind. I thought he was after your purse, dear."

"Can you describe this man, Ms. Rathport?"

She gave a description that matched mine.

"What happened next, ma'am?"

"Well, I watched him jam something into her side and make her walk with him. I followed. I'm not real fast, mind you, but with the crowds what they are, I managed to keep them in sight. Then this brave woman tried to escape. He threw her into some people and ran away."

The policeman wrote fast. "Is there anything else?"

"Oh, I recognized him, officer."

Surprise swept the policeman's face. I stared in stunned amazement. I couldn't believe it.

"You did?" I croaked. It didn't seem possible.

"You know the man's name?" he said.

"Oh, yes, without a doubt. It was Zondar of Alpha Centauri Five."

The officer stared at her with a blank expression and ceased writing.

"What?" I exclaimed in a squeaky voice. Had I heard right? I shook my head and tapped the heel of my hand against my temple.

"I've seen him many times over the last fifty years. He's one of them."

The deputy cleared his throat. "One of who, ma'am?"

"Why, the aliens, of course." She wagged a finger at us. "They're all over. You have to be very careful. He was trying to kidnap this fine Earth woman in order to breed. They've been doing it for years. They watch and wait, reading your thoughts until you're distracted enough for them to grab you."

The officer snapped his notebook shut. "Thank you very much, ma'am. We won't need anything further from you."

The lady removed her hat and turned it over. The inside was lined with aluminum foil.

"See?" she said triumphantly. "They can't steal your thoughts through the foil. Now you keep an eye out for any more of them, dear." She jammed the hat back on her head and then tottered away through the diminishing crowd.

I slumped back on the bench and closed my eyes. Terrific. The only real eye witness to the whole thing was a crazy old lady with an outlandish story, even though her description of the man matched mine.

"Theresa, are you all right?"

I opened my eyes and stared into Matt's laser-blue gaze. "I'm fine, but the man is long gone."

A few feet away, a second deputy joined the first, compared notes, and then they shook their heads.

Matt strode over. "What's being done to catch this

maniac?"

"Who are you?"

"My name is Matt Summers. I'm a friend of Miss Lennox."

"We have several descriptions, any one of which could match a thousand different men. Out of fifteen witnesses, we got six variations of what the guy looked like. The only one that agreed with Miss Lennox came from a nutty old lady. There were so many people milling around witnesses got the perp confused with innocent bystanders."

Matt ran his hand through his hair.

"This isn't the first time someone's tried to harm Miss Lennox. When are you clowns going to realize she's in danger?"

"Calm down, Mr. Summers. We're doing the best we can. The guy is probably on his way home by now, which is where I suggest you take Miss Lennox."

The crowd had dispersed, and the witnesses were released. Even the two fat women were gone. Someone had picked up the mannequin pieces. Shoppers once again strolled in and out of the store. Only one officer remained.

"Come on, honey. Let's get out of here. Did you call Jerricus? What did he say?"

Before I could answer, a bright light hit me square in the eyes. Squinting, I made out a TV camera. A woman thrust a microphone in my face.

"Miss Lennox, what went on here? Were you injured?"

"No comment," Matt replied in a brusque tone. He placed his arm around my shoulders and steered me away. They followed.

"Did this really happen, or is it a publicity stunt by your lawyer?"

I gasped and turned to stare at the obnoxious woman.

"No comment," Matt repeated, pulling me along.

We walked faster. Every yokel in the county impeded the reporter's progress by stepping in front of the camera and mugging for the benefit of the audience. Still the woman persisted.

"Do you have any witnesses?"

Yeah, but she's nuts.

"Sir, what is your name? How are you connected to Miss Lennox? Are you her boyfriend?"

We trotted and then ran. The cameraman struggled to keep up, and the reporter wore three-inch heels. Matt grasped my hand.

"Come on, Theresa. Run for it."

We raced for the exit. Dodging a knot of slow-moving shoppers, we reached the doors and muscled our way past several people coming in.

"Where are you parked?" I asked, panting.

"Two rows over, almost at the end."

I glanced over my shoulder but saw no sign of the TV people. We charged down a parking lane. The rain of earlier had left its mark. Humidity hung in the air, enveloping me in an oppressive shroud. Sweat dripped from every pore, and my heart hammered. I looked back again just as the duo emerged from the mall.

"Matt, hurry. They're looking for us."

"Bend down and keep running," he ordered.

Using the parked cars for concealment, we finally made it to the Ford. Matt unlocked the doors, and I flung myself inside. I hunched down as he started the engine, slammed it into gear, backed out of the space, and drove around the parking lot.

"You can sit up now," he said a few minutes later as he pulled into another space on the outer perimeter. "We've lost them. Let's wait a few minutes until I take you back to your car."

I brushed the hair off my face and leaned toward the air conditioning vent. The cold air gave me a smidgeon of relief.

"Damn it! Where did that reporter come from?"

"I don't know," Matt replied. "But she homed in like a guided missile. Maybe they had a police scanner in the car. Who knows? Are you all right? You look pale."

"No, I'm not all right. I'm not sure how much more I can take."

My chest tightened, making it hard to breathe. I wanted to get home and jump into the pool.

My cell rang. It was Jerricus.

"Okay, let me have it. What happened?"

I told him and waited for the eruption. It didn't come. Instead, he sighed heavily. "I thought you were going to stay out of sight."

"I know, but I hate being cooped up. I didn't think something like this would happen."

Silence on the other end told me my attorney had stopped to think. I almost heard the gears meshing in his mind.

"This could work to our advantage," he finally said. "Who was the reporter?"

"I don't know. I think the camera's station letters had a Q in it."

"Give me a description."

"Medium height, long brown hair, kind of a sharp, high-pitched voice. Asked annoying questions, too."

"Could be Rachel Johns of WCCQ. What time is it? Three thirty? I think I'll call her station and make a little statement—give them an exclusive all about how someone is out to get you."

"Do whatever you think best, Jerricus, but don't count on me and a sliver of soap again. I can't take it." Weariness washed over me.

He laughed. "I'll be in touch, and for Pete's sake, don't go out alone again. If you go anywhere with Matt, use a wig or something."

I hung up and relayed the conversation to Matt.

"I don't have a wig available, but tucking your hair under a cap and using sunglasses may do the trick."

He left the parking space and drove me to my car. I followed him home, wondering if I'd ever have a normal life again.

****

I couldn't stop my hands and legs from trembling. We walked in the front door, and I made my way unsteadily into the den. This whole day had pushed me further along toward a precipice—a precipice with a never-ending drop. The reporter showing up had been more disturbing than the attempted kidnapping. I just wanted this all over.

Matt followed and took me in his arms. Warmth and security—two commodities I desperately needed—flooded through me. Tears welled and then flowed down my face.

The sobs turned into a raging torrent. I wailed and fisted my hands in Matt's shirt while he rocked me back and forth, murmuring nonsensical words of comfort.

When I cried myself out, he handed me a tissue and settled me in a chair.

"I'm sorry," I mumbled, wiping my face and blowing my nose. "I needed to let go."

"Quit apologizing." He stooped in front of me, sandwiching my hands between his. "Theresa, when was the last time you saw your psychiatrist?"

"You think I'm going crazy?" I tried but couldn't keep the bitterness from my voice. I needed comfort, not something else to worry about.

"Of course not, but you've been under a lot of strain. It's beginning to take a toll. Make an appointment now for tomorrow. Tell her it's an emergency. Your shrink must know what's been going on. She won't be surprised to hear from you."

"Are you saying I'm on the edge?"

"You're coiled tighter than a spring. Sooner or later that spring will release."

"Jerricus described Diana as a woman on the edge. Are you suggesting I'm as tightly wound as my ex-mother-in-law?" My voice climbed a few decibels. I was afraid of his answer.

"Right now?" He looked away and rose. "Yes."

I leaped to my feet. "How dare you? How dare you compare me to that bitch? Don't ever do it again!"

"Theresa, you aren't handling the stress well. You're about to snap."

"I'll handle my stress in my own way. At least I don't reach for a bottle!"

His eyes gleamed with hurt, and guilt swamped me. I wrapped my arms around his waist and laid my head on his chest. Fresh tears flowed.

"Oh, God, Matt, I'm so sorry. I didn't mean it. I

swear I didn't. I take it all back. Please forgive me, darling."

I babbled my apology, and after a moment's hesitation his arms encased me.

"It's all right, honey. Part of stress is striking out at others, often people who are close to us."

He backed up a step and grasped my shoulders, then lowered his head and gave me a gentle, consoling kiss. Before the kiss deepened into something more serious, he broke it off and smiled.

"Come on, smile back at me."

I tried. The kiss had calmed my frayed nerves.

"Good girl."

"Thanks, Matt. You've been a rock. I had no call to say what I did."

We walked into the kitchen where he poured iced tea for two.

"Call your doctor now, and I'll tell you some good news."

"I feel like a kid who has to eat her spinach if she wants dessert," I said, dialing my cell and doing as he asked.

The receptionist told me she had a spot open the following afternoon at three. I took it.

"Now what is this good news, and I warn you it had better be spectacular. I haven't had the best of days."

Matt grinned. "I remember where I've seen The Juice."

I straightened with a gasp. "You do? Where? When?"

"It was about two years ago at the courthouse. I was waiting in one of the hallways when the doors to another courtroom opened, and two men came out. A pack of reporters surrounded them. One of the men was The Juice."

"Was he on trial?"

"No, but his boss was—Fast Eddie Piper."

"Who's he?"

"Eddie Piper is the local drug czar. He started out life as the head of the Avengers, a street gang with a reputation as being the most violent ever to set foot in Memphis."

"What was The Juice doing there?"

"He was the defense's star witness. Gave Eddie an alibi to beat a murder rap. It was a hung jury."

I gulped my tea. "So this Eddie person got off?"

"Of course. The judge may not have bought it, but all it takes is one bribe to hang a jury."

"Did they retry?"

"I went back and reread the newspaper archives. The state had to drop its case. Their witnesses either turned up dead or disappeared."

I slumped in my chair. "What a sleaze bucket. Wait a minute," I said, sitting up straight again. "You said he's The Juice's boss? That means if he was working for this Fast Eddie…"

"…then so was your late ex-husband."

The implications staggered me. The biggest drug dealer in the city had been Danny's boss?

"Oh, my God. The Juice might have not minded Danny being late with payments, but what about Eddie?"

"He wouldn't be so accommodating." Matt smiled and drained his glass of tea.

"Holy shit. He could be the one."

"During my search this morning, I also found the name of the only other defense witness. He backed up The Juice's story. His street name is Jump Drive. He's a small potatoes dealer down on Beale. I've seen him in the area before. He might give us information about where Danny fit into the scheme."

"Have you talked to him yet?"

"No, but he's easy to find."

"If I use a disguise, can I come?"

Matt hesitated and frowned. "Do you think that's wise given what happened today?"

"I'd rather face a drug dealer than be alone tonight."

"All right, but let me do the talking." He paused for a moment and then chuckled. "I watched the noon news today. They were doing a remote from Swanson Park, covering Hamilton Garrett's rally. The reporter interviewed him and Diana, going on and on about their bravery in this time of tragedy. Diana wiped the tears from her eyes, and Hamilton pontificated on the need to move on when this scrawny little guy butted in and shoved a paper in his hand, saying, 'It's a restraining order for you and Mrs. Garrett to stay one hundred feet away from Theresa Lennox, your former daughter-in-law. Her lawyer will tolerate no more harassment.' Then the guy left."

I laughed. "I thought process servers just delivered the goods. I didn't know they made speeches, too."

Matt grinned. "They don't, but I'm sure Jerricus coached the guy. His timing was perfect."

"What was the reporter's reaction?"

"She fired the usual questions at them, but their response was a terse, 'No comment.' Hamilton looked ready to explode, and Diana wore an expression that came close to insane."

I wished I could have seen it firsthand but was sure it would replay on the evening news. I had to hand it to my attorney. He sure knew how to get things done. I laughed again, and for the first time today, my spirits lifted.

****

Matt and I walked hand in hand up Beale Street, the neon signs sending a rainbow of color stabbing into the darkness. We had visited several clubs and bars over the last two hours and had our fill of club soda. So far, we hadn't found Jump Drive.

I pulled the bill of my baseball cap lower and tucked an errant strand of hair back under it, then pushed the oversized, plain-lens glasses farther up on my nose. As a private investigator, Matt had several simple disguises on hand at the house. Beale bustled with tourists, and we blended in.

"Maybe he's not here tonight," I ventured when we struck out in yet another bar.

"He's here someplace. Memphis In May is still going strong. He wouldn't miss an opportunity to sell a few grams of weed or coke. Let's try Handy Park."

Matt steered me down the street, and we entered the park. Over the years it had become an institution. Street musicians set up shop and played the best blues this side of heaven for tips tossed into open instrument cases, all under the approving eyes of the W. C. Handy statue.

Tonight, the park was crowded, and we skirted the edges of the tight-knit throng. Then Matt stopped and squeezed my arm.

"Over there," he said in a low voice.

I followed his gaze and spotted a tall, very thin black man. He wore an oversized sports jersey with the name and number of some basketball star. It hung almost to his knees. I assumed his jeans were the usual homey version belted around his thighs. A baseball cap sat backward on his head, and he sported enough gold jewelry hanging around his neck to open a store. He spoke with a young white man. I saw them trade something, then the white guy turned and disappeared into the crowd.

Matt gripped my arm, and we strolled over.

"Hey, your name Jump Drive?" he asked.

"That's my name and pleasure is my game. Whatcha need—a little weed, coke, crack, meth? I got 'em all, and it won't cost you an arm and a leg either."

I couldn't believe he openly advertised. For all he knew, we were undercover cops. But then intelligence didn't seem to be his strong point, or maybe he used as much as he sold. He had a cocky grin, and a gold tooth, embellished with a tiny diamond, flashed from between his lips. *What is it with these dealers and gold teeth?*

"What we need is information," Matt said.

The grin faded. "I ain't got much of that. You narcs? Vice?"

"No. All I want is some information concerning Danny Garrett and your boss, Eddie Piper."

"Never heard of either of them."

He turned to leave, but Matt placed a hand on his arm.

"Sure you have. You testified for Eddie a couple of years ago. I was in the courtroom."

Jump Drive turned back, his eyes wary and

suspicious, shifting between me and Matt.

"I ain't tellin' you nothin' 'bout Eddie. I like livin' too much."

Matt nodded. "Okay, then tell me about Danny Garrett."

"He got snuffed a couple of weeks ago."

"I know. Any ideas who did it?"

"Cops say it was his bitch."

"The cops are wrong. What was Danny's relationship with Fast Eddie?"

"Far as I know they never met. Danny was The Juice's boy."

"And The Juice is Eddie's boy."

Jump Drive shifted from foot to foot and scanned the crowd with nervous eyes.

"I gotta go. We been talking too long for you not to buy nothin'."

"Then answer my questions, and we'll be on our way."

Jump Drive licked his lips and replied, "All right, here's the deal. Danny sometimes sold for The Juice if he needed quick cash. When he got out of jail a few months ago, he said he wanted to go full time. He told The Juice he could sell to his buddies and all over the U of M campus. Juice cleared it with Eddie, but from what I heard, old Danny didn't pay his bills regular. He liked using, too."

"In other words, he skimmed, held out on The Juice and Fast Eddie," Matt said with a frown.

"Don't know nothin' 'bout no skimming, but he wasn't real quick in paying his debts. I think his well dried up."

"The Garretts wouldn't pay his debts anymore?"

"Guess that's the way of it. And that's all I know."

Jump Drive turned and melted into the crowd. Matt led me over to a bench. He sat silent, and I stayed the same while he thought.

Finally, I had to ask, "Do you think Eddie could have killed Danny?"

"It's a possibility. Let's suppose he put out a contract on your ex. The shooter would have to be someone Danny trusted, or he would never have met him at your place. Call Jerricus tomorrow. He'll put the theory to good use. It's another avenue the cops should be, but aren't, investigating." He paused and frowned. "A thought just occurred to me—how much did Hamilton Garrett really like his son?"

I gasped. "Are you trying to pin this on him? *Hamilton?*"

"Why not? He's pretty cold-blooded. A drug dealing son could screw up his gubernatorial chances. With Danny gone and you framed for it, he'd be rid of his embarrassing problem and garner a lot of sympathy votes in the bargain."

"Won't work. Hamilton's self-centered and single-minded, but he'd never chance doing something like that. He'd leave himself wide open to blackmail. Besides, he doesn't control the purse strings—Diana does, and she'd do anything for her son, including pay his drug debts."

"If that's the case, why would Jump Drive say the well had gone dry?"

I shrugged. "I don't know. Maybe Hamilton finally put his foot down and demanded Diana stop bleeding their bank account. Political campaigns can be expensive, not to mention brutal. It might not take long for a gubernatorial rival to unearth the payoffs."

Matt sighed and ran his hand through his hair.

"Let's get out of here. It's been a long day. I'm tired. I'll think about this tomorrow and research Fast Eddie—see if any other corpses who worked for him have shown up."

We walked back along Beale, Matt's arm draped over my shoulders. Since Danny's death, all my days had been long, scary, and frustrating. But now I had a glimmer of hope.

Maybe the cops would chase Fast Eddie Piper instead of me for a change.

Chapter Twelve

I sat on the sofa in Dr. Walker's reception area, flipping through the pages of a magazine, not really seeing or reading anything. I crossed my legs, my free foot jiggling and tapping in thin air, a sure sign of anxiety.

I'd had a restful night thanks to a couple of pills and awakened less hyper than the day before. After breakfast, I popped a tranquilizer and lay by the pool. Every once in a while, I slid into the water and worked off whatever anxiety the drug hadn't erased. Matt searched the internet for information on Fast Eddie Piper.

The story of my attempted abduction had made the late-night news, and this morning the paper saw fit to print it on page three. Jerricus wouldn't be happy until we were emblazoned on the front page.

"Miss Lennox? Dr. Walker will see you now," the receptionist said.

I nodded and muttered a thank you, then followed her through the door into the office. Dr. Walker sat behind her desk, jotting notes on a pad of paper. She looked up as I entered.

"Good afternoon, Theresa. Please be seated. I'll be with you in a moment."

I chose a chair. I never sat on the couch and refused to lie on it. It sounded so stereotyped, and I felt awkward enough spilling my guts to a total stranger, even though I'd been seeing her since the divorce.

She rose, picked up a fresh pad of paper, and seated herself across from me. A coffee table laden with an ashtray, a pitcher of water, paper cups, and a box of tissues separated us. I had used all at one time or another.

"I'm sorry to have kept you waiting. It's been a long time since I've seen you. How are you holding up?"

Louise Walker was in her mid-fifties. Tall and slim, she wore her blonde hair in a short, no-nonsense style, and her clothing of choice was pantsuits—today a conservative navy blue.

"As good as can be expected, I guess. The last two weeks have been one nightmare after another." My voice quavered. I twisted my fingers together. "I should have called you sooner."

"Why did you call me now?"

"A friend suggested I wasn't handling the stress very well."

"Tell me about it."

I spent the next thirty minutes or so detailing everything from Danny's body to the attempted abduction, including my little midnight swim and the frightening dreams.

"I…I had another one last night. It was along the same lines as the others."

"Tell me about it."

"I was standing in my bedroom, naked and dripping wet. Danny stood about ten feet away. He held a noose in his hand and curled his lips into a snarling smile. I had no trouble seeing the evil in his eyes. Panic and terror ripped through me. I shook and backed up against the wall, pleading for him to go away and leave me alone."

I gulped back a sob, not wanting to remember.

Dr. Walker poured a cup of water. "Here, drink this and take your time."

I did as she instructed, then took a deep breath. "I'm…I'm okay."

"What happened next?"

"He took a step forward, that hideous smile still in place, and said, 'But it's time, precious. Time for you to die. And this time, I'll make sure it's for real.'

"I screamed. Then a loud bang woke me. How much more can I take before my mind degenerates into madness?"

"You aren't going insane, Theresa. What was the loud bang?"

"I'm not sure. When I woke up, it was quiet. Maybe it was part of the dream."

"Dreams and nightmares are the psyche's way of releasing tension, fear, guilt, and a myriad of other emotions. Sometimes they're perceived as fact or what we think is fact."

I got it. Fact and fiction blending together. Matt had said something along those lines. But the question still remained—was I heading for a nervous breakdown or worse? Maybe, if we didn't find a killer soon.

"Are you taking your medication?"

"I just started again."

"How much are you taking?"

I licked my lips. "I took two last night to sleep and took a tranq this morning."

Her sharp blue eyes sliced into me. "Two before

bed is one too many. Take the tranquilizers as needed, but no more than three per day, two if you take the sleeping pill, and for goodness' sake, don't drink alcohol with either."

I fudged the truth a little and assured her I didn't. She made a notation on the pad, and I wondered if the word "addict" made an appearance. Dr. Walker gazed at me and smiled.

"There have been some positives in your situation. You have one of the best lawyers around."

"I know. I'm lucky he took my case. I can't afford his fees. I guess he felt sorry for me. Plus, he hates my in-laws as much as I do."

"And this private detective you hired sounds as though he's making progress," she said.

I nodded and tried to swallow the lump in my throat.

"He's—he's been wonderful." I gulped again. "But I can't help feeling so hopeless. I know all the evidence points my way, but I didn't do it. Someone wants me dead, and I don't know why. After yesterday, I'm almost afraid to stick my nose outside the front door. I mean, how much more am I expected to take?"

My eyes filled with tears and then overflowed, gushing down my cheeks in a salty avalanche. Dr. Walker pushed the tissue box toward me. I snatched the entire thing and held it in my lap, pulling out tissue after tissue in an attempt to mop up.

I sobbed and hiccupped, unable to control myself. Through it all, I babbled incoherently.

"Wish I'd never been born…So scared…Don't understand why the cops won't believe me…I don't deserve this…I can't take much more."

Dr. Walker sat silent until the hysterical storm passed. I rose on shaking legs to deposit the sodden tissues in a nearby wastepaper basket. Returning to my chair, I plopped down and held my head in my hands.

"Is that the first time you've let go?"

I shook my head. "No, I did the same thing last night with Matt."

"Theresa, allow the people on your side to help." She raised her hand when I opened my mouth to protest. "You have a wonderful lawyer. Jerricus Monroe has dozens of drones to do his leg work for him, and I can guarantee he is checking out all the leads your private investigator has uncovered. You need to put your faith in them and relax."

"That's easier said than done," I muttered.

"I know. It's simple for me to sit here and say it, but you need something else to occupy your mind. Why not call your professors? Ask for the assignments you've missed. Just because you've been suspended from school doesn't mean you can't study. See if you can take your finals anyway."

"I—I never thought of doing that."

"Even if you can't take the tests right away, the studying will occupy your mind."

"The vandals trashed my computer along with everything else in my apartment. Maybe I could buy an inexpensive one and get caught up on all I've missed."

"That's a good idea. And I want to see you again in a week. No backsliding, young lady," she said with a smile.

"No backsliding—I promise." I hesitated and then asked, "Dr. Walker, if this thing goes to trial, are you allowed to testify on my behalf?"

"If you request it, yes."

I breathed easier. Another person in my corner who could tell the world what I'd gone through at Danny's hands. Or would that be another nail in the coffin as far as the jury was concerned? On the other hand, Dr. Walker was damned good. Her testimony would be respected.

"I'll tell Jerricus. He may want to ask you some questions first. Is that okay?"

"No problem." A little bell chimed on her desk, signifying the end of my session. Dr. Walker stood and extended her hand. "Theresa, I'm glad you came in. Don't forget to make an appointment on your way out. Is next Friday at the same time convenient?"

I assured her it was and left the office, stopping by the receptionist's desk.

I walked to my car with a spring in my step. The weight of the world had lifted from my shoulders. She'd given me something positive to do. Why on earth hadn't I come in before now?

Excited about studying again, I decided to head for the university. *Might as well get started. I have a lot of work to make up.*

I parked on campus and, heeding Matt's warning about being careful, found a spot close to Southern Avenue. Before exiting my car, I surveyed the area. It was Friday afternoon, and most students had already left. A lone pedestrian with a backpack slung over his shoulder walked toward me. I held my breath. He passed two cars down, never looking my way. I relaxed and breathed.

Come on, Theresa, not everyone is out to get you.

I made the rounds of all the offices and gathered

my assignments. I wasn't allowed to take my finals, but when I was reinstated, the profs had promised to take it under advisement.

Still with the awareness of the recently victimized, I scrutinized the parking lot again on my way back but saw nothing suspicious. When the light changed, I scampered across the street, ran to the car, and flung myself inside. My police surveillance had disappeared over a week ago. It figured. I could have used them now.

Try and find a cop when you really need one.

I chuckled to myself, started the engine, and then pulled out into the thickening weekend traffic.

****

I chattered to Matt while he seasoned the steaks. "My math professor said he was glad I was continuing with my studies and that in spite of my lousy score on the last test, I'd been doing much better in the last month or so."

I gulped from my glass of iced tea, grabbed the cutting board and a bowl out of the cabinet, tore off some lettuce, and then sliced vegetables for the salad.

"I'm glad to hear you had a good day for a change. Seasoned salt?" he asked, the shaker poised over my steak.

"Absolutely. So am I. Dr. Walker was fabulous. I should have gone to see her the minute I made bail. I could have avoided all this depression and anxiety. Well, most of it any way." I peeled a cucumber and then sliced it. "Oh, did I tell you what my history professor said? My classmates are sending around a petition to have me reinstated at the university, *and* they have plans to boycott the Campus Notes Bookstore.

201

Isn't that something?"

Matt laughed. "See? You do have friends. How many fries can you eat?"

"Are you kidding? The whole bag." I chopped a scallion and dumped it into the salad bowl. "Get this, my English Lit professor told me the university had no business prejudging me, and if they allowed a teaching assistant accused of sexual harassment to continue teaching, they should allow me to continue learning. I had no idea she was such a strong women's rights advocate."

"You're flying high," Matt said with a twinkle in his eye. "I may have to spike your iced tea with one of those tranquilizers."

I stuck my tongue out. "Smart-ass. I don't care if I'm babbling. For the first time since Danny's death, I feel like things are going to work out."

The oven buzzed, and Matt slid the cookie sheet of frozen fries in, then turned and dropped a kiss on the top of my head. He leaned against the counter and snatched a cucumber out of the bowl.

"I had a good day, too."

"Oh? What happened?"

"I got the results of the voice analysis on the tapes. None of Danny's friends or The Juice is a match for the calls to you or here."

"And?"

"It eliminates a lot of people and tells us we're dealing with someone who knew Danny, but not you."

"Like Fast Eddie Piper?"

"Or Jump Drive."

My hand slicing a carrot slowed while I thought. "No, the voice on the messages was not Jump Drive's.

Of course, we're assuming the police will even be interested."

"FYI, Fast Eddie is white. I want to cover all the bases. Who knows what the future will bring?"

Matt thought of everything.

"Did you find out anything about Piper?" I asked.

"He's got a rap sheet the most hardened of criminals would envy. The police have tied several unsolved murders and disappearances to him but don't have enough evidence to arrest the guy. If he ordered a hit on Danny, he'd use someone your ex wouldn't suspect of wanting to kill him."

"But who? I mean, we've just about exhausted the list of friends and admirers." I tossed the carrots into the bowl and started on the tomatoes.

"That we know of. There may be people inside Piper's organization Danny trusted or believed meant him no harm."

"But how do we find them?"

"If we convince the cops to reopen the case, we won't have to." Matt picked up the plate of steaks and headed for the deck and the pre-lit grill. "I also caught Jerricus on the five o'clock news."

I finished the tomatoes and added them to the salad, giving it a final toss, and then checked the timer on the oven—ten minutes to go. I followed Matt out the door and watched as he slapped the meat on the grate.

"And what was he doing?"

"Giving a mini-press conference, of course. He turned it up a notch on the cops. He gave a very colorful account of your attempted kidnapping and demanded to know why the police haven't reopened the investigation. I'll bet by Monday the DA will call and offer you a deal."

"Which I will not take," I said firmly.

"Which you will not take," Matt agreed.

The sizzling fat dripping onto hot coals and the aroma that accompanied it made my mouth water. I thought while salivating. Exactly how much longer would Diana and Hamilton's influence last? My less-than-stellar rapport with them, the Memphis police, and the DA's office had rapidly become a public relations nightmare.

"What are we going to do next?"

"Just what Jerricus said—relax and stay out of sight. You have assignments. I'll watch something on TV. We'll spend a nice, quiet weekend at home."

I liked the idea. It sounded like something any normal married couple would do. But then how would I know? My marriage to Danny had been anything but normal.

****

We ate by candlelight on the deck. A small cold front slipped through during the day and the shifting wind brought a cooler breeze and lower humidity.

Done to perfection, my steak was so tender it practically melted in my mouth. I was still enthused about my day, and Matt listened during the entire meal while I talked.

After the dishes were done, he tuned in a baseball game on TV. I sat on the sofa and made a schedule for doing my assignments. The image of an old married couple, together but doing their own things, returned.

My gaze settled on Matt. A big Cardinals fan, he hadn't seen many games this season. His attention was riveted as the play-by-play man announced the score at four to three, Cardinals over the Reds. The opposing pitcher delivered a three-two pitch, and the Cardinal batter sent it flying over the outfield fence.

"Yes! Oh yeah, baby!" Matt jumped to his feet, pumping his fist in the air. "That gives us a little breathing room with an inning to go."

I wanted to laugh at his enthusiasm but didn't. I loved seeing him excited about something other than my crime. The relaxation might even erase the lines from his face.

A half an hour later, he turned off the TV and stretched, satisfied with another game in the win column.

I sat back and asked a question that had been rattling around in my mind all day.

"Matt, what do you see yourself doing say, five years from now? How long can you continue to live off the dregs of humanity in the PI business?"

He raised his eyebrows and finished his tea, crunching an ice cube as he thought. "In five years, I'll be forty-two years old. As long as private investigating pays the bills, I guess I'll keep doing it."

"But what if you had another choice? Is there something else you've always wanted—a dream?"

He leaned back in his chair. Then a wide smile split his face. "Yeah. When I was younger, I often thought I'd like to run a charter fishing and dive business."

"On Pickwick?" I asked, naming a manmade lake some ninety miles east of Memphis. I didn't know anything about fishing or scuba diving but still thought it a strange location.

"No, no. In the Caribbean."

"The Caribbean?" I'd never envisioned this. "Why

there? Have you ever visited?"

Matt locked his hands behind his head and smiled into the distance, his eyes calm. "Many times. My mother's uncle, Captain Ted, worked on tramp steamers and traveled the world."

"Sounds like he was a romantic." The thought of visiting new places and cultures had its appeal.

Matt laughed. "Not a romantic bone in his body. He just hated crowds and someone telling him what to do. Eventually, he saved enough, bought a fifty-five-foot Hatteras and a house on the beach. In those days, the Caribbean was a cheap place to live. Whenever he needed money, he'd charter deep-sea fishing parties."

"Did you know him well?"

"I spent every summer between the ages of twelve and eighteen with him fishing and boating. I loved it."

"Is he still alive?"

"No. He passed away years ago but left me his boat and the house. I still go down on occasion to make sure the money I send the caretakers is spent on caretaking, but I haven't fired up the engines in almost five years." He shook his head. "The last time I saw Uncle Ted, he was waving goodbye as he dropped me at the airport. I miss him."

"Why don't you go back? Take a little time off when this is over?"

He shrugged. "Maybe I will. I always meant to, but something kept cropping up—marriages, divorces, rehab, jobs I couldn't refuse."

"Like an abused woman accused of killing her abuser?"

"That's one I'm glad I took on. What about you? What do you see down the road?"

I sighed, set my elbows on my knees, and rested my chin in my hands.

"The psychologist thing is a start, but I wonder if I have the chops to be a lawyer. I'd like to defend poor or powerless women who feel they have no choice except to take the law into their own hands. I can see myself as an advocate fighting for women the system forgets."

"I'm jealous. That sounds better than being a charter fishing captain. And for the record, you have the stuff. You've been there, done that, and can relate." He chuckled. "Maybe you should run for office so you can be part of the lawmaking process."

I laughed with him. "Oh, God, can't you just see that? Diana and Hamilton would die."

"And this is bad how?"

I laughed again and then sobered. "Of course, this is way down the line. I have other things to worry about like staying out of prison. Those three days I spent in jail turned my stomach. I'm not sure I can take a lifetime of it."

"You won't go to prison. The state's case is so flimsy you can see through it."

"I hope you're right. If…no, when I get off, maybe I'll leave Memphis. Diana will make staying impossible. I suppose I can transfer my grades to a college in another town and start over. Diana's wrath has long tentacles. I'm afraid she'll hunt me down and cause trouble wherever I go."

"There are laws protecting you from that sort of thing. It's called harassment. Hamilton will understand even if she doesn't."

The clock in the foyer chimed midnight. I rose, stretched, and started for the front hall.

"It's getting late. I should go to bed."

Matt turned off the lights and followed, stopping me next to the staircase. The street light shone in the windows surrounding the door.

"Theresa, I know it's not much help for me to tell you not to worry—that everything's going to be okay, but I have to believe it is. You're strong. You've been through hell in the last decade and survived. You'll survive this, too." He placed his hands on my shoulders. "I think you're one special lady."

He drew me close, and a rush of heat spread throughout my body. I wanted to melt when I heard him say, "Damn, I'm going to break the rules."

He lowered his head and found my lips. Desire, white-hot and raging, ripped through me. My heart hammered, and I slid my arms around his neck. We kissed deep, hungry kisses, our tongues tangling.

Somehow, my blouse was unbuttoned and my bra unclasped. Matt's hand covered my breast, his fingers pinching the center erect.

I moaned deep in my throat. My frantic hands tugged and pulled the polo shirt from his shorts. I ran my fingers over his muscular chest covered with crisp, curling hair. God, I wanted him. I wanted him with a desperation I couldn't explain. Call it old-fashioned lust, but I had never needed anybody as much as I needed Matt Summers.

Like a stone cast into a lake, ripples of desire radiated from the pit of my stomach to every extremity. The blood pounded in my ears, and I was incapable of uttering a word. I whimpered and clenched my fingers in his hair.

Then Matt stopped, raised his head, and froze.

Not again! "No, don't stop. Please. I want you. Don't do this to me again. I can't take it," I pleaded.

"Shhh," he said, pushing me away. "Listen."

Dazed, I heard only my ragged breathing. "What?"

He let his arms drop and turned his head toward the back of the house.

"I heard something out back. The gate on the side of the house creaks when it's opened," he whispered.

I stood silent and then heard it—a faint squeaking, like the gate had opened and then been closed.

Matt shoved me toward the stairs.

"Call 9-1-1 from my bedroom. Don't come back down."

I nodded and raced up the steps, trying to dress at the same time. I tossed a glance over the banister. Matt disappeared into the kitchen. Then I heard the hutch drawer opening. That's where he kept his gun.

My heart pounded with fear. My cell was in my purse in the den. I fumbled with the phone on his nightstand. Dialing, I held my breath and waited.

"9-1-1 emergency."

"I want to report a prowler in my backyard at 1602 Willowbend Cove in Germantown."

"Your name?"

"Theresa Lennox. It's Matt Summers' residence. Please hurry."

"Stay inside. We're sending someone now. Don't hang—"

The line went dead.

Chapter Thirteen

"Hello? Hello?" I hit the redial button. Nothing happened. Then I noticed there was no dial tone.

I dropped the phone on the bed and ran to look out the window in my room. The roof of the deck blocked my view. I saw a portion of the pool, but that was all. I couldn't see the gate.

The silence from below scared the hell out of me. Matt told me to stay put, but I had to know what was happening.

I tiptoed to the top of the stairs and listened but heard nothing over the pounding of my heart. I understood the seriousness of the situation. No kid sneaking in for a midnight swim would cut the phone lines.

I started down the steps with no clear idea of what to do. I'd be useless in any kind of fight but refused to let Matt face this alone.

The sound of breaking glass and splintering wood from the deck door brought me to a halt, my hands grasping the banister like a lifeline. My knees shook so hard I feared tumbling onto the marble floor below.

Two shots boomed—one from inside and one from out. I did what every feather-brained heroine does in every romance novel. I screamed.

Matt cursed. I heard the crunch of glass grinding underfoot as he must have run for the door. A second later two more shots exploded from outside, followed by a sharp cry.

I broke free of my paralysis and found the strength to stumble down the stairs, racing through the foyer and the den to the back door, where I flipped on the patio lights. My feet hit the deck. Someone swore. The gate crashed open against the side of the house, followed by the sound of fleeing footsteps.

"Matt! Matt, are you all right?"

He lay on his side, his right hand clutching his left shoulder.

"No, I'm not all right. The son of a bitch shot me. Call 9-1-1 again."

He groaned and tried to sit up.

"Already done before he cut the lines. Don't move."

I knelt beside him, at a complete loss as to what to do. First aid had never been a high priority, and I hated feeling useless. Lights bloomed from the darkened houses around us.

"What's going on over there?" a man's voice yelled from a neighboring yard.

His head and shoulders poked over the privacy fence. He held a shotgun in his hand.

"Someone tried to break in. Matt's been shot. Our phone is out. Please call an ambulance." I wasn't going to leave Matt to look for our cells.

Sirens piercing the air told me help was already on the way. I ran down the steps and through the wide-open gate to the driveway, waving my arms to signal the first arrivals.

When told what had happened, some of the policemen set out to scour the neighborhood while others staked out Matt's house both front and back. The rest followed me to the deck.

We were questioned, but since I hadn't been an eyewitness, they concentrated on Matt. Even though grimacing with pain, he gave coherent answers.

"After sending Miss Lennox upstairs to call 9-1-1, I looked out the windows. Didn't see anything for a minute or two. Then a shadow mounted the steps. I stayed inside the kitchen. He busted in the back door. We both fired and missed. He took off. I followed. We shot again. He got lucky and nailed me."

More sirens announced the paramedics had arrived. While they worked on Matt, I sat by the table and shook. Those nasty black dots swam in front of my eyes, and I sagged in the chair. One of the men waved something under my nose. The sharp odor of ammonia made me cough and wheeze. My eyes watered, and my nose ran, but my head cleared.

The cops who had searched for the perpetrator returned with their reports. Most of the neighbors hadn't heard anything until the shots or the police sirens. Only one person verified our story.

A policeman read from his notes. "A Mrs. Kendall over on Shady Woods Lane said something woke her up. She didn't know what. A few minutes later her dog kicked up a rumpus. She investigated and saw a man limping through her front yard. He jumped into a car and took off like a bat out of hell."

"Any description?" another asked.

"Not of the man. It was too dark. He drove without headlights, but when he passed the street light on the corner, she described it as a light-colored car and 'not a clunker,' which I took to mean late model."

"Check the hospitals. If he limped, Mr. Summers may have done some damage after all."

By now the paramedics had bandaged Matt. He looked calm under the circumstances, smiling and giving a thumbs-up. Then his gaze slid past me down to the patio and at the gurney being wheeled to the foot of the steps.

"I don't need that. I can walk."

"It's just a precaution, sir. You're not seriously injured, but a doctor will have to dig that bullet out."

"It's all right, Matt," I said. "You go with them. I'll lock up here and follow in my car."

In the end, he didn't have much choice. The paramedics helped him onto the gurney. Most of the cops had left, but a couple remained on duty to guard the house and probably scour the yard for evidence.

"I'll stop by the hospital later to check on you both," an officer said.

I thanked him and took off. Since Matt's wound was not life-threatening, the ambulance took him to the Germantown hospital, less than two miles away. By the time I parked and entered, the doctors had already whisked him into a treatment room. They allowed me in for a few minutes before they got down to the business of removing the bullet.

Under the harsh light of the cubicle, I saw Matt clearly for the first time since the shooting. He resembled something out of a horror movie. The paramedics had cut off his yellow polo shirt back on the deck, and smears of dry and not so dry blood streaked his chest. Blood also stained the bandage on his shoulder, telling me the wound still bled. The left side of his olive-green shorts showed splatters of the same.

I clutched his right hand, ignoring that it, too, still bore traces of red.

"Are you all right? Does it hurt much?"

"It hurts like hell, but I'll live. In almost fifteen years of investigative work, this is the first time I've ever been shot—or even shot at. Other than the firing range, I've never had to use the damned gun." He shook his head.

"I guess you have me to thank for this. Matt, what are we going to do?"

"I don't know. The doctors will give me powerful drugs in a few minutes. It might not be until tomorrow before I can think straight."

"Will they keep you overnight?"

"I doubt it. They'll patch me up and send me home. We'll have to shove something in front of the back door until I can replace it." He frowned. "I hope the glass didn't mar the floor to much."

Why this sudden interest in trivial matters? Then it dawned on me he talked for my benefit.

"Don't talk, honey. Just close your eyes and lie back." I stroked the hair from his forehead and squeezed his hand.

He returned a feeble grin, squeezed back, and then did as I suggested. A few minutes later a doctor pulled open the curtain and walked in.

"Mr. Summers? I'm Doctor Sherman. We're going to take an X-ray of your shoulder to find out exactly where the bullet is lodged. Then I'll extract it, bandage you up, and keep you overnight for observation. How does that sound?"

"Works for me—except for the overnight business. I want to go home. The sooner the better," Matt replied in a tired, pain-filled voice.

"We'll see." Dr. Sherman turned and said, "Ma'am, I'm going to ask you to wait outside until we're finished. It shouldn't take long."

I nodded my understanding, kissed Matt, and left.

I hate hospital waiting rooms. They're usually noisy and crowded, filled with people either in pain, sick, or complaining about the long wait, especially on a Friday night.

But at two in the morning in Germantown, I was the only one present. Ah, Germantown. Even the furniture looked comfortable. I bought a Coke at a vending machine and sat on a couch, my legs crossed and my foot tapping in the air when the officer I'd spoken with earlier arrived.

"Any news?" I asked. "Did you find the guy?"

He shook his head. "No. If he was shot, he may have just been grazed and won't seek medical attention. We didn't find any blood trail, but then half the sprinkler systems in the city were watering lawns. This was no smash-and-grab job. The guy meant business."

"He was after me."

"Are you sure?"

What planet has this guy been living on?

After I gave him the abridged edition of the last two weeks, he nodded but looked dubious. "It's possible, of course, but who knows you're staying with Mr. Summers?"

"Not very many people. I guess it wouldn't take long for word to get out. Reporters can be relentless."

"Plus, we have to look at Mr. Summers' profession. In his line of work, it's not hard to make enemies. I'm sure he takes on a lot of divorce and mate-checking cases. A vengeful ex-spouse or significant other could be responsible. Do you know of any cases like that?"

I told him about the East Memphis widow with the large bank account.

The cop shrugged. "There's a possibility. How is Mr. Summers?"

"They're taking X-rays and removing the bullet. He'll be fine."

"Tell him we'll be in touch. He needs to make a formal statement in the next couple of days. As soon as you return home, the police will leave." He touched his cap and exited into the night.

I sat back, glancing at the pneumatic double doors separating me from Matt, and thought of all the times I had been in this place after Danny's loving attention. At least he had someone out here. Cabs had usually provided my transportation home.

I picked up a magazine, hoping things went fast. From the corner of my eye, something outside the entrance caught my attention. Four people, two with large shoulder-mounted cameras, perched on the curb about to come in.

Dropping the magazine like it was on fire, I rushed to the receptionist. "Please, where can I hide?"

"What?"

"Please, reporters are outside. I've got to hide."

"Reporters? Why are reporters here?" she asked, her brows drawn together in a frown.

"They're after me."

"Why? Who are you?"

I tossed another glance out the door. One reporter had hung up a cell phone. They'd enter any second.

"It's a long story. Can I go inside one of the treatment rooms? Just until they're gone?"

"Okay, use the first cube on the right. Don't move and don't interrupt anyone."

I dashed for the double doors. Interrupt? Dr. Sherman and Matt were the only ones back there. The doors swished shut behind me. Through the window, I saw the reporters enter and dodged into the cubicle, pulling the curtain behind me.

Pressing my fist against my chest to quiet my thudding heart, I opened the fabric a couple of inches and peeked out. I had a perfect view of the door window and the waiting room beyond. The reporters had set up camp. Damn. It was almost three in the morning, but I needed help and called Jerricus.

"'Lo?" a sleepy voice mumbled in my ear.

"Jerricus, it's Theresa. I need help."

"Theresa? What is it? What's wrong?" His voice sharpened.

I explained the night's events and the situation. "The reporters have taken up residence in the middle of the room. Doesn't look like they plan on moving any time soon. What am I going to do? We have to leave sometime."

My voice quavered. Tired of evading reporters and killers, I wanted to lie down and give up.

"Is there a back door out of the emergency room?"

"I don't know. Maybe. But even if there is, I'd still have to come around the front to my car. It's parked just a few feet from the door."

"How much longer before they're finished with Matt?"

"I'm not sure."

"It'll take a while what with all the paper work and such." He paused for a moment, and I heard a rustling sound as though he'd gotten out of bed. "Stay put. Stop the doctor from leaving when he's done. Tell him to stall until I get there, and for God's sake not to answer any questions from reporters. That's my job."

He hung up. I peered through the curtain and window again. The cameramen sat facing the treatment area. They looked ready to pounce. I visualized them snapping the cameras to their shoulders like gunslingers drawing guns.

The reporters paced with microphones in hand. Every once in a while, one would stop and smooth back his hair—just in case it wasn't perfect. The call letters on the cameras identified them from channels ten and eight. Why had they shown up? In view of the quick response by the media yesterday, I wondered if a police scanner *was* standard equipment in their cars.

A shaft of light shot out from the cubicle beside me, and Dr. Sherman emerged. I jerked the curtain back the rest of the way and stopped him in mid-stride.

"Dr. Sherman, wait!"

He halted and stared at me with a disapproving look. "Ma'am, I thought I asked you to wait outside."

"Yes, I know, but I'm hiding. How's Matt?"

"He's fine. I'm going to fill out the paper work. As soon as it's finished, he can sign a waiver and leave." He paused and gave me a sharp look as though my words had just sunk in. "What do you mean, you're hiding? Who from?"

"Reporters."

"Reporters?" he said, his eyebrows rising. "Why are reporters stalking you?"

"Doctor, I'm too exhausted to give you the whole song and dance. Can you avoid them and take your time with the paper work? My lawyer will deal with the press."

The doctor shrugged with a puzzled expression. "Okay, if that's what you want. You can see Mr. Summers now."

He turned and walked down a corridor while I scurried to Matt's cubicle. He lay propped up on the gurney, his shoulder bandaged and his arm in a sling. A nurse stood next to him.

He smiled and murmured drowsily, "Hi, baby. How's it goin'?" His words slurred.

I clasped his free hand, now clean, and winked. "Much better. How is he?" I asked the nurse.

"He's fine. Just a little groggy. Will you be staying with him when he gets home?"

"Yes. Is there anything I need to know?"

"We gave him a painkiller, but it should wear off in a few hours." She handed me two boxes of pills and a couple of prescriptions. "Give him one pain pill every four hours as needed and one antibiotic in the morning. Get these filled tomorrow. Make sure he takes one of the antibiotics three times a day until they're gone. If you have any questions, please call. Oh, and make an appointment with your regular doctor as soon as possible. The bandages can come off in a week. Is there anything else we can do for you?"

"No, thank you. You've been very kind."

She left. I leaned over and kissed Matt. "Thank God, you're going to be all right."

He struggled to sit up and swing his legs over the side of the bed.

"Lez get outta here."

"We can't just yet. You have to sign release papers, and there are reporters in the waiting room."

"Aw, shit. Where'd they come from?"

I told him I didn't have a clue but that Jerricus was due any moment. He lay back down, grimaced, and then yawned.

"Gonna catch a few Zs. Keep an eye open for Jerricus. Don't let the dogs see you." He closed his eyes and zonked out.

Tiptoeing back to the double doors, I peeked out again at the hounds still sniffing around like hunters to the prey.

Then Jerricus swept through the entrance. I spotted another door farther down the hall with a sign that said *Waiting Area*, scurried over, and opened it a crack.

"Good morning, gentlemen. How may I help you?"

His booming voice startled the reporters. The cameramen hustled to hoist their cameras. Bright lights instantly blazed forth. In spite of the early hour, Jerricus had dressed in tan slacks and a sport coat, the white shirt underneath crisp, as though freshly ironed, which it could be for all I knew.

"Mr. Monroe, is it true the private investigator your client, Theresa Lennox, hired has been shot?" the reporter from Channel Eight asked.

"Sadly, that is true."

Not to be scooped, the second man said, "I understand Miss Lennox is living with Mr. Summers."

The miserable slug. He made me sound like some kind of floozy.

"Due to the numerous attempts on my client's life, she has been forced to seek refuge with someone who can protect her. Mr. Summers was doing his job when the incident occurred at his home."

Well, he was sort of. Does protection include me half naked and in a sexually compromising position?

"You mean he's a bodyguard?"

"Yes."

Matt can guard my body any time.

"Is Mr. Summers badly hurt?" Channel Ten pursued.

"No, thank the good Lord. His wound is minor, and he should be released sometime tomorrow."

Where did he get that? Then I understood that if the reporters thought we'd be out any time soon, they'd never leave.

"Can we talk to him and your client?"

"Come on, boys, give 'em a break. They will answer no questions until the police reopen the investigation into Danny Garrett's murder. Now you have a statement from me, and I can't see standing here bothering these nice people any longer, can you? Let's call it a night."

When Jerricus Monroe spoke, people listened. The reporters looked satisfied. The lights and cameras clicked off. Everybody filed out the doors, except Jerricus who without anybody's permission, barged into the treatment area. I met him outside Matt's cubicle.

"That was great. But now they know where I am."

"It was only a matter of time anyway. Where's Matt? In here? Is he all right?"

He pulled back the curtain. Matt slept on. The drugs had kicked in, and the lines of pain left his face. He looked peaceful—or dead. A little dart of fear sliced through me. I slid my fingers around his wrist and breathed a sigh of relief when the strong tap of his pulse proved otherwise.

"He'll be fine. He was hit in the shoulder, but they got it out. As soon as the doctor brings the papers, we're outta here," I told Jerricus.

At that moment, Dr. Sherman walked in holding a clipboard. He raised an eyebrow at another person's presence, nodded, and then awakened Matt.

"Sign these, Mr. Summers, and you're free as a bird."

Matt barely opened his eyes, scrawled his signature on the bottom of the paper, and lay back. The nurse arrived with a wheelchair, and Jerricus helped settle Matt into it. We rolled into the now empty waiting room. Jerricus left first to make sure the reporters had gone, then signaled us the all clear. I ran to the car and pulled up in front of the hospital doors.

Jerricus leaned down next to my window. "Stay put over the weekend. Be in my office at two o'clock on Monday afternoon. We may have to let you answer questions soon. I want you prepared."

He walked to his Lexus, got in, and drove away. The hospital personnel secured Matt in the passenger's seat.

The evening had not been my idea of Friday night entertainment.

****

I unlocked the front door and, with the help of the police officers still guarding the house, steered Matt into a chair in the living room. Even though splintered and a mess, the back door almost closed. At my request, the men moved a large bookcase over the opening. I'd call someone tomorrow about fixing it.

Before they left, the cops told me they'd patrol the neighborhood on a regular basis. Feeling better, I helped a protesting Matt up the steps and into his bedroom.

"I don't need any help, damn it. I can walk. My shoulder's out of commission, not my legs."

"You're also pumped full of drugs. If you fall down the stairs, we'll end up in the emergency room again. Humor me."

He shut up and weaved from side to side, giving me a goofy grin. I pulled the covers back and guided him onto the bed. He sighed, closed his eyes, and then flopped onto his back, instantly falling asleep.

The only clothing he had left were his shorts and deck shoes. I stripped him and tossed them onto the floor, then covered him up to the waist with the sheet and turned off the lights. Picking up the bloodstained clothing, I went downstairs and threw them in the trash.

Making a quick tour of the lower floor, I double checked all doors and windows, peering out each one. Nothing moved, and while certain the shooter wouldn't return, I stared nervously into the darkness anyway. My heart hammered in my chest for a moment when headlights swept into the cove. It settled back into a normal rhythm when a cop car rolled by, patrolling as promised.

Now that things had simmered down, exhaustion seeped through every part of my body. I paused at the foot of the staircase, my feet refusing to move. The top of the steps looked a million miles away as I slowly climbed.

Finally making it, I checked on Matt. He slept with a peaceful expression on his face. Without thinking, I shed my clothes and crawled in next to him. He murmured something, shifted, and then groaned. I kissed his forehead and pulled the covers up.

Matt needed me, and I needed that. I wouldn't—couldn't—think about tomorrow.

Chapter Fourteen

In spite of my exhaustion, I had a crummy night's sleep. Worried, I awoke every hour or so, checking Matt's breathing and temperature. *He* slept like a log.

I finally surrendered and got up. Making as little fuss as possible, I jerked on my clothing of the evening before and went downstairs.

After starting the coffee, I opened the front door. The newspaper lay at the foot of the driveway. I strolled down the pavement, breathing in the fresh morning air, and bent over to pick it up when shouting voices from down the street startled me. My head snapped up. Three satellite trucks with a dozen reporters gathered at the entrance to the cove. They obeyed the restraining order, but we were trapped and under siege.

My fingers curled around the paper, and I ran for the house. Slamming the door behind me, I leaned against it, fighting tears. Damn it, didn't those vultures ever quit?

I walked into the kitchen and slapped the newspaper on the table, then spied the prescriptions Matt needed. I'd never get past those hounds in the street. Now what?

A cup of coffee helped ease my anger. A glance out the dining room window showed a woman marching up the walk. I rushed to open the door before she rang the bell. My mouth fell open in surprise when the elderly lady gave the reporters two hundred feet away the stiff, middle-finger salute. She turned and smiled.

"Hello. My name is Bette Wilson. I live next door."

"I'm Theresa Lennox. I'm sorry for all the fuss and—" She didn't give me a chance to finish.

"Nonsense. It's not your fault. They're worse than a pack of scavengers picking the remains of a carcass. May I come in? How's Matt?"

"Of course," I replied, stepping back and allowing her to enter. "Matt's doing well. He's asleep right now. It was a minor wound in the shoulder. He'll be fine. Would—would you like some coffee? I just made some."

"I'd love it."

She followed me into the kitchen where I poured her a cup and gestured toward a chair, not sure of the procedures. I'd never done a coffee klatch.

She took a sip and then patted my hand. "I'm glad to hear Matt's going to be all right. He's a good boy. When my husband had a heart attack two years ago, he cut our grass and pruned the bushes."

"He's very thoughtful," I murmured, still not sure what to say. To cover my confusion, I blew on the already cooling liquid in my cup.

"At any rate, I came over to say Harry and I don't believe for one minute that you killed your husband. We've been reading the paper and listening to the TV about all the strange things happening to you, and why the police don't arrest someone more deserving, I don't know. Last night should tell them they're sniffing down the wrong rat hole, if you ask me."

"Thank you. You're very kind." A lump formed in my throat. I swallowed lukewarm coffee to get rid of it.

She prattled on. I found myself laughing at her stories of the neighborhood characters. She had lived here for over thirty years and maintained a good grip on the gossip hotline.

Bette declined my offer of another cup of coffee. "I just came over to say hello and inquire about Matt. Can I make a grocery run for you?"

"That would be wonderful. Matt needs prescriptions filled, and I was wondering how I'd do it."

"Happy to help. Make out a list. I'll get a few groceries, too."

I gave her the prescriptions, a short list of items, and then reached for my purse.

"Don't worry about the money. Matt can pay me back later." She rose, heading toward the foyer.

"I hope you get out of the cove."

"If they try to stop me, I'll just floor my big, ole Caddy and rip right through 'em. I'll say I got the gas and the brake pedals confused. I'm an old woman. They'll believe it."

I laughed and closed the door, returning to the kitchen for another cup of coffee. Friends—what a wonderful concept.

****

We remained prisoners. The reporters stuck like glue the rest of the day. Even the pool was off limits. An inventive photographer climbed a tree in the neighbors' backyard and scrambled onto the L-shaped roof, hoping to get a shot. He scared the homeowner's wife half to death when she spotted him from a window. I apologized, but the couple waved it off, also voicing their support.

I didn't see Bette leave the cove, but since I heard no squealing tires or ambulance sirens, I assumed she made it out unmolested. She confirmed it when she returned an hour or so later with the medications and food.

Matt awoke at two o'clock. He dressed himself and, much to my annoyance, refused to take any pain pills.

"I don't need them," he said, swallowing the antibiotic. "I feel much better."

"Liar. You hurt like hell. I can see it in your eyes."

"The only thing causing me pain right now are those damned reporters."

I spent the next couple of hours hovering and treating him like an invalid. He humored me for a while.

"Theresa, will you quit breathing down my neck every time I move?"

"I'm only trying to help. You should rest."

"Why?"

"Because you've been shot, for God's sake!"

"It was a simple shoulder wound. It'll hurt for a few days and then be gone."

"Ah-ha! So you admit you're in pain."

He shot me a stern look before saying, "What's for dinner, and it better not be soup for my weakened condition."

Damn. I'd been planning on soup and salad. "Spaghetti, smart-ass."

"Good. Let's eat early. I'm starving."

That evening, most of the reporters gave up. Only

one news van and crew stuck it out. They left the next day.

I insisted Matt rest, but on Sunday afternoon he locked himself in his office. I took the hint and did a few of my assignments. Tomorrow I would see Jerricus and prepare for a possible news conference—with me as the starring attraction.

****

This time my attorney didn't keep me waiting. Doris showed me right in.

"Have you heard anything from the district attorney's office yet?" I asked, seating myself in one of the comfy chairs.

"They called this morning, but only with the news that the trial date has been set for August sixth."

"August? That's over two months away. I'm not sure I can last that long."

Jerricus smiled. "Speaking as a lawyer, I have to advise that two months in a murder case is an incredibly short time frame. I think they're rushing things because they know their case is paper thin. Naturally, I'll petition the court for a delay to mount a defense." His smile widened into a grin.

I didn't want a delay. I wanted this over—*now*. "I get it. A quick trial so the defense runs out of investigative time."

"Don't worry, Theresa. I doubt any of this will ever see the inside of a courtroom."

"I see a Garrett hand in this. Have you heard from Diana or Hamilton?"

"No, but the Worthington family mouthpiece called over the weekend to protest my public handling of the restraining order. I feigned innocence and apologized for any embarrassment the incident caused his clients."

"You *apologized*?" I didn't think Jerricus Monroe apologized for anything and was outraged he had in this case.

He waved a hand in the air. "I was lying. He knew it, but it's all part of the game."

Games. Of course. How stupid of me. Everybody played games, especially lawyers. I'd play along if I knew the rules. "Do you expect the DA to call with a deal soon?"

"Very soon. I take it you haven't changed your mind about accepting what they bring to the table."

"Absolutely not. I'm in this to the bitter end," I replied in a sharp voice. Did he really have to ask? I'd put in too much emotion to settle for anything less than complete vindication. No way would I plea bargain now.

"Don't get touchy. I have to ask. Would you like a glass of wine?"

"No, but a bottle of water would be nice."

He called Doris, and within seconds the lady appeared bearing a very expensive brand.

"How's Matt doing?" He shuffled papers on his desk, then opened a file folder, bringing out the dreaded legal pad.

"Fine. He went to his doctor this morning. There's no sign of infection, and he's thrown the sling away. He still has to take the antibiotics but says the pain pills make him dopey."

"He was damned lucky. Hear anything from the police?"

"No, other than they don't know who tried to break in. If Matt nicked him, he didn't go anywhere for treatment."

"It might not be such a bad idea for you to hole up somewhere for a while."

"You mean in a motel or something? I'd rather take my chances in Germantown. After Friday night, everybody in the neighborhood will be on the lookout for strangers. God help a legitimate delivery man."

He sat back and frowned. "I was thinking more along the lines of you and Matt staying in a suite at the Peabody. You could put his neighbors at risk by staying."

"The Peabody? Matt isn't made of money."

"Theresa, I'd pay for it and then ask for reimbursement from the state, saying it was for your protection. Nobody would screw with you at the most famous hotel in the South."

I saw his point about the neighbors but hated the thought of being cooped up in a hotel, even the Peabody. However, I liked his chutzpah at getting the state to cough up the cost.

"Let me talk to Matt. I'll see what he thinks and call you in a couple of days."

"Fair enough. Now here is a list of the possible questions reporters might ask during a press conference. They're creatures of habit and won't deviate too much."

I read through the list. Some made sense and would be easy to answer. Others appalled me.

"Why would someone want to know about my sex life?"

"Tabloid news eats scandal. They'd love it, especially if you had a boyfriend before the divorce."

"I didn't. And why would they want to know my father's name? What has that got to do with anything?"

"Trust me, honey, they'll want to know, and if you don't tell them, they'll dig until they find out. Make up a name. Say that's all you know because that's all your mother told you. They might not bother to check, especially since we've told them he's dead, but if they do, a fake name will slow 'em down. Now let's go through each question and work on your answers."

I spent the next ninety minutes fabricating answers to questions and memorizing them. Jerricus had me embellishing the vandalism, car bomb, and attempted kidnapping with a dramatic flair I found both distasteful and overblown. When I expressed doubts about my abilities as an actress, he laughed and said any time I couldn't pull it off to dab my eyes with a hankie and he'd take over.

"I'll dab frequently, but no more soap."

"You'll do just fine, darlin'," he drawled, tossing the pad of notes onto his desk.

"Don't use that moonlight and magnolias accent on me. You may have been born here, but your talk is pure Harvard."

"Touché. Good old boy is for the public. My clients, however, like to hear Ivy League educated." He laughed. "Take the answers home and study them. Practice in front of a mirror. Match facial expressions to the words. And don't forget to use a soft, quivering voice. You'll sound vulnerable and afraid."

"I am."

Jerricus leaned back in his chair and clasped his hands behind his head. "I thought you might be interested to know the medical examiner sent the results of the tox screens on Danny and the ballistics report."

"And?"

"It was your gun all right."

"Of course, it was. I know that. Was he drunk?"

"Point-oh-six, which tells us he'd had a busy morning but was still legal. He also tested positive for cocaine."

"That doesn't surprise me."

"The ME fixes the time of death as between ten and two—give or take. Danny drank and snorted breakfast, so that's as close as they can come."

My spirits lifted. "But I was on campus during those hours. How can the cops say I killed him?"

"Because you cut a class at eleven. Theresa, I told you that missing hour would be a problem. Until the police find someone who puts you where you said you were, or come up with an eyewitness who saw Danny or another person entering your apartment, you're still suspect number one."

"Even with all that's happened to me?"

Jerricus sighed and leaned forward, his arms resting on the blotter. "Those things mean someone wants to kill you, but the cops won't budge unless they have a direct connection between that someone and Danny."

My throat had gone dry, and I had the strongest urge to scream. I gulped the last of my bottled water.

"By the way, tell Matt thanks for the information he's been sending me on Danny's friends and acquaintances. I've got people checking further."

"Did he send you the latest on Fast Eddie Piper? A dealer down on Beale told us Danny sometimes dealt."

Jerricus paused and stared, a frown marring his brow. "What do you mean 'us'?"

Oops. I hadn't meant to let it slip that I helped Matt

question people. I shrugged like it was no big deal.

"I didn't want to stay alone, so I tagged along. I wore a disguise."

"I don't care. You shouldn't be accompanying Matt on interrogations. It's dangerous. Next time, stay at home and lock the doors. Better yet, check into the Peabody."

"Danny's friends all have alibis—at least most of them do," I said, ignoring his speech. "I think Fast Eddie *could* have hired someone to do it. Danny *might* have skimmed or couldn't pay and got snuffed for it."

"Maybe, but let Matt and my staff do the leg work from here on out. Friday night shows somebody is damned scared."

"Besides me, you mean?"

"Yeah, besides you. Have you heard anything more from Hamilton?"

"Not a word. I guess the restraining order did its job. He was pretty angry when Matt tossed him out of the house. It was one of the few times I've ever seen that arrogant demeanor crack."

"How come I never saw either you or Danny at any social functions?"

"Are you kidding?" I snorted. "A former cocktail waitress attending a fancy, schmancy Worthington-Garrett soiree? We were never invited."

"Don't sell yourself short. Maybe it wasn't you. Maybe your husband was the problem. Diana may have doted on her son, but if Danny, showing up stoned or drunk, threatened Hamilton's image—especially at a political gathering—then Hamilton would have refused him an invite."

I'd never considered that angle before. I'd always

assumed it was me they'd been ashamed to have meet their friends and contributors. I told him about Matt's suggestion that Hamilton could have had Danny killed.

"I can see Ham doing a lot of things for the sake of winning an election, but murder isn't one of them. Hasn't got the guts. That's more up Diana's alley, and she wouldn't harm a hair on her son's ungrateful head."

"I guess you're right, but can't you just see the headlines?"

"Of course, I can." Jerricus smiled and then rose. "Go home, and tell Matt he needs to hone his dodging skills. I'll call if I hear anything."

Jerricus's dodging joke didn't amuse me. In fact, I didn't like the way the entire meeting had gone. No way would I hide out at the Peabody or cease accompanying Matt to question people. With a vested interest in every possible suspect, I intended to continue being a quiet shadow, regardless of how dangerous the situation. If that made me too stupid to live, then it was just too damned bad.

And finally, I didn't want to participate in a press conference, answering a bunch of questions with dramatic prevarication.

But then I didn't want to go to prison either.

****

Matt greeted me with a hug and then grimaced.

"You still hurt, don't you? Have you taken anything for it?"

"No. Yes, it hurts, but not as much as yesterday or the day before that. In a week I'll be back to normal."

"Define normal," I said, irritated at the macho stance men think it's necessary to take when it came to pain.

"Nobody can define normal."

"I can define what it's not. It's not dodging bullets, car bombs, and kidnappers. It's not going over scripted press conference answers, so you can show a vulnerable side to the world." My voice rose. "It is not meeting drug dealers all over town hoping to find a killer. And it most certainly is not living here because I have no place else to go."

Matt lifted his eyebrows and had a questioning expression on his face. "Something tells me you didn't have a good session with Jerricus this afternoon." He pulled me back into his arms. "Tell me about it."

My irritation evaporated like air from a pricked balloon. "I'm sorry. I didn't mean to take out my anger at Jerricus on you."

I told him about the last few hours and the impending press conference. "I don't like lying, Matt. And it bothers me that I've become so good at it. What bugs me is all the drama and the performances will be my ticket to freedom. It goes against everything I ever learned."

" 'And the truth shall set you free,' " Matt said.

I inhaled deeply and nodded at his ironic quote. "Something like that. Apparently, truth sometimes needs embellishment. I don't see how I can survive two or more months until the trial."

"Listen to your attorney. He's right. It'll never be that long." He dropped a light kiss on my forehead. "How about I throw a couple of super-sized burgers on the grill and tell you how my day has gone?"

"With everything on it and lots of salty fries?"

"Your wish is my command. There's ice cream in the freezer, and I think I can scrounge up some chocolate syrup for a shake, too."

"You light the fire, and I'll slip into something a lot more comfortable." I headed for the stairs, calling over my shoulder, "And *lots* of chocolate."

An hour later we bit into thick, juicy burgers. I'd piled so much on top the damned thing was close to four inches high. I attacked Mount Burger.

I was amazed to taste the meat through all the ketchup, mustard, and mayo. A glob of condiments splattered onto my plate, and a rivulet of grease slid down my hand to my wrist.

I was halfway through before asking, "How was your day? Did you find out any more about Fast Eddie?"

"No, but I did come up with some other interesting tidbits," he replied through a mouthful of burger. He swallowed and shoved in a couple of fries.

"Yeah? What?"

"Remember how surprised we were Channel Twenty-two didn't have much to say about your ordeals?"

"They normally love sensationalized stuff like car bombs and attempted kidnappings."

"I've found out why they're so reticent. The station is located in rather small quarters in Midtown. They want to buy a parcel of land in a nice, wide-open area. All they need is a small change in zoning. It's before the zoning board now and comes to a vote soon. I'll give you one guess who owns the property in question."

I stopped in midchew and lowered my burger. Swallowing, I dipped a fry in ketchup and stared at him. "Hamilton and Diana Garrett."

"Bingo. He stands to make a fortune and is

bringing all his senatorial and possible gubernatorial influence down on the heads of the zoning board."

I ate a fry and drank some of my shake. "We should have figured something like that from the beginning. The Garrets own real estate all over Shelby County and beyond. Danny told me his father was one of the original investors in the first casino down in Tunica. He got out before the building boom farther north forced it to close. I understand he made a pile of money."

"I checked on the Garrett property holdings while you were gone. He's also part owner of a strip joint on Winchester called The Shake It Club. And a small percentage of it is also owned by one Edward Piper."

I almost choked. "Hamilton and Fast Eddie are *partners*?"

"Only in the strictest sense of the word. Hamilton invested money as a silent partner, but I doubt he would take the chance of being seen in the place. Politically, it wouldn't look good to his constituents who expect a church-going, squeaky-clean image. However…" Matt paused. "Danny wouldn't be so hesitant, would he?"

The implications had my heart pounding. "Hell, no. He'd demand free drinks as the son of one of the owners. He had a lot of balls in that respect. But it's also a link between Danny, Fast Eddie, and drugs. They must have met at the club. Eddie probably dealt out of it."

Matt smiled and nodded. "I emailed the information to Jerricus just before you got home. He'll check it out."

I finished my burger and fries in record time. Relief and excitement surged through me. We had the connection and a possible motive.

"How long has Hamilton been a partner?"

"Close to ten years."

During my marriage, which meant Danny had known Eddie long enough to *maybe* be granted leeway on payments. I wanted to shout with joy. It could be the smoking gun that had me taking a walk.

Matt finish his food. Under the artificial lights of the breakfast nook, the deeply grooved lines etched his face from nose to mouth and around his eyes. He looked tired and, in spite of his macho posturing, in pain.

"Why don't you go into the den and relax? I'll clean up. You've had an incredible day."

Matt stood and gently rubbed his shoulder.

"Hurt?" I asked.

"Itches. The stitches come out in a few days."

"What kind of gun did the guy use?"

"A .25 caliber semi-automatic. The cops recovered a couple of casings, but unless it was used in another shooting, ballistics will be useless. I'm hoping a latent fingerprint might have been left on the casing. People don't normally wear gloves to load a clip." He paused and leaned against the counter next to me. "I also picked up another bit of information today."

I shoved the dishes into the dishwasher. "Oh? What?"

"Did you know Danny had a girlfriend?"

Chapter Fifteen

"Doesn't surprise me. Danny had lots of one-night stands. I didn't care. It meant that was one less night I'd get the crap beat out of me."

"This one looks steady since the divorce."

"I didn't concern myself with Danny's women after the divorce. He must have moved fast because he was in jail for over six months. How did you find out about her?"

"I'd done a lot of background work on Danny, but this new information had me going over it again. I was checking when Fast Eddie may have appeared on the radar screen and noticed your ex had an arrest for domestic battery a month ago. I accessed the files and got a name—Sissy Carlton."

"Sissy?"

"Short for Cecilia. I took a chance and called her. She refused to talk over the phone but agreed to meet me tomorrow morning for breakfast at a pancake house on Ridgeway."

"Us," I reminded him.

I was kind of curious about Danny's last squeeze. He hadn't let any grass grow under his feet replacing me, but maybe he needed a new punching bag.

"All right, us, but didn't Jerricus tell you no more sleuthing?"

"This doesn't count. I'm curious to see if Danny

thought enough of me to pick a clone."

"Danny didn't think of anyone other than himself. He was a master of manipulation and a genius at finding the vulnerable," Matt said with a sneer.

"He was a regular Dr. Jekyll and Mr. Hyde. I often wondered if he had mental problems or if it was the drugs and booze that warped him."

Matt shrugged. "Doesn't matter now."

I grabbed the box of detergent from under the sink and filled the dishwasher, slammed the door shut, and set the timer.

So Danny had a girlfriend. I had ceased loving my husband years ago, admitting he'd never really loved me. He hadn't even bothered to show up at the courthouse for the final divorce hearing. He'd scrawled his signature on the papers, leaving the dirty work to his lawyer. It was just as well. I'd had no desire to see him ever again.

I felt sorry for the poor girl. Still, she'd only had to put up with Danny for a few months. Like an idiot, I'd stuck it out for close to ten years. Like an idiot—those were key words. Tears welled in my eyes. I blinked them away.

"Aw, honey, I'm sorry," Matt said, taking me into his arms. "I shouldn't have told you. I didn't think it would matter. Don't let it get to you."

"It's not that." I sniffled and rested my cheek on his broad chest. "It's just that every once in a while, the whole thing kind of overwhelms me."

I raised my head and gazed into his eyes. My breath caught at the expression on his face. Heat surged through me, and my nerves crackled with desire. Remembering the supercharged atmosphere of the other night, my heart thudded. With a groan, I slid my arms up his chest and around his neck, tangling my fingers in his hair.

"Matt? Oh, God, Matt."

He tightened his grip and kissed my upturned face from brow to chin.

"I know, baby. I want you, too."

He lowered his head and took my lips in a crushing kiss. The sparks last Friday night's shooting had extinguished burst into all consuming flames. Wave after wave of gushing heat swirled throughout my body. If I died right now, I wouldn't care. His erection stabbed me in the abdomen. I vowed tonight nothing would interrupt us.

We staggered from the kitchen through the dining room and foyer, shedding our shirts along the way. The striptease continued up the stairs into Matt's bedroom.

My bra hit the floor. Matt's mouth slid from my lips, down my throat, and across the globe of my breast until finding the aching center. His tongue and teeth produced a sharp throb from deep within. I squirmed, rubbing against him.

Incapable of coherent thought, I moaned, whimpered, and then moaned again. I shoved my hand down the front of his boxers. Silk panties fell to my ankles. I kicked them away.

Matt's hand homed in on the junction of my thighs and stroked. I cried out, pumping my hips while my hand caressed the hard heat held in my palm.

He gasped and groaned, then shuddered and pushed me onto the bed. Kneeing my thighs apart, he leaned over. In the dim recesses of my mind, I realized his gasp this time was not one of passion, but of pain. I rolled him onto his back and straddled his hips.

"Oh, God, Terry. Oh, Jesus," he moaned, fisting his hands in the bedspread.

I guided him to the entrance of my burning core and then crushed my pelvis against his, crying out when our throbbing bodies merged.

I rose, settled back, and repeated the action, then jerked upright, riding his thrusts hard.

The blood pounded in my ears, and my breath came in sharp gasps. The fire in my belly grew. Liquid flames pooled at our joining. Matt's hands found my breasts. He kneaded and pinched, sending more volts of electricity to that white-hot part of me demanding satisfaction.

Searing contractions ripped through me. I screamed, frantically riding for every little bit I could claim, shuddering and jerking as though struck by lightning.

A hoarse cry wrenched from Matt's throat. He lunged one last time. His hands held me jammed against his hips while his climax throbbed. I threw my head back, gulping air into my tortured lungs. The bed vibrated from our trembling bodies.

Then it was over. I rolled to the side, panting, waiting for the last flutter to die. The roaring in my ears ceased. Gradually, my heart regained a reasonable beat. Matt's fingers intertwined with mine. I turned my head and, in the dim glow from the streetlight slanting through the window, saw his face just inches from mine. He smiled and raised my hand to his lips.

"Wow," he said in a soft voice.

"Yeah, wow," I repeated, still a little breathless.

"I was only fooling myself all this time, wasn't I?"

"About what?"

"About keeping our relationship professional. I knew this would happen."

"We tried. I guess it was inevitable given the circumstances. I never wanted to get involved again. Our meeting was too soon after Danny. And yet…" I had entered forbidden territory talking about us and squeezed his hand. "How's the shoulder?"

"Hurts, but I don't give a damn."

I laughed. "I guess some things override pain."

"Next time I'll be more careful."

"Next time?"

"Give me a few minutes, and we'll see what develops."

Matt didn't need much time to recharge his battery. His hands and lips rekindled the flames from a warm glow into a raging fire once again.

Another climax built. He rolled me onto my side, lifted my leg over his hip, and thrust deeply inside. My orgasm spring rewound. We came together.

Matt kissed the side of my neck. Satiated, I wanted nothing more than to drift off into sleep with Matt holding me in his arms.

I snuggled closer. Tonight confirmed what I'd known for quite some time. I loved Matt Summers more than life. The realization both thrilled and terrified me.

****

Covers being ripped from my body awakened me. With the cocoon of warmth gone, I shivered and groped for the comforter.

"Up and at 'em, Miss Lennox. It's eight o'clock, and we're due to meet Sissy at nine, so get a move on," a voice said.

I growled and opened one eye. Matt stood at the foot of the bed, dressed, his hair still damp from the shower. He also grinned in a maddening way, like a man who'd spent the night making love. I sat up, grabbed the sheet, pulled it over my head, and lay back down.

"No, you don't," he replied, tugging the sheet out from under the end of the mattress. He clasped my foot and tickled.

I sat up with a yelp, jerking it from his grasp, and glared at him. "Is this the way I can expect to be awakened every morning?" I asked. Sometime during the night, I'd decided the sleeping arrangements suited me and would continue until whatever happened.

"Maybe. I haven't made up my mind yet. At least you'll start the day with a surprise." He laughed. "I'll go make coffee and get the paper in. If you aren't ready in twenty minutes, I swear I'll come up and drag you down."

I stuck out my tongue and then flopped back against the pillows. When had waking up become so much fun? When had the last time I made love been so satisfying? The answers to both questions elicited a strong response—never.

I was invigorated and eager to start a new day, knowing in my heart of hearts the end neared. When I walked away from this ordeal a free woman, then Matt and I could discuss the future. Strange—eighteen months ago such a thought would have sent me running for the nearest exit. I'd vowed never to marry or love again.

"Theresa," Matt called from the bottom of the

stairs. "I don't hear any water running. You'd better not be catching another forty winks."

"I'm up, you sleep-robbing demon," I called back. "And that coffee had better be strong and hot."

I sat up and stretched. A huge rock had rolled off my shoulders. I hadn't needed any damned sleeping pill. All I'd needed was a heavy dose of Matt Summers. *What a pleasant addiction.*

I showered, dressed, and entered the kitchen with a jaunty step. I poured a cup of coffee, grabbed the entertainment section of the paper, accepted Matt's kiss, and joined him at the table.

"You ready to meet Danny's girlfriend?" Matt asked, snatching the sports section.

"I'm looking forward to it. She might know more about his friends and acquaintances over the last few months than we do. She could give us one hell of a lead."

"That's what I thought. And this time you can ask the questions. She might open up to a woman. If that's the case, give me the high sign, and I'll leave."

I didn't find any decent movies playing anywhere and finished my coffee. We drove a short distance to the breakfast place on Ridgeway.

Inside, no single women waited. A hostess showed us to a booth. I glanced at the menu but couldn't summon my hunger bug. My eyes swung to the door every time it opened. A line of patrons waiting for seats had formed. Would she show?

I knew her the moment she walked in, a tiny thing—no more than five feet tall and not weighing much over a hundred pounds. Her dark hair was cut in a short gamin style, and her brown eyes darted around the room nervously, her slender body poised for flight.

Our gazes connected, forming an instant bond. I read sympathy, fear, along with the will to survive revealed in her eyes. We had both known Danny Garrett and lived to tell the tale. Without blinking, she made her way around the waiting people to our booth.

She looked at me and smiled, then turned to Matt.

"Are you Matt Summers?"

"Yes. Miss Carlton?"

She nodded. "Sissy will do. You must be Danny's ex-wife, the woman the police think killed him."

Her voice sounded soft and hesitant, as though expecting to be struck if she raised it. I suppressed a shudder. How well I remembered.

"Yes. I'm Theresa Lennox." I scooted over and patted the seat next to me. "Please sit down. Thank you for coming."

She sat and in spite of the good job she'd done with the makeup, I noticed the last dying darkness of a bruise on her left cheekbone.

"I don't know how I can help, but I'll try. Forgive me, but *did* you kill him?"

"No."

The waitress appeared and filled our coffee cups. "Give us a few minutes," I said when she asked for our order.

"Miss Carlton…Sissy, we'd like to ask you a few questions," Matt said.

Sissy emptied a sugar packet into her coffee and stirred it, her eyes downcast.

"Go ahead. I'll try to answer."

"I was online researching Danny's arrest records when I noticed you'd filed charges of domestic battery against him last month. Was that the first time he hit you?"

She shook her head, raising her cup to her lips with a trembling hand. "No, but it was the first time I'd filed charges. My brother insisted I have the son of a bitch arrested."

"Did your brother know Danny beat you?"

Sissy didn't answer and shifted in her seat.

"Matt, why don't you leave us alone for a few minutes? Let Sissy and I talk for a while."

Matt slid out of the booth, taking his coffee to an empty seat at the counter.

"Sometimes it's kind of hard to talk to a man about these things, isn't it?" I said.

She nodded and moved across the table to Matt's space. I understood her need to put some distance between us. Up close and personal with Danny had that effect on his victims.

"How did you meet up with Danny?"

"I was at a bar one night with a bunch of girlfriends. Annie had just gotten engaged, and we were celebrating when the waiter suddenly arrived with a bottle of champagne, saying, 'Compliments of the man in the blue shirt.' It was Danny. He came over, said he heard about the news and wanted to wish Annie good luck. He talked to all of us, but his eyes never left mine."

"I know the routine well. He made you feel special."

"He was charming and funny, and when he asked, I gave him my number. It wasn't long before we moved into an apartment in Cordova. I thought I was in love. That was three years ago."

"Three years? Then you were seeing him—"

"While he was still married to you," she finished. "He explained his time away from home as job related. Said he was a salesman for a pharmaceutical company."

A pharmaceutical company? I never knew Danny had such an ironic sense of humor. On the other hand, maybe he hadn't meant to be amusing.

"I swear I didn't know he was married until much later. I was waiting in the car for him to come out of the liquor store one night and found a receipt from Methodist Hospital on the floor in your name and dated the day before."

The waitress stopped by, but I waved her away. Breakfast could wait.

"Methodist? I remember that beating. Danny paid the bill and left me to catch a cab home. It was also the night I vowed never to take another fist in the face. The next day, I moved out, called a lawyer, and got a restraining order. Did you confront him?"

She nodded. Tears welled in her eyes. "He called me a goddamned snoop and you a cold-hearted bitch who walked out. When we got back to the apartment, he beat me senseless."

"You mentioned a brother. Couldn't your family help?"

"Most of my family lives up in Tipton County— not exactly close. Danny didn't like for me to see them. He always made me find excuses for not attending family events."

I remembered what few friends I had I'd cut off to please Danny.

"And of course, after a beating the last thing you wanted was for a family member or friend to see you."

Oh, how I related to her story.

Sissy paused and drank, then looked me in the eye for the first time since sitting down. "One night he did a number on me. With every slap, punch, and kick, he called me Theresa. The next day I called my brother. He insisted I press charges, but since Danny would soon be serving his sentence for pounding on you that last time, I declined. I blessed you in my prayers every night for having the courage to put that animal away. Thank God, he's dead. He didn't deserve to live."

I closed my eyes. Danny had beaten Sissy but seen me. How sick was that?

"Did you ever meet his parents?"

"No. He said I was just a little bar pick-up and not good enough for them. He said it so often I began to believe it."

"That's the pattern. Repeated often enough, the lie becomes the truth. You didn't miss anything by not knowing Diana and Hamilton Garrett. They knew he beat me and did nothing to stop it." I finished my lukewarm coffee and signaled the waitress for more. When she had refilled our cups, I asked, "Did you move while he was in jail for seven months?"

She nodded and bit her lip. "Yes, but he found me when he got out. I think he followed me from my parents' place."

"Why did he beat you this last time?"

"I had just moved into another new apartment up in Millington to be closer to my family. Danny showed up. He did a dance on me and left, saying he'd kill me if I called the cops. A neighbor heard me screaming and called 9-1-1. The police never contacted me about the case. I heard about Danny's death on the news."

I could believe she hadn't been notified about any proceedings against Danny. The Garrett money and influence had spoken again. Her case had been deliberately lost in the shuffle.

"My brother said if you hadn't killed Danny, he would have."

A new suspect loomed. I'd tell Jerricus about Sissy and her brother.

She glanced at her watch and drained the last of her coffee, then pushed her cup away. "It's almost ten. I have to get to work."

"Are you sure you don't want something to eat?"

"No, thanks." She rose, slung the strap of her purse over her shoulder, and held out her hand. "I'm glad I had the chance to meet you, Theresa. Neither one of us deserved what we received. I've often wondered how many other victims Danny left floating out there—victims who have families with revenge or murder on their minds."

Another thought to ponder. Sissy had provided me with lots of ammunition. I grasped her cold, trembling hand.

"I'm glad I met you, too, and hope there are no others. Find a good shrink. It helps."

She smiled and walked out the door.

Matt sauntered back over. "She had a lot to say."

I nodded as the waitress stopped by. Suddenly, I was ravenous. We ordered, and I told Matt the gist of our conversation, including the part about the irate brother and other possible victims.

"So we have another potential suspect, even though how he knew where to find your gun is a stumbling block," he said with a frown.

"If he doesn't have an alibi, I could say that in the confusion of finding Danny, I forgot I'd left my gun *on* the nightstand rather than *in* it."

"Let's not get ahead of ourselves. Has it occurred to you that in the last two weeks we've gone from one suspect to a whole herd of them?"

"I know. It doesn't make sense. Just one other would do. My money is still on Fast Eddie."

"Mine, too. This brother would have no reason to meet Danny at your place."

"The *brother* could have posed as a prospective buyer. Danny would think it funny to have a deal go down in my apartment. Perhaps, he followed me home from campus one day and waited for a time to pounce. Maybe he even planted some coke or pot. *That* could be the reason someone vandalized my place. They may have been looking for Danny's drugs."

"It's as good a theory as any. The police didn't find drugs on Danny after he was murdered. If they'd found any in your apartment, they'd have said so. Of course, they may have concentrated the search in the bedroom. A small baggie in the flour or sugar canister *could* go unnoticed. However, the police aren't usually that inattentive."

"Maybe the killer took the drugs and sorta forgot to mention it to Fast Eddie."

"I wouldn't want to be in that person's shoes. Fast Eddie has a way of settling something like that. But it's one more theory. The more we have the better. I'm sure Jerricus is working on all angles. Sooner or later, the police will have to reopen the case."

I remained convinced we could trace Danny's death back to the drug world. We had uncovered too many clues for it to be otherwise. My cell phone interrupted my thoughts.

"Hello?"

"Good morning, darlin'," Jerricus drawled. The down-home country boy had returned. He must have had good news.

"Good morning, Jerricus. You sound chipper."

Matt looked at me with raised eyebrows. I shrugged.

"I am, I am, to be sure. I just got off the phone with the district attorney's office."

My heart lurched in my chest. This was it—the call we'd been anticipating for days.

"Oh, yeah?" I tried to sound nonchalant but failed. Coffee splashed from the cup clenched in trembling fingers. I set it down.

"Assistant District Attorney Walter Haven has requested our presence in his office tomorrow morning at ten o'clock sharp. We'll show up at ten fifteen. I want you in *my* office at nine thirty to go over a few things."

I drew in a shaky breath and swallowed, hoping to wet my dry mouth and throat.

"Tomorrow, your office at nine thirty. Got it."

Matt leaned back with a smile and winked.

"And, Theresa, have you read this morning's paper?"

"Not completely. Matt and I are having breakfast out. Why?"

"Read it. Page three in the first section. The opposition is fighting back. See you tomorrow."

I hung up and drained my water glass.

The opposition?

He could only mean Diana and Hamilton.

What kind of Machiavellian tactics would I find on page three?

Chapter Sixteen

The waitress set the plates in front of us as I hung up. After she'd left, I relayed Jerricus's news to Matt.

"Don't get your hopes up," he said. "The DA may not be dropping the charges. They're probably going to offer another deal, so be prepared."

"I can't wait to get home and read page three. Wonder what my ex-in-laws said."

"We expected them to make a statement. The tide of public opinion's in your favor. You won't read anything flattering."

We ate and then zoomed home. I ran into the kitchen and grabbed the first section, ripping it open to page three. I sat down to read. Matt pulled up a chair next to me, peering over my shoulder.

Diana had given the interview. As predicted, it was not flattering. The more I read, the more dismay settled over me. The good publicity of the last few days had been wiped out. I wanted to cry.

"My son was no angel," the reporter quoted her. "He did things that were wrong. We all have character flaws. However, the allegations of drug abuse are out-and-out lies."

Next followed an unappealing rehash of my background—the trailer park, the poverty, and Newton's Bar making it sound sleazy, and me one step above a hooker.

"Miss Lennox's claims of her father's death are pure fabrication. I ought to know—I had her investigated. Ten years ago, he was still alive and living in Odessa, Texas. I tried contacting him this week, but couldn't find him—yet. I begged Danny not to marry her, but he loved her. I wanted to see him happy, as any mother would. I quickly saw that was not to be."

"Oh, my God, she had me investigated?"

"Why should that surprise you?"

I wondered how Jerricus would handle the lies we'd already told, and the ones we planned on telling, to the press about my parentage. I continued reading.

"It was obvious from the beginning all Miss Lennox wanted was money. She frequently over-extended Danny's credit. His father and I had to bail them out. She mocked him for not providing for her, provoking him into physical violence."

Yeah, right. Heat suffused my face, and I mentally hit the bitch in the mouth. She had pulled out the classic—the victim is guilty. I trembled, and Matt hugged me.

"Hang in there, honey. Nobody believes that bullshit anymore. It wasn't your fault he beat you. She's made a serious mistake. Jerricus will have a field day with this."

I nodded, reading on.

"She also attempted to cut our son off from his family."

A red haze swam in front of my eyes. "That crazy bitch! How dare she say I cut Danny off from them? I was the one isolated from people."

A tear plopped onto the newsprint. I wiped my eyes, determined to continue to the end of the piece.

The reporter concluded with a note that a memorial service for Daniel Garrett would be held next week at the First Baptist Church.

The funeral had taken place last week. Naturally, I didn't attend, but according to the news reports, mourners had spilled out of the front doors. I couldn't imagine who'd mourn Danny other than his parents, and I wasn't all that sure about Hamilton. I figured Diana must have called in every political IOU her husband had to build a decent crowd. It wouldn't do for State Senator, and possible Governor, Garrett's late son to have had a lousy turnout.

I noticed a caption at the end of the column about a related story on page twelve. I turned the pages while Matt got up to pour us each a glass of iced tea.

"Here, this'll cool you off," he said, setting the glass next to the paper.

I chugged it. A reporter had interviewed Danny's friends—the same ones we'd talked to earlier.

Richard Bartlett claimed Danny had been a nice guy who'd helped his friends whenever possible and was going to miss him.

Yeah, are you going to miss prison, too, asshole?

Joey Wheeler's comments were much along the same lines. "I felt kind of sorry for him," was a quote. He also regretted allowing the friendship to slide.

Hypocrite. You were scared to death of my husband and his friends.

Carl Wexford's comments did not surprise me. He ranted about how Danny was his best friend who didn't deserve to be killed by a vengeful ex-wife. He also claimed on one occasion to have seen me slam my own face into the wall, then call the cops.

I sat back, undecided whether to be violently ill or to throw something. "How could they?" I said, fighting tears. "How could they tell us one thing and the newspaper another? And how did the reporters even find them?"

"If we found them, Hamilton and Diana could find them, too. The 'how' is simple. Money. I'll bet all three of their pockets are lined with Garrett cash. Bartlett is an ex-con and Wheeler a struggling junior executive with a wife and baby to support. A couple of thousand dollars will buy a lot of shoes and food. Wexford will drink and snort his away in a few days."

"All Jerricus's work has gone down the drain," I protested. "And ours as well."

"Not necessarily. These interviews are on page twelve. Most people aren't interested in the opinions of Danny Garrett's friends. Conversation will be about Diana's interview."

My cell phone rang. Jerricus's ID scrolled up.

"Hello, Jerricus." My voice sounded small and disheartened.

"I take it you've read the paper," he said.

"Yeah, not too encouraging, is it?"

"Aw, don't worry. I told you, it's all part of the game. You'll notice nothing was said about the car bomb, the kidnapping, or Matt getting shot. I might reply in a couple of days, and if I do, I'll hammer home those points."

"I'm tired of games, Jerricus. I want this over."

"I know, and by tomorrow morning, it may be. I just called to warn you that Hamilton has scheduled a news conference for noon."

"How do you know?"

"I have my sources."

Of course, he did. "Which station?" I asked.

"Pick one. He's got full media coverage. It should be interesting. Ham's not a politician for nothing. He doesn't waste words. He'll come out swinging. We may have to counter fast. I'll talk to you later," he said, hanging up without a goodbye.

"Hamilton's holding a press conference at noon," I told Matt. "I can't imagine what else there is to say."

"Then I guess we'd better listen."

We'd graduated from barbs and darts to dueling pistols. Before this ended, I visualized howitzers.

****

I curled up next to Matt on the sofa. The noon news would be on at any moment. I trembled with nerves. Matt slung his arm around my shoulders, holding me tight.

The statement was the lead-off under the title of *Breaking News*. The announcer jabbered for a few seconds with the set up. Then Hamilton walked in, taking his place at the podium. Two other men stood behind and to either side of him. I assumed they were lawyers or political advisors, maybe both.

My ex-father-in-law, even with the make-up, looked haggard. The bags under his eyes could be packed for an overseas flight.

"Good afternoon, ladies and gentlemen. Thank you for coming." He paused, and the reporters settled down to listen. "In the past couple of weeks, there have been allegations made against my son that my wife and I feel we must address.

"Danny did not always do the right thing. He acknowledged it, as did we. He did hit his wife on more than one occasion. That was wrong. He paid the price in accordance with the law and regretted his behavior. In the last months of his marriage, he agreed to seek anger management counseling."

"Oh, for God's sake. Danny and anger management? What a load of horseshit! *I* was his anger management."

Matt hugged me. "I know, honey. So will anyone else who's been there."

"Theresa Lennox often humiliated him in front of his friends and us. My wife and I were deeply concerned about my daughter-in-law's mental state. She seemed to enjoy needling my son until he could no longer stand it. She also tried to drive a wedge between my son and my wife. Until this unfortunate marriage, Diana and Danny were very close. I can only assume Miss Lennox was jealous of the mother-son relationship. His murder shattered my wife, and she is suffering terribly at the loss of her only child."

Hamilton paused for a moment to sip from a glass on the podium. Matt murmured in my ear, "So far, this is the same thing Diana told the newspaper. He didn't say anything about his suffering. I thought fathers suffered, too."

"Hamilton's so self-centered I doubt he even noticed he had a son until Danny got into trouble."

Our attention swung back to the TV. Hamilton bore an expression of sorrow and oddly enough—embarrassment on his face. He cast his eyes down, the lines in his forehead deepening.

"I'm not proud of what I'm about to confess, but it's something I think the public should know concerning Miss Lennox's character. Several years ago

I tried to make amends after Danny had struck her. I offered her a thousand dollars if she would not press charges. She agreed and then demanded more. I never thought of it as blackmail but as keeping my son out of jail. It was wrong. I know that now, but please do not believe the ugly stories Miss Lennox and her lawyer have been telling. Theresa Lennox made a profit on her alleged abuse."

I gasped and closed my eyes. Matt's arm tightened, and he said something vile under his breath before turning to me. "Damn him! How does he expect to get away with a statement like that?"

"Oh, God, no!" I covered my face with my hands. I couldn't believe he'd brought up the money. I'd always known it would come back to bite me in the ass.

Matt pulled away. "Theresa? Tell me it's not true!"

I rocked back and forth, listening to the end of Hamilton's speech.

"In conclusion, I want to thank the people who have supported my wife and me in this terrible time of personal tragedy. The authorities are doing a stellar job, and I can only hope a jury of her peers will not buy into the theatrics of Miss Lennox and her attorney. I'm sure the public is smart enough to see them for what they are—cheap ploys to buy sympathy where none is deserved. Thank you."

He turned and walked away amid shouted questions but answered none. The lawyer types followed. I listened as the announcer recapped. Matt sat stone silent.

He jabbed the remote at the television and clicked the off button. "Is it true? Did he pay you hush money?" His voice was harder than I'd ever heard it.

Oh, God, can this get any worse? My cell rang. One look at caller ID told me yes it could.

"Hello, Jerricus."

"Is it true? Did you take money from the Garretts?" he asked, echoing not only Matt's words but the hard tone as well.

"It wasn't like he made it sound. He came to the house one day with an offer of a thousand dollars cash if I didn't press charges. He convinced me that I could open a private bank account and use it for whatever I wanted. He said Danny would never know. At the time, I was feeling low and confused, so I accepted. I never, and I mean never, asked for more. He came to me after every beating—always with cash—and the amount depended on the severity of the pounding. He was furious about the last beating because we were divorced. I refused his money, pressed charges, and sent Danny to jail, which is what I should have done a long time ago."

"Kind of forgot to tell me this, didn't you? I told you I don't like surprises." Jerricus's angry voice hammered against my eardrum. I didn't blame him for being mad.

"I'm sorry, Jerricus," I mumbled.

"Is there anything else you forgot to mention?"

"No, not that I can think of."

"Think harder!"

"No, there's nothing else."

"Good, because now *I* have to do damage control. Were these payoffs always in cash?"

"Yes."

"Was the account in your maiden or married name?"

"Neither. I never opened an account. I was afraid the bank might send a statement or something to the house and Danny would see it, so I rented a safe deposit box."

"Good God, is the money still there?"

"No. After the divorce, I took it out and bought a CD. It was almost fifteen thousand dollars worth of pain."

"Well, that's a blessing. Maybe nobody will be able to trace it. We'll need to talk before we go to the DA tomorrow. Come in at eight thirty instead of nine thirty. We have to plan our strategy."

I hung up and looked at Matt who scowled.

"You lied to me and to Jerricus. We agreed at the beginning—no lies! Everything out in the open so we could make plans if secrets were revealed. Damn it, Theresa, what did you think would happen? If Hamilton can take you down, he'll cover himself with Mississippi River mud and spin it so he smells good. Now we're playing catch-up."

A sob burst from my throat. "I'm sorry, okay? I'm not proud of what I did. I was too embarrassed to tell either you or Jerricus. And I swear I never touched a dime of that money until after the divorce."

He ran a hand through his hair and blew out an exasperated breath.

"Even if the bank still has a record of a safety deposit box in your name, they have no idea what you kept in it," he said, his voice calmer. "And the CD you bought with the money can be explained as part of your divorce settlement. Slide, you're home free on this one—at least for a while."

"I think Hamilton paid me in cash so Diana

wouldn't see any checks and know what he'd done. It would have pissed her off royally to think I was getting Garrett money. She screamed bloody murder when I got a two-hundred-grand settlement."

"Where did Danny get that kind of scratch?"

"Hamilton settled it on me for a fast divorce and no publicity. You'll notice he didn't bring *that* up in his statement."

"This time. Things are getting nasty."

I groaned. "Oh, shit, maybe I should just take a deal and get all this over with. I don't think I can handle much more."

Matt grasped my shoulders and gave me a little shake. "Don't even think that way. You can't change what happened. Danny is dead. Would you have it any other way?"

"No…no, I'm glad he's dead. He meant to kill me. I know it. But still, I keep seeing him lying there on the floor. I can still feel the panic, the urge to run like hell."

He folded me into his arms. "Of course he was going to kill you."

I buried my face in his shoulder. "Sooner or later, he might have succeeded, too. Have you had any luck in finding someone who could have done it?"

"I have a few leads, a couple of names to check out."

Matt's cell phone rang, and I got up to make a sandwich. I only heard bits and pieces of his conversation, but he finally hung up and joined me at the kitchen table.

"Who was on the phone?" I asked out of idle curiosity. It seemed every phone call had to do with me or my case.

"That was Fast Eddie Piper."

I choked and gulped iced tea to clear my throat. "You're kidding! What did he want?"

"A meeting—tonight at a dive called Lenny's just off Crump. I'm to meet him at nine."

"I'm going with you."

"Not this time, angel. Eddie is dangerous and the neighborhood even more so."

"Matt, I will not allow you to go alone. What if something happens?"

"My point exactly. I don't want anything to happen to you. Stay here. If I'm not home or you don't hear from me by eleven, call the cops."

"I promise to stay in the car. I'll scoot down on the floor where no one can see me, and if there's trouble, *then* I can call the police."

"Theresa, no."

"Yes, Matt." I grasped his arm. "We're in this together—to the bitter end just like we promised. I refuse to let you go alone."

He must have seen the determination on my face, for he drew in a shaky breath. "You drive. If trouble starts, get the hell out. No waiting for me. Is that clear? Out. You leave immediately."

"Absolutely," I lied. I would never take off like a whupped dog, leaving him there.

He went upstairs to his office, and I finished my sandwich. Fast Eddie wanted to meet. Maybe the last piece of the puzzle was about to fall into place.

After lunch I joined Matt in the upstairs office and read the dossier on Fast Eddie Piper.

Long and violent, his rap sheet ran to several pages. He'd been a criminal since the age of ten. On his eighteenth birthday, Fast Eddie—so named because of his blazing speed and the ability to outrun any cop on foot—turned over a new leaf, no doubt to coincide with his new non-juvenile status. He disavowed all association with his former gang and set himself up as a legitimate businessman.

The business? He sold Elvis souvenirs to tourists, first out of the trunk of his car, then from a small, dingy storefront not far off Beale. The Presley estate strictly controlled who sold what, but entrepreneurs sprang up every day and were almost impossible to shut down.

The whole thing was nonsense. He didn't get rich from the sale of souvenirs but from the sale of drugs, extortion, and prostitution. Even so, the past ten years had seen him arrested numerous times. Each time he managed to wiggle free. Witnesses had a habit of disappearing or readjusting their accounts of events, and victims changed their minds about pressing charges.

I feared for Matt. They didn't come any more dangerous than Eddie Piper.

****

I kept telling myself the street didn't look all that dangerous. People walked, and cars parked. It didn't matter that the walkers were working girls and the parked cars their places of business. And so what if every other street light had been shot out? There was still enough light to see—barely.

I pulled up to the curb about a half a block down the street from Lenny's, a seedy-looking bar on the corner. Matt wanted to wait until the last moment before getting out.

A prostitute in an orange miniskirt and pink feather

boa rapped on the window. Matt motioned her away with a wave of his hand and then opened the glove box.

"Here," he said, handing me a revolver. "Keep this on your lap, and if anyone tries to open the door, let 'em see it, but for God's sake, don't shoot unless it's necessary."

I swallowed and took the gun with trembling fingers, praying I wouldn't have to use the damned thing. I could see the headlines now—*Murder Suspect Does It Again*. I didn't want to ever see another gun.

"Okay, if you hear shots or I don't come out in thirty minutes, get the hell out of here and call the cops." He opened the car door.

I grabbed his arm. "Please, be careful."

He leaned over and kissed me, then exited. I locked the doors and watched him saunter up the street into Lenny's.

I gazed out the side windows and checked the side mirrors. The women sashayed up and down. The lack of headlights sweeping down the road indicated business lagged. I sucked in a few deep breaths, trying to relax.

He'll be all right. He'll be all right. I repeated it over and over, my gaze glued to the open door of the bar.

I dared a glance at the dashboard clock. God, had it only been five minutes? My breath quickened, and my trembling increased. I had to get myself under control. I spared a few minutes closing my eyes to visualize a meadow.

A sharp knock on the driver's side window had me damn near jumping out of the seat. A grinning black man leered at me.

267

"Hey, mama, what's a fine-looking lady like you doin' out here all by yourself? You lookin' for work? I can find some for you. Just let ole Gonzo help you out."

"Fuck off," I called through the closed window.

"Yeah, baby, that's what I had in mind."

I shook so hard I could barely grip the gun but raised it, placing the barrel against the glass a few inches from his nose. He got the hint and backed off a couple of steps, his hands in the air.

"Hey, bitch, no need to get all prickly on me. Don't need no skinny white 'ho anyhow."

I watched in the side and rear mirrors as he walked down the sidewalk behind me and turned the corner. Only then did I lower the gun and breathe again.

My relief didn't last long. Miniskirt and Feathers kicked at the passenger side door, leaned down, and hollered.

"Hey, bitch, this is my section of the sidewalk. If you want to set up shop, do it somewhere else, you hear?"

"I'm not setting up shop. I'm waiting for someone," I shouted back.

"Well, wait your skinny ass on another street. You scarin' off the few customers I got. Park on someone else's turf. And don't go wavin' that gun in my face. I'll shove it up your ass."

With that, she kicked the door again and continued her stroll up the street. The clock said fifteen minutes had passed.

"Oh, please, Matt, hurry." I'd been thoroughly intimidated by Miniskirt and Feathers.

Time dragged, and my nerves tightened. I gritted my teeth, breathing through my nose. It didn't work. I jammed my feet against the floorboards in an effort to stop my legs from shaking. That didn't work either.

I was about to drive closer to the bar when Matt emerged, jogging toward the car. He tried to open the door and had to tap on the glass. I'd forgotten to unlock it. I found the button on the armrest with trembling fingers. The lock clicked, and Matt slid into the car.

"Let's go," he said tersely.

I didn't need to be told a second time. I turned the key and shot away from the curb like a bullet from a gun. I flew down the street until we came to a better-lit area where I slowed both the Ford and my racing heart.

"Was he there?" I asked.

"He was there along with several of his associates."

"What associates?"

"Big, bad, ugly associates."

"What did he have to say?" I asked, suppressing a shudder at the image of Matt's description.

The light I had stopped at turned green. I made my way north toward Union Avenue—a nice wide street with lots of lights and cars.

"It was damned interesting. It seems your ex-husband has been a regular customer of Mr. Piper since before you were married."

"I never suspected it was that long."

"According to Eddie, the association goes back to college. He said he allowed Danny to run a tab because he knew the Garretts would pay the freight. Only the tabs kept getting bigger, so he let Danny work off some of his debt by selling to whomever he could."

"People like Richard, Les, and Carl just as we suspected," I said.

"Eventually, some of them started selling and

reported to Danny, who reported to The Juice—you get the drift."

"I get it," I replied in a grim voice. My ex-husband had been a minor link in the chain of command.

"One night, Eddie accompanied Danny to the Garrett home. It seems Hamilton refused to pay any more of his son's debts. Eddie used his own special brand of persuasion, and the tabs were paid in a timely fashion thereafter."

"Eddie *blackmailed* the Garretts? And Hamilton was his silent business partner!"

"It took balls, but he did it. He claims Garrett paid right up until you sent Danny to jail this last time. When your ex was released, Hamilton apparently told him to never darken his doorstep again. According to Eddie, Danny said there was one hell of a fight between Diana and Hamilton over it, too. So Mr. Piper put Danny to work full time, but things didn't quite work out as he hoped."

I braked for another stop light, glancing at Matt. He looked tired.

"Let me guess. Danny skimmed." The light changed, and I drove on.

"Eddie said The Juice had suspected it for several weeks but wanted to give Danny a false sense of security before lowering the boom. Here's the good part. Eddie was supposed to meet Danny at one o'clock the day he was murdered. Needless to say, the late Mr. Garrett didn't show. Ironic isn't it? Danny got whacked in your apartment in the morning when it's possible Eddie had his own hit planned for the afternoon."

I couldn't believe it. Of all the damned luck. "Do you believe him—about meeting Danny, I mean?"

"It sounds plausible. Eddie Piper doesn't do his own dirty work anymore, but he'd given your ex time to make amends. If he didn't pony up, he'd have had one of his boys do it."

"Certainly sounds logical."

"We could always theorize that Eddie planned to hit Danny in your apartment."

"If we go to the cops with this, do you think they'll buy it?" I asked.

"It's one hell of a motive. If the police do question him, he'll deny knowing Danny no matter how much he owed." Matt leaned over, took the gun from my lap, and put it back in the glove box. "Did you need to use this?"

I thought of Gonzo and the hooker but shook my head. "No. Everything was cool."

We arrived home none the worse for wear. Matt went upstairs, and I headed for the kitchen. I could have used a good stiff drink, but there was no booze in the house, and I settled for a soda instead.

Now that it was all over, I wanted to collapse. I hadn't been this tired since my release from jail. It was late, and I had to be in Jerricus's office by eight thirty. I wiped a hand over my face. I felt gritty, as though the atmosphere on Crump had adhered to my skin. I needed a long, hot bath.

I climbed the stairs and saw Matt at his desk in the office.

"What are you doing? I thought you'd gone to bed."

"I will in a minute. I just wanted to check a few things," he replied.

"Go to bed. You need your rest."

Suzanne Rossi

"Yes, Mother."

I chuckled, closing the bathroom door behind me, then filled the tub with bath salts and lit a couple of candles. An hour later I emerged to find Matt still in front of the computer, a file folder open in front of him.

"You promised," I scolded. "What's all this?"

"I'm just rereading my notes. I meant to do it last weekend but forgot."

"I guess catching a bullet screws your memory."

He held up a sheet of paper. "I never got in touch with Mr. Ferriday. I left several messages, but he's never returned them. We need his statement. I'll try again first thing in the morning." He snapped the folder shut and tossed it onto the desk.

I leaned over his back, burying my lips in his neck. My hands slipped down over his chest and pulled the shirt from the waistband of his pants. Next I unbuckled his belt. He hauled me over the arm of the chair into his lap.

"I thought you wanted me to rest," he murmured, the tip of his tongue tracing my jawline.

I shivered. A tiny spark flamed into life, sending a warm glow throughout my body.

"H-m-m," I moaned, tangling my fingers in his hair.

Our mouths met in a hot, wet kiss. The glow burned hotter. An enlarging part of his anatomy nestled against my thigh.

Bum shoulder or not, he rose and carried me to his bedroom. I was tired, but not that tired.

Chapter Seventeen

"Now is there anything else you've neglected to tell me?" Jerricus asked, his lips set in a stern line. "I give surprises—I don't receive them."

I held up my right hand.

"Honest to God, I can't think of anything else you should know. I never mentioned the money because I couldn't believe Hamilton would ever say anything. Besides, I'd invested it as soon as the divorce was final."

"And you're sure you were always paid in cash?"

"Yes."

Jerricus wrote on a legal pad and frowned.

"That'll make it harder to trace, but not impossible. It's also a bad PR move on your part. You took money for getting beat up. We'll deny the accusation, of course. Let's just hope we can get the charges dismissed before they figure out you invested fifteen thousand dollars more than your settlement."

"Can they do that?" I asked, biting my lip.

"Yes. Given enough time, they can find out anything. Now in the DA's office, don't speak unless I tell you. I don't care what Walter Haven says or how nasty he gets, just keep your mouth shut. Okay?"

"I promise—not a word."

"Look scared and confused. Visualize a rabbit hiding from a predator."

Was he serious? A rabbit? I was fighting for the rest of my life, and he wanted me to visualize a *rabbit*?

"Get that look off your face. You know what I mean. You need to look scared, humble, and nonthreatening."

Games again. Acting. I was so sick of it. For a moment my head swam. I shook it. My vision cleared, and I sneaked a glance at the clock—nine forty-five. I clasped my fingers together to stop the trembling.

"How long do you think this will take?" I had only a vague idea of what to expect, even though Jerricus had primed me.

"It could take two minutes or two hours. Where's Matt? I'd have thought he'd be here for moral support."

"He's talking to one of my neighbors. Mr. Ferriday has been gone or something since the murder. Shouldn't we be going?" The district attorney's office was a good fifteen to twenty minutes away.

"In a few minutes. I'm rarely on time for something like this. Haven knows it, but it'll irritate him anyway. I'll apologize, and he'll think he's won, but because he's irritated, he'll be slightly off his game."

If he said "game" one more time, I'd scream. He didn't. We left ten minutes later.

****

Assistant District Attorney Walter Haven sat at a large conference table, tapping a pencil on the shiny surface. He glared at my attorney as I slipped into a chair.

"Lose your watch, Jerricus?" he snapped.

"Walter, I apologize. Traffic was heavier than anticipated, and Miss Lennox felt poorly. She almost fainted in my office. I thought she should stay, but she insisted on coming. This has been a horrible ordeal for her."

I bit my tongue. Did Jerricus honestly think this guy was going to buy such drivel—or care?

Walter Haven swept hard brown eyes over me. I couldn't control the tremors sweeping me from head to toe. He looked about as friendly as a rattler. In fact, he resembled a snake with his black hair slicked back, a long nose, pointed chin, and close-set eyes. I wouldn't have been surprised to see a forked tongue flicker from his mouth.

"Spare me the theatrics. It's just us here—no jury or media to impress."

To my surprise, Jerricus laughed and took a chair next to me. *Let the games begin.* Maybe they already had.

"I take it you've called us here to dismiss the charges against my client."

"Why would I do that? The offer is man one, and she does the max."

"Walter, quit flogging a dead horse. Your case is so thin I can read a newspaper through it in a dark room at midnight."

"The murder weapon belongs to her, and her prints were the only ones on it."

"Miss Lennox went through all the tests, and no gunshot residue was found on either her hands or her clothing. Besides, most of the residue was on the pillow used to muffle the shot."

"Her bath towel was still damp. She could have showered."

"Good God, man! Lock her up. She showered

before she left for classes at the university."

Jerricus placed his hand over his heart. Sarcasm had its moments.

The assistant district attorney didn't look impressed. "There's still that missing hour between eleven and twelve. No one can remember her sitting under any kind of a tree anywhere on campus." Haven shot me a nasty glance. "And someone placed a phone call to Danny Garrett's cell from a pay phone at a gas station three blocks off campus at eleven-oh-five."

"The key word being *someone*. We know enough about Danny Garrett to know he wasn't above selling drugs now and then. Could have been a customer. Plus, nobody can remember seeing my client anywhere near the convenience store. And the surveillance cameras weren't aimed in that direction. Face it. You have a jumble of nothing."

Haven curled his lips in a mocking smile. "Your client extorted money from the Garretts to drop domestic violence charges against her husband. That sounds greedy and venal to me."

"Prove to me any payments were made. Show me a cancelled check," Jerricus shot back.

"Mr. Garrett claims to have paid in cash."

"Mr. Garrett claims? And you believe it just on his say-so?"

"What I have is a very strong circumstantial case."

"If you had that, you wouldn't be offering us a deal."

"The court docket is jammed. I'm trying to save the taxpayers a few bucks. After all, your client has the right to a speedy trial."

"It's speedy all right. Two months to trial is a new

world's record for a murder case."

The assistant DA shrugged. "The offer is on the table. What are you going to do with it?"

Jerricus looked at me and smiled. "Well, Theresa, do you want to accept a plea of manslaughter in the first degree?"

I lifted my chin, letting it quiver for a second before saying, "No. I can't accept that. I didn't do it."

I managed to choke out a sob on the final word, just as scripted. Jerricus patted my arm and smiled.

Haven clenched his jaw, glaring at both of us. "All right, I can go to man two, she does the max, but that's it."

"Not a chance," I insisted.

Someone knocked on the door, and Haven's assistant entered. "What is it, Elaine?" he asked with a frown.

"There are a couple of gentlemen outside who say they have to speak with Mr. Monroe right away."

"With me?"

I looked at Jerricus in surprise. This wasn't in the script. He kept his face impassive, but by now I knew him well enough to understand he had mastered *that* expression a long time ago. I made a mental note never to play poker with him.

"Yes, sir. One of them said he has information about Miss Lennox's case."

"Who is it?"

"A Mr. Summers and the other man is named Farris, I believe."

"Ferriday," I said, forgetting the edict about speaking unless spoken to. "That's my neighbor—the one Matt was going to interview."

Jerricus rose. "If Mr. Haven has no objections, I'd like to see these gentlemen. I'll only be a few minutes."

He left the room. I sat still as a mouse with my hands clasped together and my heart pounding. This was it—the witness I'd been waiting for. My entire future rested on Mr. Ferriday's story of what he'd seen and heard. I stood on third base about to steal home.

Neither Haven nor I had anything to say. The room was so quiet I heard him breathing. Somewhere a stray scrap of paper rustled in the breeze from the air conditioning. I stared at my clasped hands, the knuckles white, too frightened to look at him. I would do anything not to face him on the witness stand in a courtroom.

My gaze followed the wood grain pattern on the table in front of me as I willed Jerricus to return. I swallowed. My mouth had gone desert dry.

The minutes crawled by until the door finally opened, and Jerricus entered, followed by Matt and Mr. Ferriday.

"I apologize for the delay, Walter, but I think you need to hear this. Let me introduce Mr. Matthew Summers, a private investigator, and Mr. George Ferriday."

Haven nodded. "Gentlemen. What's going on, Jerry?"

"I'd like a court reporter to take Mr. Ferriday's statement."

"You want to depose your witness in *my* conference room?" the assistant DA said in an astonished tone.

"Why not? It's important. You'll hear it sooner or later anyway."

"All right, but this is a first, even for you." He lifted his phone and said, "Elaine, would you get a court reporter in here to take a statement? Thank you."

Matt and Mr. Ferriday took seats across from me. Matt smiled and winked while my neighbor looked around, taking in his surroundings. His gaze finally rested on me.

"Hello, Theresa. I'm so sorry about your apartment."

"Thank you, Mr. Ferriday. It was quite a shock."

Jerricus cleared his throat, reminding me to be quiet.

We waited in silence until the stenographer arrived and set up her machine. Haven stared at Matt.

"Summers—you're the PI the defendant hired, aren't you? You've been a busy man."

"I certainly have," Matt responded.

"I'm ready, Mr. Haven," the woman said, sitting behind the device.

Jerricus sat opposite my neighbor and smiled.

"Mr. Ferriday, do you have information about the day of the murder of Daniel Garrett?"

"Yes, sir, I do."

"Why don't you tell us about it, in your own words? Start at the beginning and take your time. Mr. Haven and I may ask questions, but you just tell us what you saw."

Mr. Ferriday licked his lips and divided his attention between Jerricus and Haven.

"Well, it's like this. Every Monday through Friday I meet my friend Elmo at the coffeehouse on the corner where we have a couple of cups of joe." He turned to me. "I never knew there were so many different ways to make coffee. Had my first double shot a month ago and damn near walked across the ceiling."

"Ah, yes, Mr. Ferriday," Jerricus said. "Go on— you were at the coffeehouse. What time?"

"Eight o'clock on the dot. I read the paper to Elmo. Elmo's legally blind. He can see to walk and get around, but reading is out of the question. At any rate, I read, and then we discuss things—sports, politics, movies."

"And did you do this on the day of the murder?"

"Sure did. Elmo was all wound up about something the mayor was doing."

"What time did you leave the coffeehouse?" Jerricus asked.

My eyes shifted from Mr. Ferriday to Jerricus and back. I didn't dare look at Matt and refused to look at Haven. My heart thudded in slow heavy beats. I bit my lips to keep them from trembling. Did my neighbor realize he held my life in his hands?

"Ten thirty, same as always."

"And did you go straight home?"

"Yep. It was Monday. I play golf Monday, Wednesday, and Friday at Audubon Golf Course. I meet three friends, and we tee off at one."

Jerricus smiled. "Okay, what time did you leave your apartment for this golf date?"

"Eleven thirty."

Haven stirred, leaning forward. "Why leave so early for a one o'clock tee time? Audubon isn't far away."

"Driving range and practice green," Mr. Ferriday said. "You don't play golf, do you?"

"No. I don't have the time."

"Well, no golfer worth his salt would hit the first tee without a little warm up."

"What time did you get home, Mr. Ferriday?" Jerricus said, bringing the man back on track.

"I'm not real sure. It was dark. The boys and I had a couple of drinks and told lies about our game at a bar, then ate dinner."

"Do you do that every time you golf?"

"No, Mr. Monroe. Only on Mondays. Makes for kind of a nice start to the week."

"Did you notice anything unusual when you got home?"

"Nope. I didn't come into the complex from the Quince entrance. I used the back way off Symington. It's not as heavily traveled, and I'd had a few beers. I wasn't drunk, mind you," he hastened to add. "Just being careful."

"When did you find out about Mr. Garrett's death?" Haven asked.

"The next morning. I was on my way to the coffeehouse and saw all the yellow tape. Scared me to death. I thought something bad had happened to Theresa. Mr. Spencer came out, told me what was what, and that Theresa was under arrest." He gave Haven a dirty look. "Bunch of nonsense. This sweet young thing couldn't hurt a fly."

Haven tried to smile. "Mr. Ferriday, I hate to be rude, but my time is limited. Exactly what kind of new information do you have?"

"I'm getting there. When I was putting my golf clubs in the trunk of my car on Monday morning, I saw a man hanging around Miss Lennox's door. He knocked and then kind of looked around—like he was seeing if anyone was watching him. I didn't like his looks, so I walked over. I was about twenty feet away when he saw me. I asked who he wanted to see, and he said a Mr. Bales. I told him he had the wrong apartment, and I never heard of nobody by that name. He kind of mumbled something and took off around the corner of the building. I started to follow but looked at my watch. It said eleven twenty, and I was already running late, so I left."

"That was over two weeks ago," Jerricus scolded. "Why didn't you contact the police earlier?"

"I did," Mr. Ferriday snapped. "An officer came out and took my statement. That's the last I heard of it."

"So the police were aware you'd seen a stranger hanging around my client's apartment during the time the murder was committed." He threw Haven a speculative look. "Why didn't you return Mr. Summers' calls? He's been trying to get a hold of you."

"I was out of town on a family emergency. My sister called the following Thursday. Her husband had a heart attack and needed bypass surgery. I hightailed it to Little Rock and stayed with her. I just got back yesterday. I called Mr. Summers this morning and told him what I told you. I ain't gonna have to tell this again, am I?"

"Only on the witness stand," Haven answered.

"I don't think it will come to that," my attorney replied.

"Mr. Ferriday, do you have a description of this stranger you claim you saw?" the assistant DA asked.

Mr. Ferriday bristled at the prosecutor's condescending tone. "No claim about it, son. I saw him."

"Yes, but can you give a credible description?"

"Of course I can. He was young—late twenties to early thirties, I'd say—medium height and kind of skinny with stringy, blond hair."

I drew in a sharp, silent breath. My God, he just described Carl Wexford. I dared a glance at Matt who lifted his lips in a tiny smile.

"Well, that only describes about a hundred thousand males in the tri-state area," Haven said. "Do you wear glasses?"

My neighbor's brows pulled together in a scowl. "Yes. I'm seventy-two years old. Most of the people I know wear glasses. I need 'em for reading, not driving or distance. I find the question insulting, young man."

"Could you pick this man out of a line-up?"

Mr. Ferriday shot a glance at Jerricus, then me.

"Well, I'm not sure. He wore a red baseball cap pulled kind of low and sunglasses."

"Don't worry. I'm sure you won't have to do that," my attorney reassured him.

"If I may interject," Matt said quietly. "That description could fit an acquaintance of Mr. Garrett's named Carl Wexford."

"We've talked with Mr. Wexford. He has an alibi," Haven said. "Thank you for coming, Mr. Ferriday. We'll be in touch.

"Why don't you wait outside with Mr. Summers while the reporter types this up? Then you can sign it. By the way, what was your profession?" Jerricus asked.

"I'm a CPA—had my own business, too. Sold it when I retired ten years ago."

"Thank you, Mr. Ferriday."

Matt, the reporter, and Mr. Ferriday left the room.

When the door closed, Jerricus rounded on Haven.

"The district attorney's office knew about Mr. Ferriday's statement and never let me know? That's withholding discovery evidence, Walter."

"It's the first I've heard of it, too. If he gave a statement, no one sent it to me. Besides, it makes no difference. He can't positively identify this so-called lurking stranger. I find his entire story suspect."

"A jury won't. He's a respectable retiree who saw a stranger where a stranger shouldn't have been."

"I am not dismissing the charges, Jerricus."

"Face reality. Your case is shredded. There's more than enough reasonable doubt here."

"The offer on the table is man two."

Jerricus stared at Haven for a moment. "What's going on here? Since when has the district attorney's office been so eager to plead down a murder case? To hear you talk, it's damn near open and shut, yet you're offering a deal that's only a step above a jaywalking fine. Is there someone outside pulling your chain—a wealthy, influential state senator, maybe?"

Haven leaped to his feet, his arm outstretched, and his finger pointing at my attorney. "Get out! I don't have to take that from you or anyone else, Monroe!"

Jerricus narrowed his eyes, jerked his cell phone from his pocket, and punched a button.

"Hello, Doris. I want you to call the judge assigned to the Lennox case, I think it's Judge Lapinsky, and ask for an immediate meeting between her, me, my client, and Walter Haven. This is urgent. Call me back."

Haven sat back down, sweat beading his brow. The confident, cool prosecutor looked nervous.

"Walter, I'm done playing games. You and this

office are being manipulated by experts."

"That's rich, coming from you," Haven said.

"Maybe, but my client is being treated worse than any slimy drug dealer I ever defended."

"Tell me, Monroe, how do you sleep at night, knowing the people you get off are guilty as hell? How do you look at yourself in the mirror and justify putting criminals back on the streets to prey on the public?"

"This may come as a shock to you, but some of my clients are innocent—like Miss Lennox. Danny Garrett was a miserable son of a bitch."

Haven snorted. "Does that make it all right for your client to murder him? And some people call surgeons arrogant. You have your fair share of hubris, too, don't you?"

A flush worked its way up Jerricus's neck and into his face. The arrow had found its mark. I shifted in my chair uncomfortably. Of course Danny had been a miserable son of a bitch who deserved to die, but then the assistant district attorney hadn't known my ex.

"Is what's being done to my client right?"

"If I didn't think she was guilty, we wouldn't be having this discussion."

Jerricus's phone rang. "Hello," he barked. "Yes, Doris…All right. That's fine with me…Good. I'll pick up Mr. Ferriday's signed and notarized statement and then take Theresa to lunch…No problem and, Doris, tell the judge thank you for me…Yeah." He hung up and glared at Haven. "We meet in Judge Lapinsky's courtroom at three o'clock. Your office is probably being notified now."

Jerricus rose and headed for the door. I followed. There wasn't much else left to say.

****

I sat at a table in a steakhouse in Peabody Place and sipped a glass of Chardonnay. Jerricus had a martini and a confident look on his face. During the ride over in the limo, he had touched base with his other clients. I used the time to call Matt and bring him up to date on the situation. He and Mr. Ferriday were having lunch, but he promised to meet me at the courthouse after dropping my neighbor off.

With no appetite, I nibbled at my salad. "So who is this Judge Lapinsky?" I'd never heard of the judge assigned to my trial. "Is he any good? I mean, is he fair?"

"Judge *Edith* Lapinsky takes a conservative interpretation of the law, but I have to admit, she's good at her job. Unfortunately, she doesn't like me too much."

"I don't need to hear that."

"She hates the abuse of wealth and power even more."

"So Diana and Hamilton wouldn't be at the top of her hit parade either?"

"Not even close."

He made quick work of his salad and flipped the little red and green card by his plate over to the green side. A server appeared and slipped a hunk of steak from a long skewer onto the plate.

"She also dislikes nonsense and hates to have her time wasted. On more than one occasion, she's dismissed the prosecution's case if she thought it looked too flimsy to fly. She likes the prosecution to win—claims it's a vindication of spending the taxpayers' money."

He shoved some steak in his mouth and chewed. Maybe I should give it a try. I finished my salad and popped my card over to green. The same server slid steak and chicken onto my plate. I cut off a piece of the former and ate. Holy cow, it melted in my mouth. Suddenly, I was ravenous.

"Do you think she'll be on our side?"

Jerricus emptied his martini glass. More steak and pork hit his plate.

"It's not a matter of whose side she's on, but who has the best case. I can tell you right now that Walter Haven is either on the phone or in the office of his boss, Bobby Lee Jefferson, begging him to dismiss."

"Matt said Hamilton helped the district attorney get elected. He and Diana contributed big bucks to his campaign."

"So did I. Matt sent the information to me."

A waiter appeared at the table. "Another martini, Mr. Monroe?"

"No, thanks, Brendan. I have to talk to a judge in a little while, but some iced tea would be good."

"Of course. And would the lady like anything else?"

"I'll take the iced tea, too," I replied. My wine would hold me a while longer.

"There goes the best damned waiter in the city," Jerricus said as the man left. "He always knows how to treat his customers."

I didn't care about waiters or restaurants. More steak, chicken, and pork popped up in front of me. Jerricus might not want to talk shop over lunch, but I needed to hear more about what to expect.

"What's going to happen in the courtroom?"

"First the judge will ask what this is all about. I'll tell her I want a dismissal. Haven will counter, then we'll each argue our points, and she'll make a decision."

"Will I have to say anything?"

"Not a thing. Just look confused."

"That won't be hard."

"Judge Lapinsky won't admit it, but she hates abusive spouses. She hands down some harsh sentences on them. The prosecution is in deep trouble, and they know it."

We finished our meal and rode over to the courthouse. Entering the elevator, we exited on the fifth floor and the courtroom of Judge Edith Lapinsky. For once Jerricus was on time. Matt had already arrived and waited outside the door.

"Don't be nervous," he whispered, kissing my temple. "Everything's going to be all right."

I sucked in a deep breath, nodding weakly.

We entered the courtroom. The door closed behind us with a thud not unlike that of an expensive cell door.

My heart pounded, and a tremor worked its way up from my legs. I quickly sat in a chair at the defendant's table and swallowed the lump forming in my throat. Matt sat in the first row of seats behind me. I clenched my jaw to keep my teeth from chattering and rocked slightly back and forth. A moment later Walter Haven hurried in with a murmured apology for being late.

"All rise," the bailiff called out, his voice echoing in the empty room.

We all rose with me grasping the edge of the table. Judge Edith Lapinsky strode into the courtroom and took her seat at the dais.

"Be seated."

This was it. In a few minutes I would know if our gamble had paid off.

Chapter Eighteen

"Mr. Monroe, I warn you that if I have been pulled from the tennis courts on my first day off in over three weeks for a dose of breast-beating or hand wringing, I'm going to be very upset. I am in no mood for your dramatic shenanigans today," Judge Lapinsky declared, firing the first salvo in this verbal war.

My heart rate increased as I winced inwardly. Jerricus hadn't lied. This woman didn't much care for him.

Edith Lapinsky didn't look like my preconceived notion of a judge. I'd envisioned an older woman with gray hair and glasses—don't know why—just did. I wasn't even close.

Her hair was defiantly red, and her blue eyes skewered my lawyer with a gaze that matched her tone. The flowing black robe disguised her height, and I wondered if she wore a tennis outfit under it. I pegged her age as anywhere between forty and sixty. No eyeglasses were visible.

"Your Honor, I swear I would not make this request if the matter wasn't of the highest importance," Jerricus stated in a calm and respectful voice.

"It had better be. Now why am I here? I take it this is your client."

She shot me a glance. I tried not to squirm. I cast my eyes down, staring at my clasped hands.

"Yes, Your Honor. I asked her here because Miss Lennox is in fear for her life, and I hesitate to leave her anywhere unguarded."

"Dramatics, Mr. Monroe, remember? She can stay provided she is mute. It's bad enough I have to listen to you. Now why did you request this emergency hearing? What is so important it can't wait another day?"

Jerricus cleared his throat and launched into the basics of my case. He'd spoken less than a minute when the judge held up her hand to stop him.

"Mr. Monroe, there's no need to go into your opening statement. Please, get to the point."

"Your Honor, I am very close to filing charges of prosecutorial misconduct against the district attorney's office. I request that the charges against my client be dismissed."

Poor Jerricus, he just couldn't help being a drama king. I had no idea what prosecutorial misconduct was, but he said it with such flair, I knew it had to be a biggie.

The judge's eyebrows rose. "That's a serious accusation, Mr. Monroe."

For the first time, Walter Haven stirred and spoke. "Your Honor, that is the most ridiculous statement I've ever heard. The prosecution has done nothing wrong to warrant such a charge. I'm just sorry we had to waste your time on cheap theatrics."

"I'd hate to have my time wasted, too, Mr. Haven, but since I'm the judge, and I'm here, I think I'll listen to what the defense has to say."

She smacked down the assistant district attorney, too. *Score one for our side.*

I listened as Jerricus went into my alibi, the time

frame of the murder, and other possible suspects. It sounded good. I visualized Matt and me living in peace and quiet, raising a family.

Then Haven answered with how I could have done it. The evidence sounded so damning, I now imagined myself behind bars for however long the judge saw fit. My spirits plummeted.

Back and forth they argued until I wanted to leap to my feet, screaming. My trembling, never completely controlled, grew worse. The voices faded in and out. Those damned black dots reappeared, obscuring my peripheral vision. *Oh, God, no, don't let me faint.*

I wanted to laugh. Jerricus would love it if I suddenly toppled out of my chair onto the floor.

"Miss Lennox, are you all right?"

I heard the voice as though from a long distance away. I looked up. The judge was saying something to the bailiff while Jerricus leaned over and covered my hands with his. A few seconds later, someone handed me a cone-shaped paper cup of water.

I drained it in a single gulp, holding it up for more. The bailiff hurried to bring another, which I also drank dry. The dots disappeared, and my hearing returned to normal. It had been a close call. The bottle of tranquilizers lay nestled in my purse, but pulling it out might not be the best of moves given the circumstances. I inhaled a deep breath instead.

"Thank you. I'm sorry," I said in a small voice.

"It appears Mr. Monroe isn't the only one well-versed in the theater," Haven said.

I glared at him with resentment. He retaliated with a smirk and a contemptuous expression.

"Mr. Haven, I will not tolerate that kind of

comment in my court room."

"I apologize, Your Honor," he said in a contrite voice that did not match the look.

She nodded and then asked Jerricus, "How do you come up with prosecutorial misconduct?"

"Your Honor, the prosecution's case is entirely circumstantial. A private investigator hired by my client has unearthed more than one other possible suspect. To the best of my knowledge, these other suspects have not been pursued or questioned." He handed several sheets of paper to the bailiff who passed them to the judge. "I have here the testimony of Mr. George Ferriday, a neighbor of Miss Lennox, who saw a man bearing a resemblance to one of the late Mr. Garrett's friends, lurking around her apartment on the morning of the murder. You will read that Mr. Ferriday gave this same statement to the police over two weeks ago. Today is the first I've heard of it."

Judge Lapinsky read quickly and then turned her gaze onto Haven with raised eyebrows.

"Well, Mr. Haven, did you receive this report?"

"I do not remember having seen such a report, and as for the lurking man theory, the witness admitted he couldn't pick him out of a line-up. Mr. Ferriday is elderly and retired with nothing better to do. The murder was an exciting break in a rather humdrum routine."

She gave Haven a nasty look. "Watch it, Mr. Haven. Not all retirees lead boring lives. I'm sixty-two and considering retirement in the next couple of years."

I enjoyed watching Walter Haven squirm.

"And according to your witness, the man in question left the premises when approached," he continued.

"It's been proven someone, possibly the assailant, entered through the back patio door. Mr. Ferriday did not pursue the man once he disappeared."

"The man in question has a solid alibi."

"The man's alibi is that he was home with his girlfriend," Jerricus said. "That excuse ranks third on the list behind mother and wife as corroborating witnesses."

"The defendant's ten o'clock class was dismissed ten minutes early—plenty of time to get in her car and make a call to her ex's cell phone from the gas station three blocks away at eleven-oh-five," Haven countered.

Jerricus answered back. "Nobody recalls having seen my client there, let alone using the pay phone outside. There are no surveillance cameras covering that area. A clerk, however, does remember a man asking about the pay phones that morning."

"But neither can anybody remember seeing your client sitting under a tree, studying for a test either. Why not go to the library?"

"Maybe she liked the peace and quiet of the outdoors and didn't want to be disturbed," Jerricus shot back.

The judge's head swiveled from man to man as though watching the tennis match she should have been playing. She banged the gavel. "Gentlemen!"

"Your Honor, attempts have been made on Miss Lennox's life from the moment she got out of jail. Her apartment was ransacked and everything she owned destroyed. She survived a car bombing and an attempted kidnapping. Last Friday night, someone tried to break into the home where she's staying and shot her bodyguard. I don't want to even go into the threatening phone calls and letters received."

"What about it, Mr. Haven? Are the police and district attorney's office investigating these incidents?" Judge Lapinsky asked.

"The letter and the calls could have been staged. The shooting occurred in Germantown, an affluent community and a target for any armed robber. As for the attempted kidnapping, the police found no one matching the description given by the defendant in the mall, and the only real witness was a little old lady who swears it was aliens."

"Mr. Monroe, you should be acquainted with the alien theory. You've defended King Titan on more than one occasion," the Judge said dryly.

I groaned. King Titan was a local character who once ran for mayor on the platform that he was an alien and therefore immune to corruption. He lost, but everyone in the city has at one time or another seen him driving a pink jeep with a pink and white fringed top.

"I have indeed, and while he may be eccentric, he's harmless. Lots of people believe in extraterrestrial beings. Luckily, my client is not one of them."

I shook my head vigorously.

"That's a plus," the judge murmured and then looked at Haven. "Do you have an explanation for the car bomb, too?"

"We concede the bomb was real. We just don't believe it was aimed at the defendant. We think her car was targeted for carjacking and that a rival gang found out, then placed the bomb, detonating it by remote control."

"Nonsense. We have an expert who will testify it

was a contact bomb."

"And I'll bring in my expert who'll rebut. It was a rival gang."

Jerricus heaved an exaggerated sigh. "Walter, a jury would laugh themselves sick at that."

"I suppose the next thing you'll do is accuse my client of planting the bomb herself in the off chance she might get carjacked."

"It may be something else to investigate," Haven said.

The judge banged her gavel again. "Order! Knock it off, you two. Mr. Haven, in my opinion, your case is paper thin. As much as it pains me to agree with Mr. Monroe, I have to on this one."

"With all due respect, Your Honor, I feel we have strong circumstantial evidence to support going to trial."

"You have bupkus," the judge replied loudly. "When I go to trial, I'd like to have the jury spend at least a couple of hours debating the issues. This Swiss cheese of a prosecution will have them making their decision in the jury box. I don't like wasting my time or the taxpayers' money. Are you investigating any other possible suspects?"

She echoed the words Jerricus had said to me over lunch. My spirits soared. Was I going to win?

"Not at the moment, Your Honor," Haven answered, his finger tugging at his shirt collar.

"Well, you should be," Judge Lapinsky snapped. "I am going to cut you some slack on this prosecutorial misconduct business. I won't pursue it because I dislike hampering the district attorney's office and the police from doing their jobs. However, I expect the investigation into the murder of Daniel Garrett to be reopened as soon as possible."

I felt faint again but this time with relief.

"Mr. Monroe, I am granting your motion for dismissal."

"Your Honor, I would like to ask that it be dismissed with prejudice," Jerricus said quickly. "The district attorney was elected with the considerable influence and money of the deceased's father, State Senator Hamilton Garrett. I feel there has been undue influence exerted over the district attorney's office by Mr. Garrett hence my concerns of prosecutorial misconduct. I don't believe it is fair for him to use his considerable means to harass and pursue my client."

"Watch it, Mr. Monroe."

"Sorry, Your Honor. I am requesting the charges be dismissed with prejudice."

"Granted. Mr. Haven, inform District Attorney Jefferson that his loyalty lies with the people of Shelby County and the state of Tennessee, not his political contributors. If the DA's office uncovers new evidence, they can refile charges of a related nature."

Judge Lapinsky banged the gavel a final time. "Court is dismissed." She rose and exited.

Haven stalked out of the room. I looked up at Jerricus. "What the hell does 'with prejudice' mean?"

A grin split his face. "That means you can't be arrested or brought up on *these* charges again."

I leaped to my feet, hugged my attorney, and kissed both of his cheeks. We'd done it. We'd won. Matt rose from his seat. I hurled myself into his outstretched arms.

Jerricus laughed and slung his arm over my

shoulders. "Come on, kid. Let's blow this joint. The party's on me."

Matt grinned from ear to ear. "Haven looked angry enough to chew nails. I don't think he even saw me sitting here."

I couldn't help it. I burst into tears of joy, clinging to Matt like a plank in a stormy sea. He held me until I regained control and then kissed me senseless. My lawyer chuckled.

I pulled away from Matt who said with a twinkle in his eye, "Let's celebrate. Party at my house. We'll stop and get plenty of champagne for you and club soda for me."

"Count me in," Jerricus said. "I'll be there around seven."

We exited the courtroom. I clutched Matt's arm, ready to dance out to the car. My ordeal had finally ended.

A sudden scream had me whipping my head around to stare down the corridor. Diana and Hamilton stood with Walter Haven and two other men, one of whom I recognized as their attorney, Simon Johns. I should have realized the district attorney's office would have notified them of our meeting with Judge Lapinsky.

In a scene reminiscent of the police station on the night of my arrest, Diana started for me, her fingers curled into claws, the crimson nails looking like bloody talons. Hamilton grabbed one arm. Johns clutched the other.

"You filthy bitch!" Her voice was a screeching shriek. "You should be frying in hell! That judge must be senile to have allowed this. Damn it, you should have been toasted in that fucking car. Couldn't you have hit one goddamned pothole? I can't believe I paid ten grand to those incompetent idiots to blow you to hell and back. And that moron, Billy Jack, was supposed to shoot you, not the drunk."

"Diana, for God's sake, shut up!" Hamilton yelled, his face ashen.

But Diana had obviously left reason far behind. She screamed everlasting damnation at me and invective at invisible hired killers. Finally, her husband slapped her across the cheek. The hysteria ceased. She glared at Hamilton for a moment and then fainted dead away.

Diana's ranting confession had been heard by everyone in the hallway—lawyers, police officers, and everyday citizens. Of the three of us, Jerricus recovered first.

"Officer, I want that woman arrested. She's just confessed to murder for hire," he demanded of a young policeman standing twenty feet away with a stunned expression on his face.

"Nonsense," Simon Johns barked. "This is Mrs. Diana Worthington Garrett and her husband State Senator Hamilton Garrett. The lady has been under a great deal of strain the last few weeks and is distraught. She doesn't know what's she's saying."

Hamilton had revived Diana and, with the help of the other man, assisted her to her feet. She alternated between hysterical sobs and maniacal screaming and had to be supported by the arms. Walter Haven stood apart, talking on his cell, no doubt telling his boss about my freedom and my ex-mother-in-law's breakdown.

The officer in question moved toward them. Diana screamed again. "Get away from me, you son of a bitch!" She tried to kick him, but Hamilton pulled her back.

"Please, let me get her home. My wife is under a doctor's care. Her medication is at the house."

The young policeman looked confused and intimidated by Johns, an out-of-control woman, and my former father-in-law. He backed away. Hamilton and the two lawyers half carried and half dragged Diana to the elevator. Haven finished his call and headed for the stairwell, distancing himself from the others. We waited until the elevator doors closed on the Garrett entourage, and then pushed the button for another.

"Holy shit!" Jerricus exclaimed when we were inside alone. "I know I called her a woman on the edge, but I had no idea she'd stepped over it."

I was too shaken to respond. The three of us exited the building before splitting up. Jerricus climbed into his limo.

"I'll see you tonight," he commented. The tinted window slid up, and the car drove away.

Matt shoved me into his car. I sat in stupefying silence for several minutes. It wasn't until we were out in the late afternoon traffic before I spoke.

"Diana? Diana was the one behind the car bomb and the break-in?"

Matt slapped his hand against the steering wheel. "God Almighty, why didn't we see it? She should have been at the top of our list, especially after what happened in the police station."

"It just never occurred to me. Not always-in-control Diana Worthington Garrett. I considered her behavior at the station the result of grief."

"And I call myself a private investigator. How

could I have missed it? I was obsessed with Danny and the drug world."

"It isn't all your fault. Diana hated me, but I never envisioned how much. I wonder who she hired. I can't see her waltzing into Lenny's and saying 'Wanna kill somebody today?' It's surreal."

Matt shook his head. "I'll look into it tomorrow. I'll also do a more thorough check into the Worthington family background. Your ex-mother-in-law has slipped way over the sanity boundary."

I shivered. I could feel the waves of her hatred washing over me, even though the woman was nowhere close.

****

The laughter and conversational babble indicated a party in full swing. Matt had invited all of my neighbors and his. Jerricus arrived late—naturally—full of good spirits and now discussed golf with Mr. Ferriday. The champagne flowed. I'd had two glasses and then switched to club soda. Matt never left my side, his fingers entwined with mine the whole evening.

I'd never seen him this relaxed, but then I was a little on the relaxed side myself. I was a free woman. I no longer feared the authorities, a long prison sentence, or the Garretts. Hamilton had his hands full with Diana, and it would be years before he could even think about me.

Someone cranked up the stereo. The dancing began. Much to my amusement, Matt's neighbor, Bette Wilson, got down and boogied with my neighbor Mr. Spencer.

I'd met most of Matt's neighbors by now. They were a nice bunch, and I understood why Matt liked living here. Everyone praised Jerricus for his abilities in getting the charges dismissed. He loved it, lapping up the honors like a cat would cream.

I marveled at the close call I'd had. For a while there in the courtroom, I'd wondered if it had all been worth it. I had come close to falling apart, and if I had had any other lawyer, I may have.

But you didn't. You had Jerricus Monroe and Matt Summers in there fighting for you.

The patio overflowed with dancing couples. Even the Jensens, whom Bette had declared standoffish, rocked with the music. Concern about the noise had me glancing at the clock. It was nearly midnight, and I didn't want an irate neighbor calling the cops on us. Then I chuckled. Anyone who could have called the police was already here.

"What's so funny?" Matt squeezed my hand.

I told him and laughed again. He leaned over to give me a lingering kiss.

"Are you tired?"

"Exhausted," I replied. "But very, very happy."

He smiled. "I told you it would all work out. I'll bet we could disappear upstairs without anybody missing us."

I tapped him playfully on the cheek. "Behave yourself. The party will break up soon."

The words had no sooner left my mouth when a big splash followed by excited voices told me someone had ended up in the pool. Matt rushed down to the patio while I leaned against the deck railing.

The impromptu swimmer was Mrs. Pendergast. She'd been swilling champagne all night, and the last time I'd seen her, she had been nine-tenths asleep in one of the chaise lounges.

Mr. Ferriday and Jerricus hauled her out of the water. She stood dripping, her party dress wrapped around her like a gauzy shroud with her hair hanging in soggy strands about her face. She resembled a drowned rat, and I suppressed a laugh. One of the men slung a jacket over her saturated body.

"I'm fine, I'm fine," she shouted. "Where did that pool come from?"

Now I laughed along with everyone else. It signaled the party's swan song. One by one the revelers stopped to thank us, congratulate me, and then leave. Matt gave Mrs. Pendergast a towel, and she stumbled into Mr. Spencer's car. As they left the cove, she sang "Ninety-nine Bottles of Beer on the Wall" at the top of her lungs.

Only Jerricus remained. "Well, kid, we did it. I have to admit there were times when I thought you'd crack, but you didn't. You hung in there and came out on top."

He leaned down and kissed my cheek, then shook Matt's hand before leaving. At first, I was touched, but then the cynic in me whispered that tomorrow morning Jerricus Monroe would be fielding phone calls from dozens of battered women.

It didn't take long to clean up. When we finished, Matt clasped my hand and led me into the den.

He held me for a moment and then kissed my lips. "Did you know I was lost from the first moment I clapped eyes on you?"

"Lost?" I wanted him to keep on kissing me. I twined my arms around his neck.

His lips feathered against my brow, down my

cheek, around my chin, and back up again. "That's right. Totally lost. You were the most beautiful, vulnerable person I'd ever met. My own life had been in turmoil for so long, I doubted I would ever recover. With you by my side, I can do anything."

"Don't talk, just kiss me," I murmured.

He obliged and the heat rolled through me. I clung, kissing him back until we had to come up for air.

"Matt, let's go upstairs."

"In a minute. Is it too soon?"

"Too soon for what?" His kiss had befuddled me a bit, and I wasn't sure what he meant.

"Are we on too much of a high right now to think straight? I hope not, because I have to tell you."

"Tell me what?"

"I love you, Theresa. I don't say those words lightly. I've said them before and been burned."

"And I've heard them before and been burned." I laid my head on his chest. "Are you sure? I mean, really sure?"

He drew a shaky breath. "I'm sure. You're warm, funny, and have twice the guts of most men. You made a decision, took charge, faced possible prison time, and outgunned the Garretts. Believe me when I say I love you."

Tears welled and spilled over. I hugged him close, not even attempting to stop the flow for a couple of minutes.

"I'd made up my mind that love was something for other people, not me. No man has ever done for me what you have. My God, you even took a bullet. I knew you were special, too. I was afraid to admit it to myself until the night you were shot." I took a deep breath before articulating what I'd known for quite some time. "I didn't want to fall in love with you, Matt. I fought the feeling because I was scared of the unknown. I'm not scared anymore. I love you so much it hurts."

Matt kissed me hard and deep. I reveled in it and gave back as good as I got. Minutes later, he broke it off. I stood in front of him, listening to my heart pound like a jackhammer.

"Theresa, I've got a lousy track record with relationships. The booze didn't help. I love you, but I'm not sure I can make that final commitment. After two divorces, I'm still gun shy. And there are times my sobriety is hanging by a thread. I don't want to screw up what we have. I need time."

"I haven't used the best judgment concerning the men in my life either. I'm still raw from Danny and this whole mess. I think we can have a future with a house and kids, but taking it slow makes sense. That doesn't mean we can't be together until we find our way."

He smiled. "You mean try on marriage like an overcoat to see if it fits comfortably?"

"I guess. We've been through too much to just walk away. I'd like to give it a shot."

"So would I."

"Do you mean it?"

He nodded. "I'm a recovering alcoholic who may sometimes fall off the wagon, humiliate myself, and embarrass the hell out of you. When sober, I'm a good private investigator, so I can provide a decent living."

"I'm not much of a prize either. There will always be some people convinced I killed my husband and got off on a technicality. I could be one hell of a handicap."

"Doesn't matter. Let's give your way a try."

I leaped into his arms and kissed him.

"I guess there's only one thing left to do," he said.

"Go upstairs?"

Matt laughed, picked me up, and then carried me up the stairs to the bedroom.

I buried my face in his shoulder. Tears of pure joy coursed down my face, dampening his shirt. There had been times when in the throes of despair I never envisioned happiness. Now that's all I *could* envision. Divorces, alcoholism, lousy judgment, and desperation, not to mention being arrested for murder aside, it was a dream come true. In a way, with all that had passed, Matt and I were already married.

Chapter Nineteen

The following few weeks passed in a blur. We had a lot of decisions to make, the first of which was to leave Memphis. It took a lot of soul searching to arrive at this accord, and we did not do it lightly.

Matt loved his job, but the shock of being shot made him reevaluate his future. Even though a damned good private investigator, Matt could not justify the level of danger to which he might expose those around him. He made up his mind to change careers. We discussed the pros and cons.

"Matt, are you sure you want to do this?" I asked.

"Yes, I'm sure, but I feel badly about your schooling. We'll be living my dream in the Caribbean. What about yours?"

I shrugged. "I probably don't have the brains to be a lawyer. Besides, I can't think of why I'd choose that profession. I don't like lawyers."

"Quit putting yourself down. I can see we have to work more on that self-esteem thing. You have plenty of smarts up there," he said, tapping my forehead. "What about the psychology angle?"

"I'm not sure I could stand listening to the problems of other people eight to ten hours a day. It's too depressing. It was a good idea, but when you get right down to it, all I want is to cook for the man I love and raise kids—if we have them—in a happy, loving house. I know it sounds old-fashioned, but it's what I want. I didn't have that kind of life as a kid."

"If we do decide to raise a family, I wonder what our kids will say in thirty years."

"That Mom and Dad were stable in a very unstable world." I kissed him.

"Okay, but if you ever change your mind, tell me, and we'll move back to the States. Promise?"

I promised but knew it would never happen. He put the house on the market.

Moving to the island of St. George in the Caribbean wasn't a hardship. Memphis may be a big city population wise, but its attitude was Southern small town. The people had long memories, and as I told Matt, there would always be some who'd side with the Garretts. I had no more desire to fight. In this case, I preferred to go quietly—the sooner the better. I was ready to start over.

Thanks to Matt's Uncle Ted, the house existed as did the boat with its potential income capabilities. The natives spoke English, and I convinced myself I'd learn how to drive on the left-hand side of the road.

Money would prove no problem. Jerricus had set me up with a financial advisor who transferred Matt's and my assets to accounts all over the Caribbean. Even Hamilton contributed to the total.

Two weeks ago we received a call from Simon Johns, the Garrett attorney. Hamilton wanted to make a deal. In return for me not filing charges against Diana, he would deposit a cool one million dollars in the bank of my choice. I negotiated and held out for two. My ex-father-in-law had no choice. What could he do? For once, I had him over a barrel, and he knew it.

We both signed papers agreeing I would never ask for anything else from the Garrett family nor bring charges against his wife. Hamilton agreed there would be no civil prosecution against me. I also gave a statement to the press through Jerricus saying I didn't for a moment hold Diana Worthington Garrett responsible for any attempts on my life. She obviously had mental problems. I pretended to agree with the police about the stupid car bomb theory of rival gangs.

As for Diana, she'd been whisked out of the courthouse and straight home. A couple of days later, her husband and her doctors committed her to Rolling Acres, a sanatorium in the quiet and peaceful setting of rural Fayette County. Hamilton, her lawyers, and doctors all claimed Danny's death had temporarily unhinged her mind. At the present, they represented her as delusional and in need of medication and therapy.

No shit. She was nuttier than a Snickers bar and had been for most of her life. She'd just learned to hide it. Matt did research on the family.

"Look at this," he said one night shortly after the party.

He handed me a file compiled on the Worthington family. It was riddled with "fragile" women and "volatile" men. Danny had inherited a plethora of his mother's genes. The family also contained a lot of inter-marriages, which probably explained everything.

"Diana's aunt killed her stepfather?" I said, looking up from the dossier.

"It was never proven. The family had the body cremated and the ashes scattered before anyone raised the word poison or had any tests performed. The county coroner was a long-time family friend. If I dig deeper,

I'll probably find he was also a relative."

"I wonder how safe Hamilton felt all these years," I remarked with a shiver.

"I'll bet he slept with one eye open."

"It says here her grandfather committed suicide."

"Hanged himself from a beam in the barn. Diana found him," Matt confirmed.

"And her great-great-aunt married her first cousin?"

"And *that* first cousin was a child of first cousins. Kind of scary, isn't it?"

"Scary's not the word for it. At one point in time, Danny raped me repeatedly in an effort to have a son. I never conceived, thank God. Danny blamed me, but now I wonder."

"Maybe sterility is God's way of saying enough is enough. Thank God, Diana only had one child."

"Isn't it funny how rich people have breakdowns and are sent to sanatoriums, while poor people are just plain nuts and end up in loony bins," I commented.

Matt laughed, giving me a kiss that curled my hair.

I doubted if Diana would never see the outside of Rolling Acres again. Hamilton would probably keep her locked up. With power of attorney he'd have complete control of the money. Even if she did get released, her activities would have to be tightly controlled and monitored.

Diana's mental breakdown had cost Hamilton dearly. A lot of old South families had eccentric relatives, and the voters didn't care. It's not all that unusual and was often a source of pride in a weird sort of way, but in this case eccentric had gotten out of hand.

With his political ambitions now dust, Hamilton withdrew from the gubernatorial race, and a week later resigned his state senate seat. He ostensibly gave Diana's long-term care as the reason, projecting the image of a devoted husband.

"I know better," I said to Matt. "He'll wait until the brouhaha subsides and will get his feet back into the political arena, probably in the city. I have visions of Mayor Garrett in a few years. Fortunately, I won't be around to witness it."

The media had a field day with Diana's actions and admissions. One of the people in the courthouse hallway that day had been a reporter for *The Memphis Scene*, a cheap tabloid paper. I think that more than anything else caused Hamilton to withdraw and resign.

Matt also kept a close eye on the police progress in regards to reopening the case. Matt had turned over most of his notes on Danny's friends, including Carl Wexford, plus those on The Juice, Jump Drive, and Fast Eddie. At present, Carl looked like the best bet.

His girlfriend, Katie, had left town, but not before admitting she'd lied about his alibi. He hadn't been with her on either the day of the murder or the night my apartment was vandalized.

I still worried, however. "I understand the district attorney's office can't come after me on murder charges again, but I'm certain a loophole can be found if they look hard enough. And even though Hamilton agreed not to pursue civil action against me, I don't doubt for a moment he'll try to get his money back."

"Fat chance," Matt replied. "But you're right. Let's get out of Memphis. We'll move to St. George. They don't have an extradition treaty with the United States.

It's the best solution."

I agreed, which explained why we now flew at thirty-five thousand feet, headed for our new home.

I gazed down from the window at the last of the neat green squares of farmland slipping by below us. Soon the bright blue-green of the Gulf of Mexico and the Caribbean would greet me. My heart pumped with excitement. For the first time since we made the decision to leave, I relaxed.

I sighed and looked at Matt. He squeezed my hand and lifted it to his lips.

"Don't worry. It's over. Everything will be all right. Nothing can happen to you or us now. We have the rest of our lives ahead of us."

"I know—don't worry, be happy."

"Don't think about it."

"It's kind of hard not to," I murmured.

"Eventually, everything will fade to an unpleasant memory."

No, some of it would always be with me, branded in my psyche forever. Matt slid his earphones on, adjusted the volume on his cell phone, and then reclined his seat. He closed his eyes, grooving to the music.

I returned my gaze to the water just now appearing beneath us. Matt was probably right. He was always right. Most of the memories would fade with time to be replaced with new memories—pleasant ones—of my new life.

****

"Ow! Goddammit," Matt swore as the wrench slipped off the nut and he skinned his knuckles against the engine block.

"Maybe you need a larger wrench," I suggested.

He threw me a look, which clearly indicated that this was man's work, and what did I know about tools? I accepted the rebuke and turned to gaze over the harbor. From the corner of my eye, I saw him sneak a glance at me and then grab a larger wrench. I said nothing.

We'd been on St. George for two months, and so far the experience had been wonderful. The house wasn't large, but Matt had plans to add on and renovate soon. The covered lanai reminded me of Matt's deck back in Germantown. We'd sit after dinner, enjoying the view and watching the sunset.

Our neighbors were a nice blend of retired Brits, island natives, and expatriate Americans, none of whom had every heard of Theresa Lennox Garrett. For propriety's sake and to avoid explanations, I now used the name Theresa Summers. Matt didn't object, and I liked it.

We found the boat in decent shape, but since we'd arrived in the middle of hurricane season, Matt decided to overhaul the engines just in case we had to evacuate to another island—hence the wrench and the swearing. The boat—recently re-christened *Smokey*—was docked at the marina in the harbor of Southaven, the capital. I found it ironic that a Mississippi town just south of Memphis bore the same name as my new home.

Matt's Germantown house had sold in a few weeks, and we'd used the money as the basis for our retirement investments, along with my divorce settlement. The two million in cash sat in a Cayman bank. Every now and then, we'd move a chunk to another bank on another island. Eventually, we'd have it all in one place.

I'd told Jerricus about the two million dollars and our agreement with Hamilton. He didn't approve and warned me about the dangers of greed. He had a point, but after the life I'd led, I craved financial security.

I turned from the harbor view and pulled my tank top away from my sweaty body. Summer in the tropics and a steam bath had a lot in common. I was still trying to get acclimatized. The house didn't have air conditioning, but Matt promised to make it a priority once he finished with *Smokey*.

"What would you like for dinner?" I asked Matt's feet, since the rest of him was stuffed headfirst down in the engine well.

He muttered something I couldn't hear.

"What?"

He pulled himself up and gave me an exasperated look. A slash of grease graced his left cheek, and another blotch smeared his forehead. His T-shirt, dark with sweat, clung to his body. Drops of moisture dripped from his nose and chin. He looked great soaking wet.

"I said I really don't care as long as I don't have to make it."

I bridled and replied, "I don't recall saying anything about you having to cook."

"Sorry, but these diesels are a pain in the ass. I've never had to work on one before. It's not as easy as I thought." He sat up, reaching for an instruction book on the seat of the captain's chair. "I didn't mean to snap."

"I'll surprise you," I said. "See you at the house."

He mumbled something as I left and walked across the dusty gravel of the parking lot. It had rained this morning, but who could tell now?

I pulled out into the traffic. I'd even gotten the hang of driving on the left-hand side of the road.

Home again, I poured a glass of iced tea and lounged on the lanai. I tried not to think about the past, but every once in a while, it sneaked up on me—like now.

Last night Matt had been online with a friend in Memphis. The police had arrested Carl Wexford for Danny's murder.

Diana was still doped up at the sanatorium, but as I'd predicted, Hamilton had come out of his shell and made a speech at a local service club criticizing the municipal government.

As usual in this quiet time when I was alone, my thoughts turned inward. I often contemplated the mistakes I'd made, mostly involving men. I never seemed to pick the right one. I lost my virginity at age fourteen to a high school dropout named Nick. A week after we'd done the deed, he was history, and my heart had been left in tatters.

At fifteen I met Kenny, age twenty and my first abuser. When I told him I might be pregnant, he dumped me out of his car on the side of the road. Luckily, I wasn't, but the experience taught me to always carry a condom.

Billy Bob, Jack, Jeff, Buddy—the list, with some of them abusive, went on and on. When Mom died, I vowed to start over in Memphis, which, of course, was where I made my biggest mistake. I met and married Danny Garrett.

Matt hated it when I dwelled on the past, calling it water under the bridge. He preferred to look upstream at what's coming. And he said I'd more than made up for my errors in judgment. He had a point, so I counted all the things I'd done right.

I moved from Walls to Memphis, found a job, and made new friends. I survived physical, verbal, and every other type of abuse at the hands of a man who once claimed to love me. I divorced my husband, and when he beat me again, I sent the son of a bitch to jail. I went to college, even if only for a short time, and found another job in a bookstore.

And of course, I met Matt. Matt—just as flawed as me and struggling to survive. We needed each other, and the need had turned into love. With his support, I knew my memories, even if they didn't go away, would recede. And as long as I was around, his need to turn to the bottle during times of stress would go the same route.

So I had made some intelligent choices after all, and I no longer feared the future. I'd hooked my star to Matt and moved here—the second-best decision I'd made.

I sighed and drained my iced tea, then watched a brilliantly colored bird I couldn't identify fly onto a branch of the mango tree in the corner of the yard. Everything was brilliant in this tropical paradise—the sky, the lemon-yellow house, the sparkling blue-green water off to the west, and the sun that blazed every day.

The bird took flight again. Yes, I had finally made smart decisions. But the smartest decision I'd ever made had been to kill Danny.

Chapter Twenty

I couldn't have pulled it off without Matt. He knew how to do things *and* how the system worked. I would have just plugged Danny, but Matt insisted we have a plan and alibis. I had every reason to believe my ex-husband would kill me. I chose to strike first.

Ironically, Matt and I first met at the courthouse. I was in divorce court with my attorney and the lawyer representing Danny. Danny didn't bother to attend. As long as it was legal, I didn't care.

Dancing into the corridor with the final papers, I celebrated my freedom and never needed to fear Danny Garrett again. In my optimism, I believed it.

Too impatient to wait for the elevator, I ran for the stairwell, jerked open the door, and then dashed down the steps. I whipped around a corner, cannonading straight into a broad masculine chest. The man teetered on the edge of the landing. His hand grasped the banister, saving him from a nasty fall.

"Oh, my God, I'm so sorry. Are you all right?" My breath caught in my throat. He had the most incredible blue eyes I'd ever seen. I ignored the funky little thrill rippling through me.

The man lifted an eyebrow and smiled a sexy, lopsided smile. The corners of those fabulous eyes crinkled.

"It's been a long time since a woman knocked me

off my feet," he said in a deep voice. "Where are you going in such a hurry?"

"I have no idea—just out of here."

"Let me guess, you're coming from the divorce courts." The smile widened into a grin.

"Guilty."

"I doubt that, or you wouldn't be so happy."

"You're right. I wasn't the guilty party."

"And now you're on your way to celebrate with your friends. You'll have tequila shooters, damning your ex-husband to hell and back until you fall off the bar stool."

I had to laugh. "No. I think I'll just have a quiet lunch somewhere."

"If you don't mind waiting an hour or so, I'd love to treat you to that lunch."

It was tempting—very tempting. It had been a long time since a man flirted with me. Then I glanced at the papers, the ink not yet dry, clutched in my hand, and common sense overruled instinct. I'd just unloaded a handsome, sexy—and violent—mate. I didn't need new entanglements.

"Uh, thanks, but I think not."

"Ah, well, my loss. Good luck, Mrs.—" His eyebrows rose.

"Garrett—no, Lennox. Theresa Lennox. I'm glad you aren't hurt, Mr.—" I don't know why I wanted to know his name or why I told him mine, but what the hell? I was divorced and could do as I wanted.

"Summers. Matt Summers."

He grinned again and continued up the steps. I started down at a more decorous pace and shot a look over my shoulder as he disappeared around the corner.

"Damn," I said, sighing.

Our paths crossed again four months later in the most dramatic of circumstances.

I tried to pick up the threads of my life and attain a degree of self-respect. I rented a little house and even had a cat—a stray I'd occasionally feed and who just stayed. Gray with white socks, I called him Smokey. On the nights he didn't go out tomcatting, he would curl up with me on the bed.

One night I came home after work and discovered a drunken Danny waiting in the shadows. I tried to run, but he caught me and proceeded to pound me into jelly.

"You call the cops, and I'll fuckin' kill you, do you understand?" he'd snarled when leaving.

I understood all right. I crawled to the phone and called anyway. Within hours, I was in the hospital and Danny in jail.

I spent two days in intensive care before moving into a semi-private room. Another day passed until I was off the painkillers and able to talk to my roommate. Due to be discharged the following day, she looked forward to seeing her husband and kids again.

"My husband is up to his ears in work, so my brother is picking me up. I can hardly wait to get out of here."

I didn't pay much attention, but my interest was piqued the next morning when her brother arrived. It was Matt.

I recognized him, but it took a few seconds for him to remember me. Why should he? I looked like hell with two black eyes, a broken nose, and a fat lip.

"Good God, what happened to you?"

I told him. His eyes darkened with anger. "I hope

you had the son of a bitch arrested."

"Yes, and this time I won't drop the charges."

"Good girl."

I figured I'd seen the last of him. I was wrong. He visited every day and drove me home after my discharge.

We took the relationship slow and easy. Occasionally, we'd go out to dinner or to the movies. He didn't pressure me into having sex, nor did he ask questions about my marriage. I didn't probe into his past either, although he did admit to a drinking problem now under control. We talked about movies, books, our favorite foods, and the St. Louis Cardinals.

I found myself liking Matt Summers a whole lot.

I walked on eggs for two months after my release from the hospital. Danny had made bail and moved in with his parents. After a lot of legal wrangling and stalling, not even the Garretts could postpone the inevitable. Rather than go through a trial he was sure to lose, my ex took a ridiculous plea bargain of assault and a year in jail.

Matt insisted we go out the night before Danny's official surrender and allocution. We arrived home from dinner and a movie in good spirits. I entered the house laughing and flipping on lights.

"Would you like a glass of iced tea?" I asked.

"Love one." He picked up the TV remote. "Mind if I channel surf?"

"Go ahead. I'm beginning to like sports."

I flipped on the light in the dining room and stopped dead in my tracks. Hanging from the chandelier, a noose wrapped tightly about his neck, was Smokey. A note had been cruelly pinned to his chest and read—"You're next, precious."

"Precious"—Danny's signature endearment right before he beat the crap out of me.

I screamed. Matt ran into the room and cursed, then held me close as I cried. He steered me into the living room and dumped me in a chair where I couldn't see the dining area.

He cut Smokey down, carried the pitiful body outside, and buried it. He returned, scooped me out of the chair, and sat on the sofa, cradling me in his lap.

"I'll kill him," I sobbed. "I swear to God I'll kill the fucking son of a bitch. Why? Why kill poor Smokey?"

"Because Danny knew it would hurt you. We should have stayed here, ordered in a pizza, and rented a movie."

"He means it, you know—about me being next. Do you think he'll come back tonight?"

"I don't know. We'll call the police and have him picked up right now. This ought to tack on a few more months to his sentence."

"Don't bother. No one ever heard him call me 'Precious,' and the note was crudely printed. He'd deny he was here, and Diana will give him an alibi."

"To be on the safe side, I'm sleeping on your sofa tonight. Tomorrow, he'll surrender and be shipped off to jail. Then I want you to find a new place to live. Officially petition the court to take back your maiden name and get an unlisted number. Better yet, pay cash for a pre-paid phone. He won't be able to trace it."

I cried myself to sleep that night. I missed the furry body curled up on the bed, his rumbling purr like a gentle vibrator massaging my feet.

Danny was duly carted off to jail the following morning, and I began apartment hunting. I sought out the kind of place Danny would never think to look when he got out, finally settling on the Quince Gardens.

My lease on the house still had a couple of months to run, and rather than lose the security deposit, I elected to stay. I couldn't pass the dining room without seeing Smokey. My bitterness grew. I wanted Danny dead.

Hate and anger—two of the strongest human emotions—festered. I plotted how to eliminate my ex-husband. None of my schemes had any practicality, but I couldn't stop thinking about it and was determined to kill Danny before he had a chance to kill me.

One night, Matt treated me to dinner. I sat withdrawn and quiet, staring at my food and wondering if I could poison Danny in some way.

"You'll never get away with it," Matt said in a low tone, leaning forward after the waiter had cleared our table.

"Get away with what?"

"Killing Danny."

How the hell had he known? His gaze skewered me like a sword, pinning me in my seat, unable to move.

"What do you mean?" I asked.

"You're plotting how to kill him, aren't you? Well, you'll never get away with it."

I licked my lips and took a drink of water from the glass on the table to dampen my parched throat.

"Theresa, talk to me."

"All right, so what? If I don't kill him, he'll kill me. You saw the note. He means it. I can't just sit back and wait for him to do it once he gets out. Sooner or later, he'll find me. And don't give me any song and dance about justice, the system, or restraining orders. I have one of those. They don't work."

His eyes scanned the room as the waiter brought the check.

"Let's not talk about it here."

Matt paid, and we left, driving to a strip mall where we parked on the outer perimeter.

"How do you plan on doing it?" he asked.

"I bought a gun after I got out of the hospital. You advised me to do that, remember? I could shoot him and then drop the gun in the river."

"As soon as his body's discovered, the cops will be on your doorstep. Then you'll have to explain why you no longer have the gun."

"I'll say I lost it, or it was stolen."

"That's the oldest excuse in the world." He paused and gazed out the window for a moment. "No, we have to think this out very carefully—down to the tiniest detail."

"We?"

"We."

And that's how we became coconspirators.

****

"Are you sure you want to do this?" Matt asked for the hundredth time.

"Yes."

With the decision made, Matt turned into a complete detail paranoid. He insisted I move into my apartment as soon as possible. Once settled in, I would then get to know and establish a good rapport with my neighbors.

"I can't be seen at your new home," Matt

323

maintained. "And once he's dead, we have to pretend we've never met before. Can you do that?"

I inhaled a shaky breath. "I think so."

"And all public conversations follow the same line, just in case a third party is listening. That includes my office, your apartment, and our cars. Bugs can be placed anywhere. I don't want to take a chance on a slip of the tongue screwing us."

I'd thought this extreme until the day I arrived at his office to "hire" him. Carleen overheard every word we said, and so did the cops in the diner. He even made me go through my story on tape, so that if he had to hand it over to the police, it would sound authentic.

"Any halfway decent PI would make a recording," he said. "It's called covering our asses."

Matt also decided to roll the dice by using my gun and leaving it at the scene of the crime. It was illogical and a point for the defense. No one is that stupid.

"Go to a firing range a couple of times a week. Learn how to shoot the gun and get to know whoever works there," Matt told me.

Now I needed an alibi. A job might not be convenient since it could involve schedules not of my choice. He brought up enrolling at the University of Memphis, scheduling my classes for a specific time, and then working from that.

Throughout all the planning, we only had one argument—who would pull the trigger.

"I'll do it," Matt said.

"No way. Killing Danny is my idea, and I'll take the heat. My prints should be on the gun anyway."

"Absolutely not. You need to be at school establishing your alibi. I'll do it."

"No. *You* haven't earned the right."

He looked at me with concerned blue eyes. "Are you sure you can pull the trigger?"

I relived every minute of that last savage beating and imagined Smokey's horrible death. I nodded, clenched my jaw, and swallowed.

Matt stared and then sighed. "All right, but if at any time you have second thoughts—let me know. Promise?"

"I promise."

Where to do it also posed a problem. All of my ideas involved witnesses. I had to get Danny alone—one on one.

"My apartment," I said one afternoon as we ate sandwiches on a park bench overlooking the Mississippi.

Matt damn near choked. "Are you nuts?"

"No. I kill him, go to school, establish my alibi, and then come home hours later to find the body."

"That's crazy."

"No, it's not. I'll do what every innocent person does," I replied, my thoughts in fast forward.

"What? Panic?"

"No, call the cops, but panic is a good idea and probably inevitable."

"And why would he go to your place?"

"To kill me."

"And how will he know where to find you? You can't make any calls from your phone to his. They can be traced."

"You call him. Give him a load of shit about how I dumped you, and now you want revenge. He'd understand that. Danny always understands revenge. He just won't expect me to understand it."

I also observed the daily routines of my neighbors. Most of them were over sixty and rarely deviated from their set schedules. Timing was crucial. We had to make sure nobody witnessed anything until we wanted—namely, Mr. Ferriday. His golfing habit was the perfect answer.

Matt spent hours in different library branches, researching Danny on the internet. If something went wrong, no one could tie Matt's hard drive to Danny prior to his death. When he finished, we thought we had a handle on things. We knew my ex had been into drugs and chose Lester Meeks—the most violent and useless of Danny's friends—as the fall guy.

From the beginning, the plot had problems.

First of all, Danny turned out to be a model prisoner. Go figure. Coupled with Hamilton's influence, it bought the creep a get-out-of-jail-free card after serving only seven months. We had to move our schedule up. My accidental meeting with him on campus played right into our hands but also told us we needed to stop talking and commit. Taking another human's life—even Danny's—was the hardest decision I ever had to make.

"It's not too late to back out. We can just leave town," Matt said when, in a moment of doubt, I questioned our right to do it.

"Danny will never give up. He'll have Mommy search until she finds me." I shook my head and swallowed hard. "No, he has to be stopped. If I leave, and he beats some other poor woman to death, I'd never forgive myself, knowing I could have prevented it."

I didn't sleep at all the night before. I lay awake

rehearsing my part over and over in my mind, sometimes getting up to go through the motions.

Matt called Danny early on Monday morning from a disposable cell phone with the story we'd concocted. Matt recorded the conversation so I could hear it as we drove to the apartment my first day out of jail.

"Mr. Garrett?"

"Who wants to know?" Danny's voice had sounded slurred, like he'd gotten an early start on the beer.

"Name's Gerald Watkins, and up until a few weeks ago, I was your ex's main man. She got sassy, and I had to smack her one, then she called the cops. I just got out of jail."

"Sounds like the bitch. Where can I find her?"

"That's why I'm callin'. She's scared shitless of you. I wish I could be around to see her face when you show up."

"I'll take a fucking picture. Now where is she?"

Matt gave him my address, ending with, "The patio door is real flimsy and should be easy to jimmy. If you show up between nine and nine fifteen, she'll be in the shower and won't hear a thing. And do me a favor, hit the fucking bitch once in her smart mouth for me."

The tape ended. Matt later destroyed it.

By eight o'clock, I paced the floor like a caged tiger. My stomach rebelled, and I threw up. I shook so hard I had momentary doubts I would be able to hold the pistol, let alone shoot it straight.

At nine I took up my position, the gun concealed by a bed pillow in a shaking hand. I'd stripped naked so any gunshot residue or blood would not be found on my clothing.

I waited, trembling like a leaf in the wind and

fighting the urge to be sick again. My heart pounded away at ramming speed, and my breath came in short little gasps. I clutched the gun and pillow to my stomach.

Danny arrived at nine fifteen. I tensed when the patio door broke, then slid open. Footsteps advanced through the living room and down the hall to my bedroom. He entered, stopping ten feet away, a sick grin on his face when he saw me.

"Hey, precious, just the way I always imagined it." He laughed and grabbed his crotch, a gleam of anticipation in his eyes. In his left hand, he carried a length of cord. He meant to kill me just as he had Smokey.

My trembling ceased as did the nausea. My heart still raced, and the blood thundered in my ears. I lifted the pillow-wrapped gun and fired twice. Even muffled, the shots reverberated throughout the room.

Danny took both bullets in the chest, then dropped like a stone. He made no noise. Just died, his sightless eyes staring at the ceiling.

I tossed the pillow on the unmade bed and pitched the thirty-eight onto the floor next to the body. I had no idea if the bullets had gone through or lodged inside. I figured one of them must have scored a direct hit in the heart.

The roaring in my ears receded, and I heard voices. My heart lurched in panic before I realized the sound came from overhead. We had counted on Mrs. Pendergast's TV viewing habits. I had been too terrified and focused to hear a thing before pulling the trigger.

The trembling and the nausea returned. I ran for the bathroom and vomited again, then sobbed.

Forcing myself to remember the script, I turned on the shower and scrubbed my body from head to toe, including my hair. Then I dressed, picked up the cord he'd carried, grabbed my backpack from the coffee table, and ran from the apartment.

I sat through my classes in a daze, trying to appear normal to anyone who'd notice, which explained why I failed my math test. I couldn't concentrate.

Walking back into the apartment that afternoon was awful. Even though I knew what I'd find, I still had a moment of panic when I peeked into the bedroom.

The aftermath with my arrest went pretty much as expected, although Matt's backsliding into alcohol did give me a few anxious moments.

"I was so damned scared for you," he explained later. "I kept visualizing everything that could happen in jail and lost control. The sweetest sound I ever heard was your voice talking to Carleen."

Firing my public defender hadn't been on the books either. Luckily, I had lied, telling him the same story I had the cops.

Nailing down Jerricus was a stroke of genius on Matt's part. The moment I shook hands with the most powerful attorney in the state, I knew I'd found my man. I *did* tell him the truth. He had defended so many guilty clients I figured he'd heard more true confessions than a cheap tabloid. He never turned a hair at my guilty status.

"All we need is to convince a jury of reasonable doubt for an acquittal, but I don't like dealing with juries if I can help it. I'll go for a dismissal instead. Keep in mind, however, *that* won't protect either of you if the facts are ever uncovered. The DA could reindict you both on conspiracy to commit murder and a few other charges to boot."

Of course, Diana threw the biggest monkey wrench into our plans. I still shiver at how close she came to succeeding.

"We assumed the white car following us on Thursday night belonged to the police. It was Diana's minions," Matt explained a few days later. "They guessed we'd go back to the motel, so they slipped into the old mall property and took a shot at you."

"What about the tan car?"

"Legitimate police surveillance."

The vandalizing of my apartment forced us to realize we had a major problem. Unbeknownst to me, Matt hired a former PI friend to do several things we couldn't.

"I gave him the key to your patio door and told him to just toss a few things around."

"Why didn't you tell me?" I asked.

"I wanted you to have a natural reaction in case one of your neighbors was nearby. Diana's goons were a bit more aggressive. I knew immediately Bob hadn't done it."

The private investigator also made the phone call from the gas station to Danny's cell and left the threatening messages on our answering machines. Answering machines are old-fashioned and not used much anymore, but since we both had landlines, they served our purposes. Matt mailed the letter to himself.

Matt also orchestrated the kidnapping. He referred to it as an incident.

"What kind of an incident?" I questioned when he told me he'd devised a plan to help me look like a victim.

"I haven't decided yet, but that's all I'm going to tell you. It needs to take place out in the open with a large crowd where my man can blend in and get away fast."

"How about the mall? If you pick a day near the end of the month, the place will be packed with people trying to get a bargain on sale items."

"That might work. Let me think on it for a while."

I knew something would happen, but given the car bomb and everything else not in the plans, I was a nervous wreck. Suppose whatever occurred was the real thing?

Matt's friend also posed as my kidnapper. The crazy old lady was his grandmother. And the description I'd given the police of my abductor didn't come close to what the guy looked like. Matt had suggested keeping it simple, especially since I wasn't sure what would happen.

"He was medium height and weight with short dark hair and wore a white T-shirt and blue jeans," I told the officer.

Matt had scripted it so both the grandmother and I would tally. Any other descriptions would be discarded as a case of mistaken identity.

The alien thing threw me for a while until I saw the genius of it. I hadn't seen it coming, and my reaction was perfect.

Matt also used Bob to lurk around my apartment the day of the murder so Mr. Ferriday could see him. When Matt interviewed my neighbor, he skillfully convinced him the man he'd seen bore a strong resemblance to Carl Wexford. With Lester's demise, we had moved him to the top of the fall-guy list.

The car bomb scared the crap out of us. Knowing how deeply my ex was involved in the drug trade, we both assumed someone thought I had access to either Danny's drugs or money.

The police never apprehended the man who shot Matt.

"Thank God, Diana hired morons," I said to him a few weeks after my dismissal. "She reminds me of that battery bunny—she just keeps going and going. She's probably still working on eliminating me, even from Rolling Acres."

"She's crazy enough, but there are other things that concern me."

"Like what?"

"There's a theory in forensics that was first formulated by a man named Locard. It states that whoever commits a crime takes something from the scene, but more importantly, leaves something of himself behind."

"I'm not sure what you mean."

"Let's say the police arrest Carl for the killing. If he were in the room with Danny, he should have taken something forensic with him when he left, like carpet fibers or blood splatter."

"It's been a long time. That stuff could have easily been lost."

"True, but evidence is kept for a long time, too. He should have left something behind—a footprint, fingerprint, hair—hair falls out all the time. The forensics people would have vacuumed the place and found it."

"And because Carl was never in my apartment,

there's nothing. Is that what you're saying?"

"Exactly, there's nothing, but there should be. Sooner or later, when the case is reopened, the police will go over the evidence collected the day of the shooting and realize what *isn't* there."

"And come right back to me. They may also take a closer look at you, too. So what do we do?"

That's when he came up with the St. George angle.

"But you've worked so hard on this house," I protested.

"It's just a house. Besides, if they get around to investigating me, they'll uncover that we knew each other before the murder. I was at your place a lot. One of your neighbors will remember. No, we leave."

Looking back, I marveled we'd pulled it off. We made so many mistakes, and one loose end could have unraveled the whole thing. We got lucky on two counts.

"The Garretts were their own worst enemy," Matt declared at the airport before boarding our plane. "They were arrogant as hell and thought they could use the legal system indefinitely."

Nor had they counted on Jerricus Monroe. During the celebration party he pulled me aside.

"Lady, I defend *real* murdering scum on a daily basis, but I look at your case and see an act of mercy. If Danny Garrett hadn't killed you, he would have killed someone else sooner or later. He was as psychotic as his mother. Look on it as getting a flu shot to prevent the disease."

I found him paraphrasing the words of The Juice ironic to say the least.

Did I feel remorse for setting up Carl as the fall guy? Not really. I didn't care one way or the other if he got acquitted or rotted in jail. Matt predicted he'd get off.

"No fingerprints on the gun. Even if he used gloves, how did he know where you kept it? And what was his motive? Why kill the golden goose?" he explained.

"It would be great if he worked for Fast Eddie, too, and was ordered to it."

Matt shook his head. "Not even Fast Eddie would hire someone as dumb as Wexford. No, we move. We can't take the chance old Carl's case doesn't go the way yours did with a dismissal for lack of evidence."

I shrugged. Cut from the same cloth as my ex-husband, Wexford deserved whatever the jury decided. On more than one occasion, he'd made sexual advances to me while Danny had laughed.

Smokey II jumped up into my lap and settled down for a nap. I scratched behind his ears, and he set up a deep, steady purr. I loved this black and white Smokey but still kept a photo of the original in a silver frame on the dresser.

I sometimes wondered what the hereafter holds for us. Even though not a church-goer, I still had enough Southern Baptist in me to think about it. Would we be forgiven? When I asked Matt, he'd shrugged.

"I don't know. We did what we had to do. It may not have been right, but it was necessary for your survival."

"You mean like soldiers in a war?"

"Something like that."

I hoped God would understand.

I gazed over the verdant hillside to the stretch of turquoise water with the rolling waves beyond and sighed. The sun lay low on the horizon. Matt would be home soon. He'd shower while I cooked a simple dinner, then afterward as we sat on the patio, I could tell him the news I'd planned on telling him at the boat this afternoon.

First thing tomorrow morning, I'd insist we make our living arrangement legal, although, in truth, we'd been pledged to each other the moment I pulled the trigger. I'd once heard it said that criminals are married to their alibis, and Lord knew, Matt and I had depended on each other to make things work.

We might as well make it official. Our future was about to take yet another course.

I was pregnant.

A word from the author...

I was born in Indianapolis, Indiana, but have been fortunate enough to live in several diverse cities—St. Louis, Missouri; Rockford, Illinois; Memphis, Tennessee; and Fort Lauderdale, Florida. I have two adult children and seven grandchildren. My husband and I recently moved back to Memphis to be nearer to family.

Much of my spare time is used to indulge in my guilty pleasures like floating around in my pool on a hot summer day. And if I happen to think up a good plot line while doing so, all the better. I also have little containers of ice cream stashed in out-of-the-way places in my freezer.

I love writing and hope readers enjoy the journey of my stories along with me.

Thank you for purchasing
this publication of The Wild Rose Press, Inc.

For questions or more information
contact us at
info@thewildrosepress.com.

The Wild Rose Press, Inc.
www.thewildrosepress.com

To visit with authors of
The Wild Rose Press, Inc.
join our yahoo loop at
http://groups.yahoo.com/group/thewildrosepress/